THIS TIME
THE SHOT WAS NEARER...

Frantically, Royce signalled aft, and the tub-shaped smoke float thudded into the water, the black, greasy vapour already pouring out in a steady stream, low across the wave tops. The wind plucked at the fringes of the pitiful smoke-screen, and tore the life from it, leaving only the core, and a fast-moving vaporous mist between them and the Germans.

"Open fire when your guns bear!" ordered Royce, and following on his words came the clatter of the starboard Oerlikon, as Able Seaman Poole sent a stream of tracer spinning through the smoke, the shells seeming to bounce across the waves as they groped for the enemy....

Also by DOUGLAS REEMAN
from Jove

THE GREATEST ENEMY
THE LAST RAIDER
PATH OF THE STORM
THE PRIDE AND THE ANGUISH
RENDEZVOUS—SOUTH ATLANTIC
TO RISKS UNKNOWN

DOUGLAS REEMAN

A PRAYER ★★★★★ FOR ★★★★★ THE SHIP

A JOVE BOOK

Two previous printings
First Jove edition published February 1981

10 9 8 7 6 5 4 3 2 1

Printed in the United States of America

Jove books are published by Jove Publications, Inc.,
200 Madison Avenue, New York, NY 10016

Author's Note

A Prayer for the Ship is the story of the Royal Navy's Light Costal Forces during the last war. A lot of it must necessarily be my own story too, and the events which I saw and shared I can never forget.

The world we knew was fast-moving and violent. The men who fought and often died in the English Channel and North Sea were young. Some were very young. So immediately after the war had ended, and that small desperate world had gone forever, the memories were still too real, the circumstances often too vast, to interpret without bias. Recently, as I read proof of the book for the American edition, I realized that, had I left it any later, my viewpoint might have been similarly distorted.

I found myself asking: were we really like that? How in a space of weeks or months could untried amateurs become professionals—men who carried war into the enemy's territory, usually with little regard of the risks involved? Maybe the story chose its own time, when memory and substance had become clearly blended—like a gunsight, blurred to the eye on either side of the correct setting, which all at once becomes stark and vivid.

Some of the relationships and ideals included in the story seem simple and out of touch with the world around us. But in those times life did become simplicity itself. Someone with whom you had shared your hoarded rations or discussed home and family was gone in the blink of an eye. A handshake, a brief smile, and the next day he might be dead.

To the little ships and their crews this story is humbly dedicated.

1973   D. R.

1

THE whole of the naval anchorage seemed subdued and cowed by the relentless, sleety rain which drove across the estuary, whipping the grey waves into a turbulent, white-capped frenzy. As the wind moaned through the mean little streets around the port, and swept the soaking jetties, the various ships-of-war strained and tugged at their cables and wires, while huddled figures in glistening oilskins sought cover and protection behind the gun-shields or flapping canvas dodgers. Across and beyond the boom-gate, a few barrage balloons plunged and staggered like drunken whales, as their cursing crews somewhere in the muddy fields fought with the creaking moorings. The sea itself looked even greyer than usual, and it was difficult to discern the break with the racing clouds which was the horizon, where a lone trawler fought into the teeth of the gale, one minute hidden by the steep, jagged waves, and the next instant showing her streaming keel, more concerned with staying afloat than listening for a prowling U-boat.

The tall, rust-streaked sides of the Coastal Forces Depot Ship *Royston* shuddered as the gale punched her, but she remained the steadiest vessel in the harbour, her cables fore and aft stretched bar-taut, and her deck-planking patterned with little humps of blown salt. Her charges, Motor Torpedo Boats and Motor Gunboats, were strung in uncomfortable trios around her, banging and lurching together, rope fenders and old motor tyres doing their best to ease the jolting motion. Up on the main deck, the Quartermaster peered out towards the railway wharf, and cursed unsympathetically at the ship's motor-boat which had just left the shelter of the wall, and was bounding over the stream towards him. He saw the Coxswain lift his hand in a half-hearted sign and then withdraw into the tiny wheelhouse. The Quartermaster turned to the other figure sharing his vigil, the Officer-of-the-Day, who was endeavouring to read a signal, already soggy with rain, in the shelter of his oilskin.

'Motor-boat returning, sir,' he yelled. 'One officer aboard.'

Lieutenant Pike waved the tattered signal in acknowledgement.

'Turn out the Duty Watch, I am going to bring the boat aboard, no more trips today.'

As the Quartermaster pulled out his silver call and switched on the Tannoy microphone, Pike watched with narrowed eyes as the motor-boat swung up to the main gangway and hooked on with its usual precision. His glance shifted to the nearest Motor Torpedo Boat, the only one showing a sign of life, as a handful of the Depot Ship's maintenance party scurried round repairing and replacing the scars of a running battle two nights before, when the young First Lieutenant had been killed, as so many had been from this flotilla.

As usual the replacement was arriving in the motor-boat. Pike returned the salute of the slim officer who stepped over the gangway, his too-new greatcoat gleaming with rain.

'Sub-Lieutenant Clive Royce, come aboard to join,' he shouted.

They shook hands, and Pike ushered him to the first doorway, while two disgruntled members of the Duty Watch collected the baggage of the latest arrival.

'Go below to the wardroom,' said Pike. 'The Commander is in there at the moment and he'll want to see you right away.'

Royce nodded, and stepped into the passageway. Immediately, the sounds of the storm were muffled, and a feeling of security surrounded him. He stripped off his greatcoat and cap, straightened his uniform, and had a quick glance in the mirror outside the old-fashioned door marked "Wardroom". He had a pleasant face, with eager, grey eyes, and a firm but generous mouth. His hair, now flattened by cap and rain, was dark almost to the point of being black. Taking a deep breath, Royce slid the door to one side and stepped in. The wardroom had once been the first-class saloon in the old ship's early days as a small passenger and cargo vessel, and had a prosperous, rather Edwardian look about it. The sides and deckhead were oak-panelled and carved in ornate designs, and a long, polished bar completely lined one end. The whole room was littered with dumpy, red-leather chairs and sofas, all well-worn but comfortable looking, and most of them were occupied by youthful officers who lounged about reading magazines, listening to the radio, or just dozing.

A round-faced, cheerful-looking Commander leaned against the bar listening to a serious Lieutenant, who kept pounding the bar as if to emphasize a point that was beyond anyone else's comprehension.

Royce coughed nervously. 'I was told to report direct to you, sir. My name is Royce.'

'Well now, I'm Commander Wright, and I do all the "crewing" of the boats here, so I'll get you fixed up right away.' He beamed. 'And this is your Commanding Officer, Lieutenant Harston, so I'll leave you to get acquainted, while I arrange your orders.'

At twenty-three, Harston was already a veteran of the East Coast and Channel warfare, and the first signs of strain were beginning to show on his pale, rather artistic face. Coolly he offered his hand in a surprisingly strong handshake.

When he spoke, it was with a soft, careful deliberation.

'I've taken the trouble to look up your particulars in advance, because in this racket we don't seem to find the time as we go along.'

He paused while he made a gesture to the barman with his glass, which was ignored in favour of two elderly officers at the other end of the bar.

With a shrug, he continued, 'Terrible service here. Now, let me see. You're twenty years old, been commissioned three months. Sea experience, three months in an Asdic trawler. You'll probably notice the difference when you find three and a half thousand horsepower under your feet. Correct me if I'm wrong, but I believe you were beginning to be a marine draughtsman before you joined, any connexion?'

9

'Well, I've always been keen on the sea, small boats, and that sort of thing,' finished Royce lamely.

'What you mean is, you haven't a clue, but you're a hard-working boy, and willing to learn. I only pray you get longer to learn than your predecessor,' he added grimly.

At the sight of Royce's crestfallen expression, he relented, in fact his whole personality changed, and a warm, friendly grin spread across his face.

'Never mind, tomorrow morning I'll take you over the boat, and tomorrow night I'm afraid we go out again. In the meantime, we'll grab this blasted steward and drink to War Savings, or something!'

As that first evening wore on, Royce had plenty of time to study his superior, and to observe his quick, breath-taking changes of mood and manner. He would re-tell some of his experiences in the flotilla on the East Coast convoy routes, or the mad dashes through the night with the enemy coast only a few yards abeam, telling how and why each operation was a success or a failure, speaking in his soft, precise voice, his blue eyes distant and apparently unseeing, then with a jerk, he would become a boy again, as he recounted incidents like the occasion when he and his friends stole a fire-engine and drove it madly round the town, hotly pursued by the military police. He lay back in his chair and gave his queer, high-pitched laugh, 'There was hell to pay over that. But they never caught us. In fact, old Benjy over there has still got a hose in his cabin.'

Every so often he introduced Royce to his new team-mates, as they drifted in and out of the bar, and he appeared satisfied with the way that he answered the very mixed selection who made up the flotilla's Commanding Officers. There was Ronnie Patterson, a young, red-faced north countryman, whose language was apt to appal strangers, but who was obviously a great favourite with everybody. Artie Emberson had been a barrister, and looked it. When he spoke in his drawling voice to the steward on the question of drinks, it sounded as if he was questioning a rather dumb witness. "Benjy" Watson was the inevitable practical joker, who had missed many a court-martial by sheer good luck—the last occasion being when he dressed in a captured German officer's uniform and went to a local cinema. His pointed, pink face split into a beaming smile as he re-told the story.

'Not a blessed soul took any notice of me,' he roared, 'and if I hadn't given a Nazi salute when I passed two army types, it would all have been a waste of a run ashore!'

Jock Murray was another whom Royce liked instantly. A small, hard-faced ex-fisherman from Aberdeen, whose family had been trawling the North Sea for generations, he was a man of few words and only one interest, the sea.

One thing they all had in common, they were old before their time, aged by experiences that Royce could only guess at, and imagine.

When the bar-shutters fell with a bang that brought a roar of protests, Royce floated, rather than walked, down to the tiny, box-like cabin which was to be his home while in harbour. A newly cleaned and emptied place, where his predecessor had once slept and thought and hoped, and although only dead forty-eight hours, the last of his earthly traces had already been swept away.

So Clive Royce went to war, and with the relentless rain lashing the side of his cabin, he fell into a deep, dreamless sleep.

* * * * *

Royce's first morning with the One Hundred and Thirteenth Flotilla dawned fresh and clear, the gale had blown itself out during the night, and only the smell of damp oil-skins and a few puddles on the canvas awnings gave a hint of the torrential rain. The whole harbour bustled with activity, as if to make up for a lost day, and as motor-boats and harbour launches scurried to and fro between their parent vessels, ships' companies and base staff got down to the daily business of preparing their charges for sea.

As he swung himself down the catwalk from the depot ship on to the first M.T.B., Royce was aglow and eager to start, inspired perhaps by the easy confidence of the other officers at breakfast, plus a somewhat ponderous speech delivered by the base Operations Officer about the "nation depending upon these young men in its hour of need", while Royce shifted impatiently at the top of the gangway. Ah, there she was! Low, grey and sleek, Number 1991 painted in large numbers on her bow, her decks crammed with overalled figures, one of whom straightened and saluted. A short, chubby, little man, with a battered Petty Officer's cap tilted rakishly over unruly ginger hair, he put down an enormous wrench.

'Petty Officer Raikes, sir, Coxswain. I expect you'll be the new officer?'

He had a faint Liverpool accent, and seemed amused by Royce's immaculate uniform.

'The Captain's aft at the moment, sir, I think he's expecting you.'

Was there a hint of sarcasm in his voice? Royce couldn't be sure. Perhaps it was the hidden bitterness of a junior professional to a senior amateur.

'Very well, Cox'n,' he nodded, and stepped aft. "That was it," he thought, "be brief and to the point."

He found Harston sitting on a smoke float, deeply engrossed in a conversation with a large man in a bowler hat, the sign of dockyard authority.

Royce smiled, 'Reporting for instruction, sir, and a fine morning it is too, after the drenching I got yesterday.'

Harston stood up quickly, like a cat: 'When I want your views on the weather, I'll let you know,' he snapped. 'It may interest you to know that I've been here since six thirty, trying to get these repairs finished, and while you no doubt have been indulging in a bit of gossip, and enjoying an excellent breakfast, I've also been arranging your duties for you!'

Royce flushed and stammered, completely taken aback by this unexpected attack. 'The Operations Officer stopped me, sir, he was telling . . .'

'I'm not interested. If you want to be a big pin in a little ship instead of tea-boy in a battle-wagon, you'll have to get down to it, and forget this barrack routine stuff. We don't start at nine here, with three hours for lunch,

12

we keep going till the job's done, and the job right now is to get this boat ready to go out at 2000 tonight!'

He swung back to the stolid dockyard manager, who had taken a sudden interest in the guard-rails during this tirade.

His voice now sounded heavy and tired: 'Righto, Angus, you'll do that for me, then? Bless you.' And without a further word, he strode to the catwalk. As he heaved himself over the other M.T.B., he turned and called for the Coxswain.

'Get those men at work on the guns as soon as you can, I don't want any more jamming. And get some overalls for Sub-Lieutenant Royce, and then show him the boat, every bit. I'm going to have breakfast, if there's any left now.'

Royce watched him scramble up the ladder and out of sight; he was completely shattered.

'Phew, was that the chap who told me last night not to worry,' he muttered. 'Well, I can see this is going to be just fine.'

The portly Angus coughed at his elbow, 'I'm off, just got to see about some new bolts, an' that. Now, don't you worry about him, son, he's the best that comes, I've seen a few, too. Trouble is, he's been at it too long. I think the poor bloke's just about had it.' And with a heavy thud on the shoulder, he too disappeared.

For the next hour, Royce and the Coxswain crawled and scrambled over every inch of the M.T.B.'s eighty-five feet, the latter pointing out this and that he felt would be of immediate interest, but reserving his more personal observations until he found out with what sort of an officer he had to deal.

As he confided to the Petty Officer Motor Mechanic, "Pony" Moore, later in the morning over their "tots", 'You never know with these Wavy Navy types, some of 'em listen like babes while you try to stop them making fools of themselves, and the next thing you know you're on Defaulters 'cause you haven't done the job to their liking!'

'When will you learn, Tom, all officers are bastards,' was Moore's only comment.

Royce did find out, however, that the flotilla was engaged in assisting the two other main East Coast groups operating from Harwich and Yarmouth, with the result that their patrols were more varied and uncertain, and the whole base was kept on a mobile footing.

Eventually they arrived back at the tiny, open bridge. The Coxswain pointed to a speaker in one corner.

'That's our latest bit of gear, sir, an R.T. link between the group. It enables the Senior Officer to get right on to you at once about the form of attack, etc. It's a big help at night, I can tell you, 'specially when you can't use lights, and most likely can't even see the next ahead.'

'Have any of the boats got Radar yet?'

'Blimey, no, sir!' laughed Raikes, 'there's a queue from Pompey to Benghazi for that lot. The next war'll be over before we even get a smell!'

He suddenly tensed, 'C.O.'s coming aboard, sir, I'll be off after the guns' crews, the starboard Oerlikon is bloody bad!'

Harston stepped briskly on to the bridge. 'How's it going, Number One?' he drawled. 'All buttoned up?'

'Yes, sir,' said Royce coldly, 'I'm trying not to make an ass of myself.'

He received a searching glance. 'Take it off your back, Number One, we've all got to learn. Now shove off to the depot ship and get your issue of special clothing, and then report to the Flotilla Commander's office at eight bells. He likes to meet all his new boys. Before they make asses of themselves,' he added drily.

The office was situated in what had once been the Purser's room, and he was shown straight in to the presence of Lieut.-Commander Arnold Paskins, R.N.V.R., ex-author, yachtsman, and mountaineer, and now in command of the flotilla, with twenty skirmishes and two D.S.C.'s to his credit. He rose from his desk, littered with signals, serial photographs, and charts, a tall, lanky, but wiry figure, topped by a sharp-featured, well-formed, aristocratic face, with clear, steady eyes.

'Sit down, Royce,' he offered. 'I thought that it would be only fair for you to get to know as soon as possible the sort of job you've landed in. There's no other branch in the Service where so much responsibility falls on the most junior officers, chaps like yourself, who only a few months ago were at home doing respectable jobs, or going to school, or like me,' he grinned, 'just enjoying life. I've studied your reports and I'm satisfied with what I've read, so provided the Hun gives you time, there's no reason why you shouldn't make the grade. As you know, we're going out tonight, and if anything goes badly, you might find yourself in command by morning. Could you do it?' Those piercing eyes bored into him.

Royce thought to himself, "After this morning's episode, I think it would be comparatively simple!" But he could only answer: 'I'll do my best, sir.'

The interview was ended, and as he left the cabin, Paskins returned to the endless mass of the paper war.

* * * * *

The Operations Room in *Royston* was crowded and noisy as was usual before every sailing-time, and the chairs which were lined in front of the big wall-maps and charts were already filled with Commanding Officers and their "Number Ones", chatting, or shouting lustily to each other, or making notes and alterations on their own charts. Harston and Royce found a couple of chairs at the front, and having greeted everybody and settled down, the former pointed out the patrol areas on the big master chart. A hush fell on the gathering, and the officers rose to their feet as Commander Wright, Paskins, and an R.A.F. officer entered the room.

'Sit, gentlemen,' boomed Wright. 'You may smoke.'

There was renewed rustle of scraping matches, and clicking lighters, and when all were settled and the pipes were going well, Wright continued: 'This is the patrol area for tonight.' He pointed with a long cane. 'You will observe that at approximately midnight the local coastal convoy passes the main north-bound convoy about here, and as it shows every sign of being a dark and cloudy night, you can expect some trouble.'

15

The R.A.F officer was next. Royce discovered that he was the representative from Coastal Command who gave details of the local flying and air cover in the area. He had a dull, uninteresting voice, and as he droned on, Royce thought over the events of the day, and in spite of himself, he had to smile. The C.O. had been more than helpful and friendly all the afternoon, and had apparently forgotten the morning's clash of temperaments, and he now sat hunched forward on the edge of his chair, listening intently to everything the officer on the rostrum had to say, his face alight with boyish enthusiasm and keen understanding, apparently unaware that he had nearly caused Royce to lose faith in himself.

The Air Force officer sat down, and the irrepressible Commander Wright jumped to his feet. 'Any questions, gentlemen?'

One by one the various Commanding Officers rose and fired their queries. Weather report, enemy shipping movements, recognition signals, and a score of other details, which Royce and the other "second-hands" scribbled on their pads. Eventually the conference ended, and in groups they hurried back to the boats which now rode easily in the gentle swell, as if resting before their ordeal.

As Royce changed into his one-piece, waterproof "Ursula suit" he felt himself trembling with excitement, his mind awhirl with the instructions and taut with a determination to give his C.O. no new cause for complaint. There was nobody he could turn to for advice or guidance now, all that was behind him, this was it, the "front line", and right at that moment he would not have changed places with any other living creature, even considering the great overshadowing sinking feeling caused by fear. Fear of what? He couldn't be sure whether it was of death, or of not making the grade. He gave the zip-fasteners a final jerk, clapped on his cap, and stepped out on deck.

Harston leaned over the side of the bridge, having a shouted conversation with Artie Emberson in 1993, moored alongside. The latter waved a copy of the *Daily Mirror*.

'I see that some chappie in the House of Commons says

we are expendable, so we will have to keep our petrol engines, diesels are too expensive for us apparently. So in future, old man, when you burst into flames, remember, nobody loves you!'

Hartson grinned: 'I'd like to have had some of those perishers with me on the last trip, they might have learned what it's like to float about on top of a time-bomb!'

'Come, come,' drawled Emberson, 'you really mustn't be so bitter, don't you realize there's a war on?'

Harston's next remarks were drowned by a deafening roar, as Emberson's engines came to life, and Royce smelt the powerful fumes of the high-octane spirit, as smoke enveloped the boats, then the roar toned down to a steady pulsating throb as they ticked over confidently. Emberson wound a bright yellow scarf about his throat, and giving the thumbs-up sign to Harston, he turned away to make final preparations for sea.

'Right,' snapped Harston, as Royce appeared. 'Single up to springs and stand by to slip.' He smiled briefly: 'Old Artie's got the fastest boat in the flotilla, and won't let you forget it, but we'll show him when we get out.'

On the cramped fo'c'sle, Leading Seaman Parker, a tough, capable man in oilskin and thick leather gauntlets, was supervising the business of preparing the wires for a quick get-away, as he had done so often before, and he shot a steely glance at the new First Lieutenant as he came forward. Like the Coxswain, he wondered how the new boy would behave.

Royce returned the casual salute: 'You're Parker, I believe,' he said. 'Carry on and single up to springs, and stand by to slip.'

He was going to add that he wouldn't interfere with Parker's routine task, but at that moment he felt the boat shake, and with a series of coughs and snarls the main engines shook themselves awake. He had no idea that these frail craft would stand such a shaking, and he noted with some amusement that Parker's whole burly frame quivered like a jelly on a plate.

Parker waited until the engines settle to a steady rumble, then shouted: 'Is it right we're goin' to get a refit after this trip, sir?' His hoarse, Cockney voice easily drowned the din, and Royce was even able to appreciate the slightly anxious note in his tone.

'Worried, Parker?' laughed Royce, and the three other seamen who lounged against the guard rails, chuckled.

'I've been in this boat long enough to be bleedin' worried,' answered Parker defiantly, and spat over the side.

Royce coloured at this unexpected outburst, and saw the other seamen tense with expectancy.

'That's enough of that,' he barked, surprised at the sound of his own voice. 'You've obviously not been in it long enough to learn to control yourself, now just you stand by those wires!'

'Aye, aye, sir,' answered Parker heavily, and turned his angry eyes away.

Royce turned to the bridge, where the C.O. was peering through his glasses at the signal tower, furious with Parker, and himself. It was becoming more and more obvious to him that there was a great deal more to being an officer than just wearing the uniform. How could he show he wanted to learn, without appearing stupid, and how could he adopt Harston's easy manner with the crew if it only made him seem weak?

His jumbled thoughts were cut dead by the insistent winking of a powerful lamp from the tower, and Harston's terse orders.

'Let go springs, bear off forward,' and to the voice-pipe at his side: 'Slow ahead together. Starboard ten.'

As Royce watched, the greasy wires were released by the depot ship hands and splashed briefly into the water, from where they were eagerly snatched, before they could wrap themselves around the churning screws, and with a quickening vibration at his feet, the boat swung away from her moorings in a wide arc, to take her place at fifth in the line of the eight boats which were all manoeuvring into an orderly procession heading for the boom-gate. Lieut.-Commander Paskins, the Senior Officer, led in his newly-painted craft, her bold 2001 shining in the setting sun. Royce could see him scanning the flotilla through his glasses, and felt vaguely reassured by his presence.

As he returned to the bridge, and reported that the boat was fully secure for sea, the R-T speaker crackled into life.

'Hallo all Captains, this is Leader calling. Keep close station on me, and watch for convoy recognition signals round about midnight. No moon tonight, so don't creep on to my quarter-deck!'

The speaker popped and went dead. Harston grinned, he seemed more at east now that he was at sea again.

'What a useful gadget, much better than the lamp. The blessed signalman always gets excited in action anyway, and squirts the signals all over the place!'

The boats slid over the full but gentle swell, into a glorious blood-red sunset, that painted the glittering waters with a million rich and changing hues, and as it grew darker, the boats became dull, uneven blobs on this heaving travesty of colour.

'I'm going to get a couple of hours shut-eye now,' said Harston. 'That'll give you time to get the feel of her, and I'll be fresh later on when I'm needed.' He smiled: 'Alright, Number One, she's all yours.' And suddenly the bridge was a lonely place.

Royce peered over the darkening fo'c'sle, where the pom-pom crew, in their bulky clothing, hunched around the gun, and away over the bows, at the twisting stern of Emberson's boat, and the white froth which seemed to link all the boats together.

From out of space, a tinny voice rattled: 'Able Seaman Lewis relieving on the wheel, sir.' Royce groped his way to the now invisible voice-pipe, and acknowledged the message. That meant that the reliable Coxswain had left the wheel and handed over to the usual Quartermaster.

'Cocoa, sir?' a youthful murmur at his elbow steadied the wave of nerves which threatened to make him recall the Captain to his aid, and the signalman, Mead, a slender, seventeen-year-old who had joined the boat only a month before, thrust a steaming mug towards him. Royce drank gratefully, and felt the thick chocolate radiating through his whole body.

'I needed that, "Bunts",' he smiled. 'You're new here too, aren't you?'

'Yes, sir, finished my training last month, and came straight here. I had hoped for a chance to get a commission, but I suppose nobody thought I was the right type,' he grinned ruefully.

Royce, determined to make a success of this encounter, reassured him hastily, and was on the point of promising to take the matter up, when he happened to look ahead again, and with a sickening shock, realized that Emberson's boat had vanished from view. With a hasty glance at the compass, which told him that they were on the correct course, he yelled down the voice-pipe:

'Full ahead together, and watch your course!'

To the horrified Mead he barked: 'Make to the next astern. Increase speed and keep station on me.'

Even as the lamp began to clatter, the boat leapt forward with staggering force, throwing up twin banks of foam from either bow, as the high-speed hull lifted from the water like a dolphin. He peered out ahead into the darkness, straining his eyes, and sweating with fear. If he lost the rest of the flotilla on his first trip out, Harston would definitely get rid of him. Damn the cocoa, and the signalman, if only he had . . . a frantic shout came from the pom-pom.

'Boat dead ahead. Dead ahead!'

And there it was, fine on the port bow, with the distance shortening at an alarming rate. His head was suddenly clear, and he felt strangely resigned.

'Hard a-starboard. Stop. Full astern together.'

The boat reeled round to starboard, and the engines screamed in protest. Vaguely from below he heard the crash of breaking crockery, but still they rushed on, until every detail was visible on the other boat. Then, when a crash seemed inevitable, the engines began to tell, and with maddening slowness she slewed round and glided up along the other boat's starboard quarter.

Saved! He licked his lips, now trembling. 'Slow ahead together, Quartermaster, resume previous station.'

Emberson's loud-hailer clicked on: 'Mother, there's someone at the back door!'

Royce waved to him with relief, and watched anxiously as the other boats astern sorted themselves out and resumed patrol in an orderly line.

He was then aware of Harston's dark figure below the bridge, and he stiffened for the onslaught.

Instead: 'Well done, nothing like livening things up a bit!' and he was gone.

When the Captain returned to the bridge, just before midnight he found the new Number One with his eyes glued to the next ahead, his lesson learned. He smiled to himself, it would not do for Royce to know that the Coxswain had shaken him awake to inform him that the new officer was rushing at full speed into the rest of the flotilla, apparently out of control!

In the far distance, a pinpoint of light stabbed at the blackness, and the Senior Officer replied to the challenge, which had come from one of the convoy's escorts, and the next instant the slowly moving merchant ships were looming past. Coasters, oil tankers, freighters, and all the rest, huge, and yet so helpless, and dependent on the anxious escorts which dashed backwards and forwards around the convoy like ferrets smelling out a rabbit.

Harston jerked his head in their direction. 'Rather them than me. Look at those blessed escorts. One destroyer, vintage about 1917, two converted trawlers. It makes you sick; you've got your politicians to thank for this state of affairs.'

In a few moments, the convoy was swallowed up by the night, and the anxious business of station-keeping began again, but now Harston remained on the bridge, which was now whipped by a keen breeze that removed all traces of drowsiness from the watchkeepers, and with an unlit pipe clenched between his teeth, he constantly swept the starboard beam through his night glasses.

'Not much to worry about with that little convoy,' he observed. 'It's the big northbound we've got to watch out for. They break up the convoy here to take it through the swept channel, and the E-boats sometimes have a go for the stragglers.' Then he stiffened. 'Ah, there she is, right on time.'

And there was another light flashing, far away on the starboard bow, and soon the familiar, hulking shapes of the groping merchantmen were gliding past, their empty hulls rising like giant forts, and their half-exposed screws churning white patches of froth against the inky back-cloth. Again the escorts raced back and forth, through their cumbersome charges, but a stronger guard this time, two destroyers, and some corvettes—taking no chances.

Ship after ship rolled past, till Royce lost count, and then, with a final protesting hiss of steam from an ancient freighter, they too were gone.

The flotilla swung about to steer north-east, the "top leg" of the patrol area, slackening speed over the dark swell, so that their engines just seemed to be ticking over, and it was again possible to talk without shouting above the din.

Harston rested his chin on folded arms, as he leaned across the screen. 'Sorry you joined, Number One?' he grinned.

The other looked up quickly from the dimly-lit compass. 'I guess I'll be alright,' he said thoughtfully. 'I must say I wish I had the knack of being fierce enough to get things done without worrying about their feelings.' He nodded towards the huddled gun's crew. 'It's difficult to get people to look up to you without giving them the impression that you're looking down on them, if you follow me,' he finished lamely.

'Heavens, what a complicated mind you've got.' The muffled figure shook with soft laughter. 'But I think I know what you mean; it happens to all of us at first. Take my advice, don't try to be too definite in your ideas until you've got to know the lads as individuals, you'll be right on top line then.'

They lapsed into contented silence as a can of hot, sweet tea was heaved on to the bridge, the scalding liquid running through Royce like a fresh confidence.

One of the bridge lookouts lowered his glasses. 'Leader's turning, sir, comin' back down the line.'

Paskins' boat cruised slowly down the line and as he came abreast of them, he shouted through his megaphone, 'We'll stop here for a bit, in case Jerry's sending anyone across to intercept the convoy.' And as he raced back to the head of his flotilla, the boats cut their engines, and rolled uneasily in the freshening breeze. With legs braced, the two officers stood back to back with their glasses trained into the blackness, Royce noting with sympathy the dismal retching of the young signalman as he fought his private battle with the sea.

Half an hour passed. Their eyes smarted, their bodies ached with the constant readjustment to the irregular pitching of the slender hull, and only Harston seemed cheerful and alert. Without warning, a bright orange flash lit the horizon, and seconds later a dull boom echoed across the water, yet before it had died away, the R-T speaker crackled into life.

'Leader calling. General chase!'

Harston's orders jerked Royce back to reality. 'Full ahead, steer due West.'

All round, the eager engines coughed and roared to life, and with a mighty flurry of foam they were off, their graceful high-speed hulls surging and leaping over the steep, little waves towards the distant fire which slowly ebbed and then died, as if extinguished by a giant hand. Emberson's boat was well out ahead of the pack, throwing up two solid sheets of spray as she tore into the night like a grey avenger.

Royce scrambled down to the pom-pom platform on the bucking fo'c'sle, as the gunners stripped off the spray shields, and trained their weapon round. His heart thumped madly, and he felt the sour taste of vomit forming in his throat, the icy fingers of real fear clutched at his inside, until he felt his head reeling. With an effort he steadied himself against the rail, and then noticed that Leading Seaman Parker was the gunlayer, his face hard and set, his large, red hands controlling his gun with ease

23

and practice. For a moment their eyes met, and Parker's heavy face twisted into a grin. 'Now d'you see why I want a bloody refit?' he yelled, and Royce found himself laughing crazily in return, his voice sounded unnatural too, as he called back, 'I'll need one myself after this!'

He found himself falling through space as the boat rolled to her beam, the tiller hard over, but Parker's vice-like grip pulled him up with a jerk, and as if in a dream he caught a brief glimpse of a lump of wreckage in the water that Harston had narrowly avoided, and two up-turned white faces that were immediately lost in their boiling wake. As they swung back on course, they caught up with the rear ships of the convoy, and Royce had many blurred impressions of gleaming black hulls and rusty plates skimming past within feet of his touch. A destroyer was firing rapidly across the head of the columns at a twisting, silver-grey shape brilliantly framed by a well-placed star shell.

'E-boat, Green one-one-oh!' yelled the rating wearing the head-set, and the pom-pom swung round farther still, but the target was blotted out by a madly zig-zagging tanker, which broke away from the neat line of ships.

'For Christ's sake, what's he doing?' cursed Parker, and as if in answer, a fresh explosion rent the night in two, and a blinding flash lit up the stricken tanker's bridge and rigging like a hideous monument, and a searing pain shot through Royce's eyeballs, as he cringed from the shock. Already the ship was rolling in her death agony, and in the light of the fires on board they could clearly see small, pathetic figures scrambling down the sloping decks. As they crossed her bows they saw the killer turning towards them, the long, low shape gleaming in the flickering light from the tanker. With a deafening rattle the starboard Oerlikon opened fire, the red tracer clawing over the rapidly shortening range, then the heavy thud, thud, thud of the pom-pom joined in, as the two boats closed each other. Then Royce saw the green tracer climbing, apparently lazily, from the E-boat's guns, and pitching down straight for him. He felt a sudden, hot breath on his cheek, and heard the clang of metal behind him, while somewhere on the bridge he heard Harston's cool voice shout: 'Watch your steering, Coxswain, there's another ship dead ahead!'

At the swing of the wheel, the M.T.B. swerved again across the path of the E-boat, the range dropping to twenty yards, before another looming merchantman hid the E-boat from view. In the distance, they saw Emberson's boat take up the chase, and the tracers intermingled in a fresh, deadly pattern, as the German captain twisted and turned in desperation to break off the action. Yet another M.T.B. burst out of the convoy and opened fire immediately, and in the concentrated cross-fire, they saw the enemy stagger and lose speed as small orange flashes rippled across her bridge and decks, and pieces of the hull broke away as the cannon shells struck home. Without warning the E-boat ploughed to a stop, and burst into flames, burning petrol spewing out of her like life-blood. Within seconds she flopped on to her side, and with a searing hiss slid under the surface. The silence which followed seemed to burst the eardrums, and even the racing engines appeared quieter. Shakily Royce drew his glove across his cold, wet face, gulping in the keen air to rid his throat of the tang of cordite and fire.

'Alright, sir?'

He was aware of Parker peering at him through the gloom, a look of concern on his large face. He nodded shakily, feeling incapable of speech, and only dimly conscious of his surroundings.

Parker rounded on his gun's crew who were watching Royce with interest. 'Come on you lazy lot!' he bawled. 'There may be some more of the perishers about yet, so don't look so ruddy cocky!'

The pale blob of Harston's head appeared over the bridge screen. 'Very nice shooting,' he called. 'You can secure now and get rid of the empties; Jerry has broken off the action. Come on to the bridge, Number One.'

As Royce clambered over the glittering shell cases to the ladder, he forced himself to think straight, and to try to piece together the violent events of this unreal and nightmarish encounter with the enemy, and immediately his mind was assailed with fresh doubts as to his competence in such a terrible situation.

Making a great effort to keep his voice steady, he nodded in the direction of the convoy, 'What happens now, sir? Do we stick with them, or press on after the E-boats?'

Harston was studying him keenly. 'Well, I'm happy to say, neither. They'll be quite safe now, and Jerry got a bloody nose. One E-boat sunk by that lucky old lawyer, Artie, and the destroyer mauled another. Pity about those two ships,' he added, 'but at least they were empty, except for their crews, and God only knows where they are now, poor devils. There are a couple of trawlers looking for them.'

He glanced up at a pinpoint of light ahead, and focussed his glasses. After a moment he turned, his face suddenly tired. 'Make a signal with the lamp to the next astern, "Resume formation". We're returning to base.'

Royce forced a smile. 'Bunts still seasick?'

Harston stared at him for several seconds before replying, then waved vaguely to the darkened corner of the bridge. 'Afraid he's bought it,' he said harshly.

Royce lurched over to the small figure sitting awkwardly against the signal locker, and knelt down at his side. The young signalman's legs were sticking straight out in front of him, his hands still clutching his Aldis lamp against the oversized duffle coat. His face was thrown back, and the fair, curly hair rippled gently in the cold breeze, as the glazing blue eyes stared up at the scudding clouds, as if amazed at what he saw. Through the thin plating at his back was a small, round hole.

Royce, suddenly ice-cold, choked back the lump in his throat, very gently prized the lamp from the stiff, chilled hands, and blindly triggered the signal to the dark shape astern.

As the flotilla reformed into line, Harston swore softly out to sea. 'Damn them to hell! He was just telling me that he wasn't afraid!'

He pounded his fist on the rail, then seemed to go limp. 'You did well, Number One, but don't ever worry about

26

being afraid, the man who says he isn't is either a liar, or a bloody lunatic!'

The Coxswain stepped out of the darkness and touched his cap. 'Everything's secure below, no damage,' he reported. 'I'll get a couple of the lads to give me a hand with young Mead here.' He fumbled under his oilskin, and produced a bottle and two enamel mugs. 'I brought you a couple of tots of neaters, sir. I reckon you can do with it up here.'

Harston downed his rum with one gulp, and walked stiffly to the compass. 'I'm going below to write my report, Number One. It saves a bit of time when we get in. Do you think you can handle her now?'

Royce nodded.

'Call me when you sight Outer Spit buoy, that'll be about 0500.'

He paused as he passed to the bridge ladder. 'It's all so bloody futile, isn't it?' and then he was gone.

Royce checked the course, and leaned against the screen, his chin pillowed on his hands, suddenly desperately tired and cold, his face stiff with salt spray, and the towel wrapped around his neck soggy and raw against the skin. On and on thundered the boats, and still he stood as if in a trance, only once stiffening when he heard the Coxswain supervising the removal of Mead's body, his watchkeeping companion of how long ago? Only four hours, it seemed like a lifetime.

Far ahead he saw the steely grey fingers of the dawn creeping almost cautiously across the horizon, and the dim shapes of the other boats took on a hard realism. Up and down the weaving line, red-rimmed eyes peered out for friends, and weary, muffled figures waved and sighed with relief. As far as Royce could see, Emberson's boat was the only one with visible damage. A line of holes above the waterline, and one larger gash in the deck just aft of the port torpedo tube, not too bad, in fact.

'Outer Spit buoy on the starboard bow,' reported the lookout, and Royce peered at his watch, 0445.

He leaned to the Captain's speaking tube. 'Captain, sir,' he called. 'In position, Outer Spit ahead.'

27

Harston joined him, and silently, side by side, they stood and watched the landmarks taking shape in the growing light. First the dull hills at the back of the port, then, more sharply defined, the long, low harbour walls, the boom-gate, now open to receive them, and a couple of outward-bound trawlers, jauntily thrusting their blunt bows into the choppy sea, their spindly funnels belching smoke, their tattered ensigns fluttering defiantly as any cruiser. The hands fell in for entering harbour, silently this time, only dimly aware of their surroundings, and only thinking of sleep, the sailor's cure for everything.

Through the harbour mouth, and up the stream, past the heavy cruiser *Leviathan*. On the cold morning air they heard the shrill notes of a bugle sounding Reveille, "Wakey, wakey, lash up and stow," and as they threaded their way between the moored vessels, unnoticed, except by the vigilant signal tower, the anchorage roused itself for another day.

First to the petrol jetty to take on fuel, then, while the other boats made for the depot ship, they pulled over to the railway wharf, where Royce saw a khaki ambulance waiting to take young Mead on his last trip. They watched it drive away, then slipped once more, and in the harsh, bright morning sunlight they tied up alongside the *Royston*'s catwalk. Seven o'clock exactly.

The depot ship's maintenance men, wide awake and freshly shaved, hurried aboard and went to work. Royce dismissed the hands and sleepily watched them scramble up the steep side and disappear. Then, together, the two officers went over the main gangway, where Harston handed his brief, scribbled report to a messenger, and they were confronted by Artie Emberson, his reddened face creased into a smile. He slapped two hands on Harston's shoulders, and pulled him towards him.

'So you're still here, you old devil, and I thought I'd be able to have your breakfast this morning!' But his obvious relief shone in his eyes.

Breakfast was a hurried, silent meal, as the grubby officers mechanically warmed their chilled insides with the carefully prepared food, and then, with a tired smile here, and a pat on the shoulder there, they dragged themselves to the sane, quiet privacy of the little cabins. As Royce closed his door behind him, he caught a glimpse of himself in the mirror and was shocked at the grey, lined and suddenly aged face which stared back at him. He didn't remember undressing, or dabbing his sore skin with the steaming water, he just managed to heave his body between the gentle sheets and switch off the light, and the next instant he was safe from the sea, from patrols, and from himself.

2

IN the months that followed, the war at sea, as far as Royce was concerned, pursued a regular, wearying pattern. Night after night they patrolled their scattered areas of the North Sea, covering the vital convoys which crept up and down the East Coast, and sometimes there was the variation of the hit-and-run dash across to the mud flats of the Dutch coast in search of the enemy's supply ships. Like the men who manned them, the little ships knew every stress and strain as the momentum of war quickened, and the carefully-laid rules were overlooked or savagely broken. Often in foul weather, and always at faster speeds than their engines were expected to tolerate, they pushed into the night, their wooden hulls twisting and bucking, while the cold North Sea winds moaned through every crack and crevice, making the watch below groan, and clutch their damp blankets closer to their chilled bodies. On watch, these men fought against sleep, and off watch, rest was denied them by the cold nights, and the uneven motion of the mess-decks, which took every opportunity to bombard them with crockery, wet clothing, and the ever-penetrating sea water, which slopped about them, and made their lives a misery. Even the prayed-for refits became scarcer and shorter, as the cry went out for more ships, and more men. In the middle of these confused circumstances, Royce grew up, and became a useful and efficient member of their little world which was cut off from the rest of the fleet, and, in fact, from any other way of life. He now knew the life history of every member of the crew, their likes and dislikes, and their weaknesses. Their hopes and fears he shared.

It was not, as he repeatedly told himself, quite as they had said it would be when he left the training establishment at Hove. Apart from that breath-taking encounter on his first patrol, he had not caught even a smell of the enemy. His war so far had mainly been against the weather, plus a steadily mounting struggle with the boat's technical and domestic affairs, of which the latter was becoming rather out of hand. It was, as far as he could see, a case of a good crew overworked and pushed to breaking-point, with little prospect of improvement. His opposite numbers in the flotilla assured him that all would be well in action, but as that seemed a cruel justice to him, he painstaking carried out his duties ashore and afloat, in a great effort to avoid a queue of defaulters at the Captain's table, or the miserable collection of leave-breakers and deserters, which some First Lieutenants were having to contend with. The result, although not startling, was gratifying, and was not unnoticed by Harston, who left more and more tasks to his assistant, in the safe knowledge that they would be carefully and intelligently carried out, without the fear of an aftermath of furious signals from base, or disgruntled comments from the Coxswain. The other result was that Royce's social life was now at a standstill. With the exception of brief visits to a giant Nissen hut in the harbour limits, lavishly called the Officers' Club, he had confined his activities to the depot ship. With these thoughts in mind, he sat in his cabin half-heartedly concocting a letter to his parents. He found it difficult to write in a matter-of-fact way that would please his mother, and yet find suitable information about the war, of which he knew little, for the sake of his invalid father, who was, in his own way, a keen strategist. In addition, he knew that any one of these letters might well be his last. Both the other East Coast groups had been encountering heavy opposition of late, and it seemed likely that their turn would come again soon.

He finished the letter with a flourish, and a sigh, and reached for his pipe. At that moment, the door slid open, and Harston and Artie Emberson were framed in the light.

'Well, well, well,' drawled the latter, 'so this is where your little slave hangs out!' He surveyed the spartan cabin, which resembled all the others in the ship to an exact degree.

'Hmm, most tastefully furnished too. As you have stated, John, this is a very adaptable lad.'

Harston grinned. 'Sorry to upset your solitude, Number One, but you'll doubtless be horrified to know that S.O.O. has granted the flotilla a night in harbour. Apparently they want the whole area cleared of small fry so that our larger friends can get in some sea time!'

Emberson interrupted. 'And as the junior partner, we thought you might be interested in having your education extended by a run ashore to the old White Hart with us. You like?'

Royce was already buttoning his jacket, and searching for his respirator. 'Thanks very much; two pieces of good news in one evening is more than I can resist.'

Emberson winked. 'Not only a keen lad, but eager!'

The White Hart was situated half-way along the port's High Street, between the food office and a musty-looking restaurant, its high, ornate façade giving the appearance of vulgar opulence amongst the other neglected and weatherbeaten buildings. As the three officers pushed open the swing doors and fumbled through the heavy blackout curtains, the brassy, cheerful noise, coupled with the mixed aromas of beer and tobacco, overwhelmed them. The evening was young, but already the bar was half filled with early drinkers, mostly naval officers from the local flotillas, with a pale blue sprinkling of the Air Force Coastal Command base nearby. Here and there, in the odd corners of the vast lounge, were the seemingly misplaced regular customers, their dowdy suits making a sharp contrast with the uniforms. They too were mixed, either elderly, sitting quietly with their friends and watching the young sailors' friendly horseplay, or young and loud-mouthed, the product of the port's reserved occupations. These latter were usually overpaid and, therefore, overconfident of their new surroundings.

The long bar of dark wood, shiny with bright lights and spilt beer, was ably controlled and easily dominated by a cheerful barmaid of supreme proportions, who scurried to and fro with pots and glasses, her plump face split into a permanent grin, and her speedy service punctuated with giggles and nods to her thirsty court, and a hurried, 'Sorry, love, no spirits', to any strange face which hovered near her domain. The landlord, a rotund and grizzled little man, in a shabby tweed suit, remained at the end of the counter, passing the time with his cronies, and keeping a watchful eye on the busy scene.

Emberson shouldered his way through the crowd. 'Ah, Grace, my beloved,' he called, 'could my friends and I have three large pints, and three halves of your very best cider.'

Grace beamed. 'Oo, sir, I thought you'd be out tonight, what a nice surpise.'

'So much for security,' said Emberson, with mock sadness.

Royce eased his way through the crush, and plucked at his sleeve. 'I don't like cider, thanks, the beer'll do.'

'Shurrup, nitwit!' hissed Emberson. 'It's Scotch! What do you want to do, start a riot in here?'

They found a small table, conveniently abandoned by the R.A.F., and sat back, stretching luxuriously.

Harston drank deeply. 'The friendliest joint in the town,' he smiled, 'and with Artie's influence over the queen there, we are more or less well in for the duration.'

'Dear me,' replied the lawyer. 'A most unfortunate expression. When will you realize that my feelings for the wee Grace are just platonic.' He regarded Harston solemnly. 'You, sir, have no soul. How can you keep the respect of young Clive here, if you can't learn to moderate your approach to the fair sex.'

Royce relaxed in his chair, enjoying the wrangling of his companions, and feeling for the first time accepted into the close fraternity which he had chosen a year? a lifetime ago.

The evening wore on, and the bar filled to its uproarious capacity, while from the radio Vera Lynn did her best to comfort the nation's young men elsewhere. Here in the White Hart her efforts seemed wasted. Royce's mind swam happily, and he seemed vaguely unable to prevent his face from slipping into a vast smile of good fellowship. His detached thoughts were shattered by a mighty slap on the shoulder which made him cannon into the table, nearly causing a disaster.

Benjy Watson's shiny pink face floated over them, and behind him two other officers of the flotilla struggled manfully with a large parcel.

'My dear old soaks!' he boomed. 'I've had the most ghastly night; these two dreadful characters have been leading me astray.' He silenced their protests with a wave of a huge fist. 'You know I wanted the "Save for Victory" banner from the post office to go round my bridge? Well, these silly baskets got me so flustered, I got the wrong one. It's all about a Dog Show! I ask you, a Dog Show! I haven't got a dog!' He pulled a bottle from one jacket pocket, and a glass from the other, while the others howled with laughter at this latest crazy episode.

'You lunatic!' roared Harston. 'No wonder we're always at sea, this town isn't safe from you!'

With the arrival of the irrepressible Watson and his accomplices, the quiet party was shattered, and Royce's sides ached, as he found himself caught up in an act that would have made a small fortune on any variety stage.

The lights had just been dimmed to herald "Last Orders"—shouted announcements would have been useless, when the curtains parted, and above the milling bodies, a blue steel helmet, with the word "Police" painted on the front, could be seen making its way to the bar.

Benjy's jaw dropped, and a look of complete horror crossed his face.

'Christ! I've been rumbled at last, and caught with the loot too!'

He wheeled rapidly to his grinning companions. 'Don't stand there like a shower of silly oafs, get rid of that banner, and let's get out of here!'

As one man they downed their drinks, the parcel skidded beneath the legs of two startled airmen, and in a compact, if unsteady, body they forced their way to the doors. Even as they reached the curtains the policeman yelled out above the din, 'An air-raid warning has just been sounded, so be careful you don't show any lights when you leave.'

Benjy was hustled protesting up the street.

'But what about my banner?' he implored. 'All that trouble for nothing. I'll do that silly copper if I ever see him again.'

Harston chuckled. 'Time for bed, little man, it definitely was not your day for carrying the banner.'

Still laughing, they arrived at the barbed-wire enclosure of the harbour area, and automatically straightened themselves as they produced their identity cards to the weary sentries. Benjy was still muttering and bewailing his loss when they reached the windswept pier, and only when they split up and went to their cabins on the depot ship did he start to smile.

'You just wait, I'll get you something really worthwhile next time,' he promised.

Royce was past caring. He was happy, and the Navy was just too wonderful for words.

❋   ❋   ❋   ❋   ❋

The flotilla swept gaily through the boom-gate, weaving and dipping in the easy swell, as they picked up their stations on the Leader. A keen breeze swept over the tiny bridge of M.T.B. 1991, as Royce listened to the hands in the various parts of the boat reporting that they were 'Closed up to exercise action', the normal practice when leaving harbour, to ensure that all sections were working correctly. As the last reported, 'Port Oerlikon closed up, sir,' Royce informed the Captain that all was well.

Harston hardly seemed to notice, he was visibly excited, and in fact, new life seemed to have crept into the whole crew, as this was not just another patrol, not another aimless battle with the weather. The sweep by the destroyers on the previous night had broken up three enemy convoys off the Dutch coast, and the R.A.F. had reported that they were making an effort to reform and press on up the coast, doubtless loaded with vital supplies for the armies in Denmark and Norway, and for the German Baltic fleet. The flotilla's job was to intercept and destroy the rearmost convoy. All morning they had laboured with the maintenance staff to get everything in first-rate order, and extra care had been taken as the long, evil-looking torpedoes had been greased and slid into the tubes on either side of the boat, and now, as the low coastline was swallowed up in the dusk astern of them, they all knew that this was to be another supreme test of their skill in the handicraft of war.

'Defence stations now,' said Harston, 'and make sure everyone gets a good whack of food during the next two hours. And we'll get some corned beef sandwiches laid on for the return journey too. I think they'll have earned it by then.'

Harston went below for his customary cat-nap, and half of the crew followed his example, in order that they could be fed in two watches. No longer did Royce tremble at the loneliness of the bridge, in fact, he enjoyed the feeling of complete power that he had over the lithe, trembling hull beneath his feet. As Harston had told him that first day, he now knew the difference between a trawler and this three and a half thousand horsepowered killer.

On and on they went, and as the sky darkened they met a solitary destroyer on patrol, creeping along like a great grey shadow, in the hopes of surprising a raider, or assisting some convoy straggler.

The new signalman, Collins, a stolid north-countryman, turned his head, 'Signal sir, from destroyer, "Should you be out alone so late?" Any reply, sir?'

'Make, "If we had been E-boats, we'd have been picking you out of the drink by now"!' snapped Royce.

There was a chuckle, as the lamp clattered away in the corner of the bridge.

'No answer, sir.'

An hour later they were reinforced by a strong flotilla of Motor Gunboats from Harwich, the "pocket battle-ships" of Coastal Forces. Their purpose was to cover the withdrawal after the attack had been pressed home. Signals flashed, and the boats jockeyed to and fro, until the M.T.B.s had formed into two parallel lines ahead, with the M.G.B.s three miles astern, then silence enveloped the flotilla, and no more signals were made or required, as each captain knew what was expected; it was all just a matter of time. The mighty engines purred obediently as they were throttled down to a minimum speed, and the tiny ships crept stealthily forward, searching, probing. Royce swung his night-glasses in a wide arc, and decided it was time to call the Captain, and seconds later Harston climbed up beside him, fresh and apparently unworried. He took in the situation at a glance. His boat led the starboard column, and Paskins in the leader, led the port column at a distance of about a thousand yards.

'Action Stations,' he said quietly, and Royce pressed the button that had called sailors from their rest, and to their deaths, the world over.

Even before the bells stopped ringing, the last man heaved himself into his allotted space, which, for the next few hours at least, would probably decide the fate of the whole boat. The slim barrels of the Oerlikons, and the menacing muzzles of the pom-poms swung back and forth through their maximum arcs, as the crews tested them, and reported automatically to the bridge. The steel hatches clanged shut over the engine room, imprisoning the mechanics in what was at best a shaking, roaring helter-skelter of noise and fumes, and at worst a blazing hell from which there could be little chance of escape.

'If we can pull this off all right tonight, Number One, I think we can get that refit you want so badly, plus a bit of leave, of course.'

'That'd be really something, sir,' replied Royce feelingly, for he knew that the boat's maintenance was becoming a little bit out of hand. A good slipway in the dockyard was what she required now.

At the prospect of leave, they lowered their glasses and grinned at each other like schoolboys. Royce had long ago decided that Harston should have a rest from active service for a bit.

'Enemy coast ahead!' sang out the bridge lookouts together, and as they peered across the dark, oily water, they could make out only vaguely the black finger of land

38

which was the start of the low-lying mudflats which abounded in these waters.

For another half-hour the boats felt their way forward, but no convoy steamed out to greet them, no targets loomed before the gaping torpedo tubes, and the tension on the decks could be felt. Here a man rubbed his eyes savagely, and stared again into the sombre blackness, and there another cursed his mate softly as their bodies touched on the gently rolling gun-platform.

Royce was not the least affected, and he felt a childish rage consuming him, causing him to rebuke the signalman for lowering his glasses for a few seconds.

'Those damned airmen have made a mistake,' he muttered. 'There's no convoy, and if there was, they slipped out this morning, blast them!'

'That'll do, Number One!' The voice was mild, almost disinterested.

Royce swore again under his breath, and peered over towards the Leader's blurred shape on the port beam, and then he saw a shaded signal lamp blinking astern: he must be worried too, to use a lamp so close to the enemy coast.

'Leader's signalled supportin' gunboats to sweep to the south-east, and to report if there's anything at that end of the coast,' reported Collins. His voice sounded doubtful.

Still Harston seemed unsurprised and apparently preoccupied with his own thoughts. Royce could faintly make out his outline in the front of the bridge, leaning across the screen on his folded arms, an unlit pipe clenched between his teeth, which suddenly gleamed white in the gloom as he smiled.

'Number One,' he spoke softly so that the lookouts and signalman should not hear. 'Don't let this sort of thing get you down; this war's like a great, stupid puzzle. If we work like hell, and have lots of actions, the boats crack up, and we need boats, more and more of them. If we don't get a shot at anything, and have month in and month out of peaceful but damned monotonous patrols, then it's the crews who go round the bend. You just can't please anybody.'

He paused and studied his First Lieutenant's gloved hand as it pounded the rail, softly yet viciously, in a steady rhythm.

'It's not that I'm a crack-brained, death-or-glory character, or that I don't realize that ninety-nine per cent of finding and knocking seven bells out of Jerry is just plain luck,' explained Royce, the words tumbling out of him. 'It's just this constant waiting, and not knowing.' His voice trailed away, and he shrugged his shoulders helplessly.

Harston moved swiftly across the bridge, with his quick, cat-like step and gripped his sleeve urgently, pulling him close to his pale face. When he spoke again, his tone was strange, quite unlike anything Royce had heard from him before, almost fanatical.

'Never, never feel that you're wasting your time. Everything we do helps to tie them down, even when we're not killing them! That's why I rode you hard when you were sent to me, war is a hard business. Now you've made the grade, our grade, otherwise I wouldn't be telling you this.' Here he paused and waved his arm towards the hidden coast, and when he continued, he spoke slowly as if spelling out the words: 'But I hate those bastards more than any other crawling creature on this earth. I've seen what they can do, have done, and'll keep on doing until we——'

He broke away with a jerk, as a dull boom and blue flash lit the slowly cruising clouds. Immediately the R-T speaker crackled into life: 'Leader calling, the M.G.B.s have struck oil, maximum speed!'

The night split open as the engines roared into life, and Royce saw their own bow lift before him, as all boats raced off in perfect twin lines, throwing up the great, curving streams, their stems slicing through the water. He flung himself down the ladder to the gun platform, with a brief impression of Harston hanging over the bucking torpedo sighting mechanism. He seemed to be laughing.

Now the sky was criss-crossed with tracers, and a small fire blossomed into a full, orange glow, showing a small ship burning and listing on to her side. As they closed the battle, they saw the M.G.B.s circling four trawlers, firing rapidly, and even as they watched, another of them burst into flames, throwing up a fountain of sparks.

Harston leaned over the screen, beckoning urgently, and as Royce climbed up, he shook his fists wildly. 'For Christ's sake, what are those fools doing? Look at them! They've broken formation, and for what?' His voice rose almost to a scream. 'Four bloody trawlers! There's your convoy, Number One! Are you satisfied? No? Well *they* apparently are!'

Royce was dumbfounded. 'But I don't see——'

'Do you want me to spell it for you? They are a decoy! A decoy, and our so-called escorts fell for it, and now we're in the trap!'

Royce's heart went cold as he realized the implication of this new menace, and tried to force his mind to function, but he seemed numb, until Harston seized his arm roughly.

'Get aft and stand by to jettison smoke floats, and get ready for some fancy shooting.'

Paskins too fully realized their position, and unless he acted promptly, there was nothing to prevent the hunters becoming the hunted. Frantically he signalled the jubilant gunboats to reform and cease fire, and then formed the torpedo boats into one line, his own boat leading, and Harston's now fifth, with Emberson following in the rear. There was only one thing to do now, get out into the open sea as soon as possible.

It was at the very moment of decision, even as the boats began to move off, that the trap was sprung.

There was a sullen detonation astern of the flotillas, and many thought that it was a trawler blowing up, but doubts were short, as a star shell burst with savage brilliance in the sky at their backs. In a split second the night became day, as they were silhouetted and sharply defined to anything that lay ahead. Blinded, the gunners hugged their weapons, a lifetime passed, in fact four more seconds,

41

then the black wall ahead of them flamed into life, a mad, whirling cone of red and white tracer shells, that screamed overhead and hissed into the churning waters around them, with such a crescendo of noise that they were stunned. Two second, later, Paskin's boat reached the maelstrom, and was ablaze from stem to stern, sharp little flames licking out of the bridge superstructure joined those which were eagerly consuming the upper deck. There were two sickening explosions which shattered the craft into a hundred sections, and sent flaming wreckage whirling skywards, and she was gone! Before they could recover from this awful spectacle, they were all in it, twisting and turning to avoid the probing, searching avalanche of fire which flew about their ears! Royce sent the smoke floats thudding into the sea, and soon a pall of smoke would be forming to provide cover or confusion for friend and foe alike. He scrambled to the gun platform, as the twin pom-poms groped blindly for a target, his head splitting with the crash and rattle of the enemy salvoes. Then, for the first time, they all saw their hunters, for the sea seemed full of them. E-boats, their long, dark hulls gleaming with spray as they tore down towards them, and astern of them were half a dozen armed trawlers, not in the accepted sense, but floating gun batteries, protected by steel plates and huge blocks of concrete, behind which the German gunners fired and reloaded as fast as a combination of training and hatred would allow.

'Open fire, first trawler!' yelled Royce, and the pom-poms joined in the tattoo with a steady bang-bang-bang, their twin tracers lifting and dropping towards the hunched, menacing shape of the trawler. The range closed rapidly, five hundred yards, two hundred, one hundred, until they saw their shells rippling along her sides. The Oerlikons and machine-guns added their ear-shattering rattle, as if in desperation, but still the trawler came on, her decks a mass of spitting muzzles.

Royce felt the boat lurch beneath him as white-hot metal tore into her sides, and something clanged against the gun-shield and screamed away into the night. Another violent flash illuminated the boat, and he saw the mast and aerials stagger and pitch across the bridge. Simultaneously a deafening explosion came from aft, the shock sending him spinning to the deck. He scrambled to his feet, dimly aware that the pom-poms had ceased fire. Leading Seaman Parker sat moaning softly by the ready-use ammunition locker, his face a bloody mask. The other gunners were twisted together in a distorted embrace by the guns. With horror he saw a white hand on the already darkening decks, like a discarded glove.

Of the trawler there was no sign, although her gunfire roared and whined through the steep bank of smoke forming astern, which was tinged with pink and orange hues, making it look a real and solid thing.

He realized too that they were maintaining their speed, but turning in a wide circle. Forcing his way behind the port Oerlikon gunner, who fired steadily into the smoke, he pushed his way into the shuttered wheelhouse. Even as the door opened, he smelt the cordite fumes, and above the rattle of the guns, he could hear a persistent, shrill screaming.

As his eyes became adjusted to the feeble light, he realized that the interior of the wheelhouse was a complete shambles. Pieces of equipment were scattered about the deck, and he could see the flashes from the starboard Oerlikon's intermittent bursts through a six-foot gash in the plating. Petty Officer Raikes was on his knees by the wheel, hard at work with a screwdriver, which he was using like a jemmy, as he used all his strength to free the steering gear, which was jammed tight by a corner of a steel plate, bent over like wet cardboard. Royce noticed that his unruly hair was speckled with little pieces of paint which had been torn from the deckhead. Lying pinned under the twisted metal of the gash in the bridge side was the wretched creature whose spine-chilling screams made Raikes fumble and curse, and turn an imploring eye to Royce.

'Can you stop 'im, sir?' he gasped. 'God knows what's keepin' 'im alive!'

Indeed, there seemed little resemblance to a man in

43

the twisting bundle of rags which caused Royce to step back with horror. Able Seaman Lund, already wounded, had been dragged to the bridge for safety, only to be pounded into human wreckage by the last salvo of cannon shells, which had raked the boat from stem to stern. With a final jerk, the Coxswain freed the wheel, and clambered to his feet, spinning the spokes deftly in his scratched and bleeding fingers, and as if that was the awaited signal, the awful cries ceased, for ever.

'I'm on course, now,' shouted Raikes, 'but if you can get me a relief, I'll give you a hand on deck.' He sounded cool and confident.

Royce nodded dumbly, and went outside into the cold air, to pull his aching body on to the bridge. With despair he saw the tangle of wires and halyards wrapped round the mast, which pointed over the side like a broken limb, and under it, the shattered chart table, wood splinters, and the upended signal locker spewing out its cargo of coloured bunting. Harston knelt in the pose of a runner waiting for the starting pistol, moaning softly, and trying to pull himself to the voice-pipe, each movement causing him to clench his teeth and close his eyes with pain. In two strides, Royce reached him, and eased the weakly protesting body back against the screen.

'It's all right, Skipper, just take it easy, we'll have you fixed up in no time. Now just you lie quiet.'

Harston seemed to hear, but he couldn't be sure, and he glanced wildly round for assistance. For the first time he saw the large sea boots of the signalman protruding from beneath the chart table. One of them twitched faintly, and then, with a sudden heave, Collins rose from the wreckage like a huge dog, apparently unhurt, but shaking his head, and repeating slowly, 'Gawd, what 'appened?'

Royce yelled madly: 'Quick, Collins, relieve the Coxswain, and steer!' He twisted round to the compass which was, by a miracle, intact. 'Steer north-west, and send him up with the first aid gear.' He stared at the signalman anxiously. 'Can you do that?'

'Yessir, I'm okay, just a bang on the 'ead. Gawd!' and he limped down the ladder.

Harston's eyes opened, and he seemed to be trying to focus on Royce's worried face. A gloved hand patted feebly at his shoulder, and a small voice croaked, 'Leave me, Number One, I've had it. Get the boat out of here.'

His chest shook to a violent fit of coughing, and Royce held him close, hugging him until it stopped.

The pale face twisted into a smile, and Royce bent his head to hear.

'You're all right, Clive, the best I've ever——' He coughed again.

Royce felt a sudden fierce grip on his arm as Harston tried to pull himself forward.

'Look after my boat, and the lads for me, will you?'

Royce nodded. 'Don't say it, I'll get you back,' he choked.

'Tell Artie he can have my breakfast, and tell him that . . .' He quietly lowered his face on to Royce's shoulder, and he felt his body give a long shudder and go limp.

For several seconds he sat holding him, until the Coxswain appeared with two seamen. Then he turned his head away, so that they should not see his tears, and rasped, 'The Captain has just died. See to the others.'

Gently he freed himself from the embrace, and stood stiffly at the rail, then he called down the engine room voice-pipe, 'Everything all right down there, Moore?'

The tinny voice rattled back, 'Aye, aye, sir, no damage. There were two holes forrard below the waterline in the mess-decks, but I've had 'em plugged. I can still give you maximum revs, if you're wanting to get out of it, sir.'

Royce could well imagine Moore squatting down in the smoke and din of the engines, surrounded by tanks of high-octane spirit, and wondering what on earth was happening above his head, but taught by his nine years in the navy to ask no questions.

'Very good, stand by for full speed after the Coxswain has made his report.'

Ten minutes later, Raikes reported the findings of his hurried tour. 'Five dead, including the Captain,' he paused and lowered his eyes. 'Three wounded, one seriously, that's Banks, port Oerlikon,' he added.

Royce then remembered the huddled gunner firing wildly into the smoke screen. Alone, wounded and frightened, he had fired until his magazine was empty.

'As to damage,' continued Raikes, suddenly brisk. 'Two shot holes below the line, now plugged. 'Bout two hundred holes in the port side, and half that on this side. Pom-poms jammed, machine-guns smashed, and motor dory in bits. Most of the gear below is buggered-up too.'

'In other words, she'll float but not fight. Right, keep the Oerlikons closed up, and try to get the wounded comfortable. Oh, and a good cup of rum all round.'

He turned to the voice-pipe. 'Steer west-north-west, full ahead!'

He was aware that the Coxswain was still standing there.

'Well?'

'I just wanted you to know, sir, that I'm sorry about the Captain. He was the finest man I've ever served under.' For once he seemed at a loss for words.

Royce nodded. 'Thank you, 'Swain, I know what you mean.'

Collins had resumed his place, and was sorting out his flags in an aimless and fuddled manner, and as he worked, muttering and humming to himself, Royce stood looking at the empty corner of the bridge, the dark stains on the planking, the cruel pattern of bullet holes in the thin plating that had plucked down a man, a leader, who even at the gateway of death had thought of his duty to others.

Furiously Royce dashed his hand across his face and eyes, and stared hard across the grim, heaving waters, the reaction of the last soul-tearing hour causing him to tremble violently, and his stomach to heave until he felt faint and ice-cold.

Of the battle there was no sign, in fact, as far as he could ascertain, there was no other vessel at sea, and a

46

great peace had replaced the flaming crescendo which had nearly engulfed them. Far across the dim horizon the sky broke, and displayed the silver fangs of the dawn, which were reflected and magnified by the twin sheets of white foam cascading from each side of the sharp bow, as it lifted and pointed towards home. Beneath his feet he felt the thud of hammers as the Coxswain's party shored up the splintered planks, and sorted out the usable gear from the debris and confusion. The sounds of their activity, and the smell of cocoa from the galley steadied his nerves, and he felt himself stretching, and exercising his taut muscles for the first time. Wearily he raised his glasses, and as he swept the bleak area on the port side he tensed as into the lenses flitted a small, white feather, surmounted by a fast moving hull, and even as he watched, the shape shortened, turning towards him, moving fast.

Already his hand groped for the button which caused the alarm's clamour to call its urgent message throughout the boat, and brought the men running once again to their stations, except that this time there were only the two Oerlikons, with little ammunition, the huge torpedoes that lay in their tubes like useless passengers, and of course, they were quite alone.

'It's one of the gunboats, sir!' Collins's keen eyes had recognized the speeding shape, even at that considerable distance.

And a gunboat it was, flashing a challenge, which Collins promptly answered. She tore down in a wide arc to run parallel with them, but fifty yards away.

'Reduce speed, and keep station on me,' boomed the loud hailer, and Royce caught a glimpse in the grey light of the Senior Officer of their escort surveying their damage through his glasses.

As Royce made no comment—his own loud hailer was in several pieces—the sharp voice crackled again: 'The rest of your flotilla are coming up astern. You are the last one to be accounted for.'

Royce waved heavily, and ordered the Coxswain to reduce speed. The Senior Officer had set him wondering.

'The last one to be accounted for.' What did that mean? That all but Paskins' boat were safe? But what of the casualties? At that thought, a fresh pang of grief shot through him, as he saw starkly in his mind's eye Harston groping weakly across the deck where he himself now stood, and he remembered anew his helplessness as he felt the last spark of life die, the vital, ever-boyish spirit vanish in a split second.

It was all so unreal, so nightmarish, that he shook himself violently, without realizing that this nightmare would live with him forever.

He suddenly observed that all the terrible scars of battle were now visible on the gallant little ship's upper deck, and the horizon had taken on a hard, grey line, as a new day broke, slowly at first, as if reluctant to display the night's tragedy, then with the full, bright glare of a watery sun, it was upon them. And with it came the little band of brothers, limping painfully out of the early morning mist, one behind the other, closely bunched, seeking comfort and protection in what, at any other time, would be a dangerous formation.

Emberson's boat led, and as she drew near, an intricate pattern of holes could be seen down the side, and the barrel of one Oerlikon was missing. From the bridge, a bright yellow scarf waved like a defiant banner. Next, Benjy Watson's 2007 came into view, towing another boat stern first, and making very heavy going of it, as the reluctant charge, which was Jock Murray's 3007, yawed awkwardly from side to side. Watson stood high on the bridge screen, watching the tow-rope with red-rimmed eyes, and constantly barking changes of speed to his Number One, who sat on the chart table, having his hand bandaged. Murray's boat was a mess, blackened by fire, riddled with shot, she was down by the head, the pumps clanking monotonously to stop the sea which poured hungrily through the torn planks. The Captain slumped moodily by the compass, breathing heavily, and cursing the slow passage. Half his crew lay dead below, and his Number One had been blinded.

Still the procession came on, M.T.B. 1815, commanded

48

by Lieutenant Deith, the suave, dark ex-car-salesman from Kensington, was steering a very erratic course; her rudder gone, she was using just the engines. She too, had plenty of debris, human and otherwise, to show as evidence of defeat.

Lieutenant Cameron's 2015, the flotilla's newest addition, was least damaged, except for a torn upper deck, and hovered in the rear, keeping a watchful eye on her companions.

And that was all; two boats missing, Paskins's and 1917, Lieutenant Ronnie Patterson, the youngest of the captains.

By this time, Emberson had drawn close alongside and was waving happily with a megaphone.

'Get John up here, will you!' he yelled. 'I knew you'd turn up all right.'

Royce swallowed hard, and gripped the rail with desperation. 'I can't,' he faltered. 'He was killed last night.'

He wanted to say so much, but what was there to add to this bald statement, that now sounded so cold and indifferent?

Emberson's smile of welcome vanished, and he seemed turned to stone.

'I see,' he nodded slowly. 'I see.' And he added something which sounded to Royce like, 'my friend'.

He pulled off his cap, and lowered his head, his hair ruffling in the cold breeze. He stood like that for some seconds, but it seemed a frozen eternity. Then with a brisk jerk he replaced his cap, and squared his shoulders.

'You and I'll have a talk later,' he called. 'I'm glad you're safe.'

With a roar of engines he swerved away to lead the line again.

Royce never forgot the voyage back, every little detail, and each crisis forcing him to strain himself to the utmost of his ability, and by the time they were challenged by the destroyer patrol sent out to guide them to safety, he was near mental and physical collapse.

In silence they landed their dead at the railway jetty

and handed over the boats to the waiting dockyard men. Then, bundled together in a harbour lighter, they made their way back to the *Royston,* unaware of the curious and anxious faces that lined the rails, feeling nothing but a deep despair of pain and defeat.

3

THE hard, bright glare of a spring morning sent a powerful shaft of light sweeping across Royce's tiny cabin, as the steward deftly unscrewed the deadlight, and laid down a large cup of tea at the side of the bunk. The bunched figure wrapped in the blankets lay quite still, like the others that the steward had been busily tending, and even the scattered array of salt-stained clothing, sea boots, and other gear bore a marked similarity. Gently but firmly, in a manner born of long practice, he found a shoulder, and shook it. The figure groaned, and stirred slightly.

'Morning, sir, pusser's tea for one!' he chirped brightly, and then stood back to await results. Like the rest of *Royston*'s ship's company, he knew quite well about the last battle of the M.T.B. flotilla, and of the losses sustained. He knew, too, that this young officer had refused help and rest after his ordeal, until he had made sure that his crew were safe in their hammocks. And even then, he had forced himself to write letters to the relatives of the dead, and telephone the hospital to inquire of the wounded. As he had handed in his report to the Operations Officer, he had been told that fourteen days' leave would be granted to all the boats' crews, as from the following morning. This morning.

Royce blinked, and heaved himself on to one elbow. Dazzled by the bright sunlight, he squinted at the steward. 'Thanks. What's the time?' His voice sounded thick.

Swiftly the steward moved into the attack. 'Now don't you worry about a thing, sir,' he said quickly. 'It's eight o'clock now, and it's a lovely morning to be starting your leave. I've pressed your best uniform, and Stripey Muddock has done four shirts real smashing for you. Oh, and I've looked up the trains to London just as you asked.

Breakfast is spam, but Cookie has doctored some powdered eggs, special. I'll bring it in to you.'

Royce didn't remember asking about trains, and suspected he was being pampered, but the door closed before he could muster a comment, so he rolled off the bunk, and sipped the sweet tea.

Later, as he munched his breakfast, he thought about leave, and wondered if his parents would see any difference in him, or whether his mother would persist in treating him like a schoolboy. The thought of the Surrey woods, now green and fresh, the feel of springy turf under his feet, and the excited barks of old Bruce as he lumbered about in the bushes, sent a queer thrill through him, and a warm excitement made him determined to close his mind tightly on the previous forty-eight hours.

As he dressed slowly and carefully, his ear picked out the usual shipboard noises which he had come to know so well. The measured tread of the Quartermaster above his head, the clanking of a winch, the appealing mew of the gulls, and the twitter of the pipes throughout the ship, as the hands were invited to muster on the fo'c'sle to perform a task.

In bustled the little steward, and surveyed his charge carefully, then nodded. 'Very smart, if I may say so, sir, and just in time for the nine-ten to London. Gets in at about eleven thirty, and there are plenty of trains out from Waterloo for your manor.'

Royce thanked him, and picked up his case and respirator.

'Tell the Quartermaster to hold the post-boat. I've just got to call in to the Wardroom.'

The handshakes were firm, and the good wishes genuine, as he parted from his friends, all of whom were looking forward to their leave, as a starving man sees his first meal. Emberson followed him on deck, and together they looked down into the duty boat, hooked on at the main gangway, the Coxswain obviously impatient to be off.

'Well, so long, Clive,' he said quietly. 'Have a good

leave and forget everything else. I'm following you in about an hour.'

Royce watched the lonely figure at the guard-rails until the motor-boat turned the railway jetty, and the *Royston* was hidden from view.

He made a smart figure in his best doeskin jacket, the gold wavy stripe gleaming on the sleeve, as he strode briskly up the ramp to the station. A naval patrolman hurried from the R.T.O.'s office, and saluted.

'Beg pardon, sir. Sub-Lieutenant Royce is it?'

When the officer nodded, he continued: 'Dockyard gate 'ave just 'phoned through to say there's a Wren trying to get through to see you. I don't know no more, the line's gone dead again, but I expect it's some message from the Signal Tower.'

Royce paused, one eye on the clock. 'Hm, I guess it'll wait till I get back. I don't want to wait an hour for another train.'

'Aye, aye, sir. I'll tell them you've gone if they get through again.'

Royce settled himself in an empty compartment, and proceeded to fill his pipe with duty-free tobacco. Ten minutes to wait, and then the war and the navy would be left behind.

His line of thought was interrupted by a screech of brakes in the station forecourt, where he saw a grey dockyard van jerk to a halt, and immediately a small figure in blue jumped out, and hurried up the platform, apparently peering in each window, to the obvious delight of the sailors in some of the compartments.

'Good God,' he thought. 'It must be an urgent message after all.'

He went cold at the thought of a possible recall to duty, but in order not to prolong the agony, he thrust his head out of the window.

'Are you looking for me?' he called.

She reached him, and stood looking up, breathing fast. He saw by her badges that she was in the signals branch, but at once his attention was taken by the girl herself.

53

She had quite the most attractive face possible, he thought. The eyes, which were now looking anxiously into his, were of the darkest brown, which contrasted with the smoothest skin Royce had ever seen. From beneath her jaunty cap, dark curls were rebelling against naval uniform, and completed this enchanting picture.

He realized he was staring, and coloured slightly. 'I'm Royce,' he explained. 'Are you looking for me?'

'Yes, I wanted to ask you about Lieutenant Harston,' she said quickly, her voice soft and warm. 'I was hoping you could wait for me.'

Royce tensde, taken aback. 'I didn't know he had any friends outside the flotilla here.' He felt vaguely angry. 'I expect the *Royston* can tell you the full details.'

The rather sad little face tightened. 'I'm Julia Harston, his sister,' she said quietly.

Royce was completely shattered, this unexpected turn of events made his mind whirl, and he struggled to put right the damage his hasty words had done.

'I, I'm terribly sorry, I didn't understand,' he stammered. 'You see I thought, I thought Harston had no relatives . . .' He coloured when he realized he had referred to her brother by his surname.

'I thought a great deal of him, he taught me everything about this job, and when you came up to ask about him, well, I just felt I didn't want to share . . .' He broke off helplessly.

She studied his face for a few seconds, and when she spoke it was with slow deliberation, as if she wanted him to feel the impact of every word.

'We have no parents, they were killed in an air-raid on London last year.' She paused, and for a split second her lower lip trembled. 'Now I'm the only one left.'

Somewhere down the platform, a hundred miles away, a voice shouted: 'Hurry along there! Close all doors!' And a warning whistle sounded.

Royce was torn by violent and previously unknown emotions. She stood there alone and small on the now empty platform, and he felt he wanted to jump down and hold her close to him, to comfort her, and to protect her.

The words came tumbling out of him. 'Look, can I see you again? I'll be back soon; I can come back earlier.'

'I shouldn't think so. I'm going on draft tomorrow,' she answered simply.

A shrill whistle called urgently, and the engine gave a violent hiss of steam, and the train shuddered.

'Please, I must see you,' implored Royce, leaning right out of the window, until her face was but a foot away. 'Where will you be going?'

The train jolted, and began to trundle out of the station.

Her small chin jutted defiantly. 'I expect the Powers That Be can tell you the full details!'

With that she turned and walked quickly down the platform, and as the train gathered speed Royce still hung precariously from the window and watched the tiny blue figure until smoke from the ancient engine blotted out the station, and the scenery became squalid rows of small houses on the outskirts of the port.

He sank down on the worn cushions, a feeling of helplessness overcame him, and he knew for the first time the ache in his heart. All the way to town he sat restlessly staring out of the window, picking out the old landmarks, and trying to free his mind of the large brown eyes of Julia Harston. Julia: he repeated her name over and over in his mind, until it kept time with the clickerty-click of the wheels. If only he hadn't sent the telegram to his mother saying what time he'd be arriving, he could have stopped just a little longer. When the train pulled up with a last protesting lurch, he had determined to find her, wherever she was, whatever she thought of him.

He only vaguely remembered Waterloo as he struggled across its busy concourse, the blaring loudspeakers, and hundreds of hurrying servicemen. The joyous reunions, and the brave and tearful farewells, that were commonplace in a Britain at war.

An hour later he stepped down from another slow train on to the little station on the edge of Oxshott woods that he knew so well, and, as if in welcome, the daffodils in the station-master's garden made a colourful fanfare. The next instant, his mother's arms were about his neck, and his father pumped his hand, while Bruce, older and fatter, but just as boisterous, lolloped about his legs. In the background, old Arthur the porter, who had been there for a lifetime, nodded and smiled.

'You're looking well, Clive,' said his father gruffly, and his mother merely nodded, her eyes shining.

And so, in a specially hired taxi—they had never gone in for a car—arms linked and Bruce perched on a suitcase beside the driver, Clive Royce came home. Not the callow youth in the proud uniform who had set out less than a year ago, full of worried anticipation and eager hopes, but a quieter and older person, self-confident, an officer.

The first week of his leave was made up in dashing round visiting old family friends, as much to please his parents as anything else. In the evenings, he walked contentedly through the woods, smoking his pipe, and throwing sticks for the dog, but always at the back of his mind lurked the fears of the previous week, and once in the night he sat up in bed sweating, hearing again the rattle of the machine-guns and the awful cries of the dying. When he thought of Harston, he thought of Julia, and when he thought of her, he was always filled with the same desperate longing. He had to find her, to see her again.

The second week dwindled all too quickly, and as the days passed, his mother seemed to shrink, and become more and more attentive, and although he had never told her of the horrors of battle, she was quick to understand what had changed her son.

On the last Thursday they sat round the fire in the evening, after a late dinner, Royce feeling sure he had been forced to eat half of their rations, and talked of the future, after the war, when his father glanced at his watch, and reached for the radio.

'Won't do to miss the news, will it, dear?' he smiled. 'Clive'll feel he's getting out of touch.'

It was all the usual information, an advance here, a retreat there, air raids in the Midlands, air raids on Germany. And then at the end. 'During the night, our light coastal forces have been active off the Hook of Holland, and actively engaged a number of enemy E-boats. One E-boat was sunk, and several damaged. Two of our vessels sustained some damage and casualties. Next of kin have been informed.'

His mother switched it off, and said too cheerfully, her face averted, 'What about the last of the sherry. I'll go and get it for you lazy old things.' And she hurried out to the kitchen.

The two men faced each other, then his father patted his knee. 'You mustn't mind Mother, you know how she worries,' was all he said.

But the next day on that same platform, he thought of those words, as they stood in silence until the train was actually running into the station, then the good-byes were hurried, the hugs so brief, and as he was borne rapidly away from the sun-drenched little station, the picture of the two seemingly frail figures, and the rough worried-looking dog, were imprinted firmly on his mind.

After many wearisome hours of travel, consisting mainly, he thought, of changing trains every few minutes, and trying not to leave his respirator on the rack, he observed the now familiar landmarks of the low-lying Essex coast, and soon the deserted marsh flats, and the rich, fresh fields began to give way to scattered houses and cottages, and eventually the train ground to a stop in the bustling harbour station.

As he strode to the barrier, he picked out several faces from the flotilla, who either saluted or smiled, according to their rank or disposition. Petty Officer Moore, spruce and dapper in immaculate uniform and gold badges, so unlike his usual greasy overalls and woollen cap, was apparently loaded down with mysterious parcels from doting relatives—he came from a vast family—and seeing Royce, he nodded awkwardly, and fell in step beside him.

'Afternoon, sir,' he greeted affably, 'I 'ope you 'ad a good leave?'

Without waiting for an answer, he plunged into the full story of his own achievements, which appeared to consist of mainly visiting as many pubs as possible, with his family, all of whom were employed at the docks, and as he put it, 'the bleedin' cash was flying about like peas on a pusser's blanket!'

As they strolled along the railway jetty, they saw the boats lying once more alongside the depot ship. In two weeks the dockyard had done marvels. Planking patched and replaced, all the hulls repainted a very dark grey, which improved their rakish lines, and even now, their decks swarmed with overalled figures as the maintenance staff completed the work of restoring and putting final touches to their craft.

In the *Royston*'s wardroom, the bar was just opening as Royce hurried in, and soon he was firmly embedded in a tight circle of old friends, and eagerly they exchanged gossip, and pumped the other officers for the latest news of operations,

A small, wizened R.N.R. Lieutenant, bearing the purple stripe of an Engineer, and known to all affectionately as "Fixer" Martin, because of his magical powers with the M.T.B.s' engines, looked sadly at his empty glass, and shook his head.

'I'm afraid you poor boys have a shock in store.' He sighed deeply, and continued: 'Have any of you fly-by-nights heard of a Lieutenant-Commander Aubrey Kirby, Royal Navy?'

He made "Royal Navy" sound like an illuminated address.

'Good Lord, yes,' answered Benjy Watson, who looked rather haggard after a violent leave spent chiefly in the West End of London. 'He's the Captain of the old destroyer *Wycliffe,* a bit of a bastard to all accounts. Why?'

Martin smiled crookedly. '*Was* the Captain of *Wycliffe*.' He paused. 'You will be delighted to learn that this strait-laced, regimental, self-opinionated lump of peace-time navy is now Senior Officer of the flotilla!'

He was not disappointed by the gasps of amazement.

'And as our plump friend here says, he is one big bastard!'

'But look here, old man,' drawled Emberson, 'we've

58

always had an R.N.V.R. chappie, that was the whole point, I mean, with all due respect to our regular brothers, we don't want a fellow who's thinking of his career all the time. Dash it all Fixer, you must be mistaken.'

Deith, the quietest of the flotilla's commanders, pondered thoughtfully, and signalled the steward to fill Fixer's glass. As he wrote out a chit for another round of gins, he smiled.

'Well, thank you so much for cheering us all up, you old pirate, he may not be as bad as all that, why he might even get to like us.'

Martin laughed outright. 'I heard him talking to the Operations Officer, by accident of course, and he said, quote: "Coastal Forces are an important arm to the Service." Wait,' he warned, as a cheer was raised. 'He then said, quote: "It's too important to be run by a lot of irresponsible yachtsmen and week-end sailors." Unquote! What! no more cheers?'

'Hm, and I see that there's a conference in the fore-noon at two bells tomorrow. I imagine that's so we can get acquainted,' said Emberson, rubbing his chin. 'Steward! Same again, and we'll drink to a short war!'

* * * * *

A blue, choking haze of tobacco smoke swirled and eddied around the operations room, as the flotilla officers made themselves comfortable for the conference, and as Royce glanced about him he saw everywhere the visible signs that the fortnight's leave had performed wonders, and a new life had been pumped into the fresh, eager faces. He felt a quick pang inside when he remembered that no longer would he sit with his ear cocked for Harston's quick and witty observations, and the careful and patient explanations of these conferences, and he wondered sadly what his new C.O. would be like. It was strange that he had not yet met the replacement, as he had already seen several new faces who had taken the places of the wounded and the dead. Except for his own boat, the flotilla was again up to full strength, with two new Vosper boats in the place of those which had become tombs for their crews. Even Jock Murray's 3007 was back, complete with a new bow, and as the slow-speaking Scot had said, 'It was the neatest bit of plastic surgery you could wish for!'

A hush fell, as two figures strode on to the raised platform.

'All right, gentlemen,' said Commander Wright cheerfully, 'carry on smoking, and I'll bring you up to date.'

But all attention was rivetted on the other officer who sat down briskly behind his superior. Lieutenant-Commander Aubrey Kirby was all that you would expect a regular naval man to look. His uniform neat, a gleaming white shirt, its starched cuffs protruding sharply from beneath the sleeves bearing the two and a half gold symbols of authority. He was so true to pattern that it was difficult to determine the man himself. He was rather short and stocky, with a pink, round face. His hair, which was cut short to regulation length, was brushed straight back, but it had no definite colour, and even his features were very ordinary. But the eyes, they were a different matter. Like two pieces of pale blue glass, and as he sat erect and self-contained, with his small hands folded in his lap, he looked for all the world like a smug siamese cat, or so Royce thought.

He was not alone in this somewhat discouraging opinion. Benjy leaned over his shoulder, his warm breath smelling faintly of gin.

'Don't you feel sorry for the feller? The pekinese in the pigsty!'

He shut up quickly, as the cold eyes flickered in his direction for the briefest instant.

Commander Wright rambled on, apparently unaware that anything was amiss, and Royce realized that the speech of introduction was coming to a close.

'And now, gentlemen, I'll leave you to your new S.N.O., who will tell you about the next operational patrol.'

With that, he withdrew, a trifle too hastily.

Kirby rose slowly, and walked to the middle of the

platform, exactly the middle, and stood with his hands behind his back, like the guest conductor at a promenade concert. When he spoke, his voice was sharp and clear, but unexpectedly high, and he got straight down to business.

'In a few moments we'll go over the plan of action for tomorrow night, but first I want to bring a few points, merely matters of personal discipline, to your notice.'

He paused, and a twinge of uneasiness ran through his audience.

'Firstly, some of you appear to imagine that uniform is unnecessary in Coastal Forces. Those of you who feel this way will most certainly be crossing swords with me in the near future. From now on, aboard the depot ship, and at any time in harbour, number fives will be worn, without the trimmings. No fancy scarves, or funny hats, and not battle dress. If you are personally neat and smart, you will set a good example to your men.'

Emberson stood up quickly, his face half amused and half angry.

'But, sir, you can't treat the men here as if it was barrack routine,' he drawled. 'Why, it can be dangerous in this job, and a little laxity in some ways helps a lot.'

For the first time a gust of laughter ran round the officers. Kirby was unmoved and quite expressionless.

'My orders stand,' he snapped, 'and I'll trouble you to keep your personal opinions to yourself.'

Emberson cursed under his breath, and sank down to his seat.

'That scuttled you,' grinned Benjy. 'First round to the Little Admiral!'

Kirby then proceeded to list the orders and regulations which would in future be enforced in every boat of the flotilla, which seemed to cover every eventuality from the colour schemes of the hulls, to the lengths of beards worn by the crews.

He finished up his offensive in the same unemotional, crisp tones, pausing only to flick a speck of dust from his sleeve.

'Remember,' he ended, 'you have not been outstanding

in the past. I intend to see that this is the best flotilla on the East Coast, and if you all co-operate, my task will be easier. If not,' he shrugged, 'some of you will have to be transferred.'

Royce only vaguely heard the details of the patrol for the following night, his head was whirling with indignation; he felt hurt, not for himself, but for his friends, who now sat silently listening, while the clear, flat voice continued to rattle off the facts and figures, as if they were a crowd of backward schoolboys.

'One final point. I shall be taking over 1991, with Royce as my Number One, so all my personal orders will be passed through him. That is all, gentlemen, I trust you will see to your duties.'

They rose and moved for the door, but the voice had not quite finished.

'Sub-Lieutenant Royce report to me.'

Royce was left in the empty room facing his superior, and a feeling of resentment filled him, but he took the proffered hand, which was cold and soft.

'Well, Number One,' said Kirby cheerfully. 'Took it well, didn't they?'

'They're wonderful chaps, sir,' mumbled Royce hotly. 'They've been through hell, and I wouldn't wish to be with a finer lot.'

Kirby's face hardened.

'Let's hope you don't have to. In the meantime, I want a list of all defects from the engineer over the last six months, and the results of all practice gunnery shoots over the same period. On my desk tomorrow morning.'

He turned on his heel and strode off. Royce felt as if the whole private, happy atmosphere of his little kingdom had been suddenly shattered by this interloper. When he reached the wardroom he found that the others were of the same opinion.

'Strewth!' roared Benjy. 'If I tell my boys to put number threes on, there'll be a ruddy riot!'

Emberson smiled quietly.

'Not to worry, I think I can say without offending any greybeards present, that I am now the oldest inhabitant here, and I can further pronounce that within a few months this chap will be as good as gold, after all, be patient, he *is* R.N.!'

'Oh yes,' nodded Murray from the corner of the bar, 'I've heard of them. They look after the navy in peacetime!'

A howl of laughter went up, and the ice was broken.

The following afternoon, however, Royce stood uneasily on the bridge of the M.T.B. awaiting his new Commander, and having slaved for twenty-four hours to get the boat ready, he was in no mood for laughing. The boat gleamed from stem to stern, the smell of new paint pervaded everywhere, and all visible signs of the last action had been wiped away, like an unpleasant drawing from a blackboard. When he had first mounted the bridge, he had not been thinking about Kirby and his regulations, but wondering how he would react to going into action again, and whether his nerve might have gone, like so many, who had been labelled "bomb-happy". In the warm sunshine the bridge looked quiet and peaceful, and the fresh steel plates gleamed dully in their grey paint, while the brass of the binnacle and voice-pipes shone cheerfully in welcome. It was difficult to imagine this place as the roaring, shell-torn hell that it had been just a couple of weeks ago. He had checked the charts, the stores and ammunition. The guns had been tested and the torpedoes stripped and prepared, until he was quite satisfied. He had even done the returns that Kirby had wanted for some purpose or other, and he was feeling the strain now of waiting to see his superior's reactions to his efforts. He had not long to wait. Kirby, in a spotless new duffle coat and white scarf, swung over the side and marched up to him, and even as he returned his salute, his eyes darted everywhere, taking in every small detail.

'Quite good, Number One,' he conceded at length. 'We proceed to sea at 1630 as ordered. Make a signal to that effect. Although it's a more or less routine patrol off the Dutch coast, we might be lucky, and in any case it'll get the cobwebs blown away.'

The Coxswain mounted the bridge to report all hands

aboard for sea, and Royce was pleased to see that he had made a special effort to smarten his appearance. His cap, usually worn after the style of Admiral Beatty, perched carefully on the unruly, carroty hair, and his sweater was almost white.

'I understand that you, at least, are a regular?' questioned Kirby. 'That is a good thing indeed.'

'Yes, sir,' answered the Coxswain, cautiously, 'and I bin in this boat for two years, since she was built.'

'I see.'

And as Raikes turned to leave, 'See that I'm piped aboard on every occasion in future, and I don't want to see the men lounging on the guard-rails. Keep them busy. A busy ship is an efficient one. I shall be watching you, Coxswain.'

'Aye, aye, sir,' answered Raikes, in apparent amazement.

'Good,' thought Royce, 'even the R.N. aren't used to this sort of thing.'

In due course the time of departure drew near, and with special care Royce watched as the hands singled up the wire springs, ready to slip. Around him the other boats were busy, and Royce felt a glow of affection as he watched the familiar figures scurrying to and fro. On the bridge, Kirby stepped from one side to the other, swinging up his glasses and examining his flotilla from every angle.

Collins, the signalman, lowered his glass. 'Signal from tower, sir, "Preparative, five minutes".'

Kirby rang down "stand-by" to the engine room, and listened angrily, as the other boats began to rev their motors vigorously.

'If the engines are in proper order,' he barked, 'you don't need to start them until that Preparative is lowered.'

With a rush the tiny flag dipped, and Royce yelled, 'Let go all lines. Bear off forrard!'

Fortunately for Petty Officer Moore, the engines roared to life at the crucial moment, but as he said later, 'Never before, and never agin!'

Carefully, and gracefully, the eight boats swung into

line and picked up their distances, making a proud picture in the bright sun. The new ensigns fluttered defiantly from the gaffs, and on every deck the crews stood in neat lines for leaving harbour.

As he stood on the fo'c'sle with his men, Royce's heart lightened with pleasure at the sight, and he felt bound even closer to these wild young men, upon whom so much depended.

Through the boom-gate they threaded, and round the bell-buoy, towards the inviting but hostile sea, over which a million shimmering lights sparkled, and not even the faintest breeze ruffled its gleaming surface. He wondered what it would be like in peacetime. The small beaches packed with perspiring families, no doubt. Sand castles and toffee-apples. Laughing girls and carefree men. It was a world that didn't exist. He sighed, and dismissed the hands, and returned to the bridge.

'As soon as it's sunset, the flotilla will go to action stations,' ordered Kirby, 'and as I said at the conference, nobody fires a shot or breaks station without a signal to that effect from me.'

Royce took over the watch, realizing it was useless to argue or make suggestions, and Kirby retired to his cabin. It seemed obvious to him that Kirby still thought he was running a destroyer, and didn't really grasp the significance of this close fighting, where individual action counted for so much.

As the light faded, and the boats bowled forward at a steady, medium speed, Royce leaned pensively on the screen, and thought again of Julia. It was wonderful to have someone to think about in that way, and he decided that as soon as he could get ashore, he would start making inquiries to try and trace her, without making it too obvious. He wished that there was someone he could consult about such matters, someone who would be able to give him the benefit of experience that he himself lacked. Before he had volunteered for the navy, he had been far too wrapped up in his work, and studying for seemingly impossible exams, to even consider investing some of his meagre allowance on the pursuit of the opposite sex. It was all very worrying; she might at this moment be getting engaged, or even married, without his getting another look at her. He shook himself, this was absurd, he told himself, why, even if he ever found her again, she might be quite unlike the girl of his constant thoughts, and he would make a fool of himself once more. But the image of the large brown eyes persisted, and again all doubts and appeals to reason were dispelled.

Two ungainly corvettes, their sides streaked with rust and red lead, steamed sedately past, no doubt on their way back home from convoy duty, and as is the custom of the navy, the signal lamps got busy.

'Signal from *Rockrose,* sir,' grinned Collins. ' "What yacht club are you?" '

Royce laughed. 'Make "East Coast Cruising Club. What are you doing?" '

For a few seconds the lights winked back and forth across the darkening water.

From *Rockrose,* "Joining the Wrens, Good night!"

With a cheery toot on the siren the battered pair made off towards Harwich.

Kirby stood by his side, apparently drawn from his cabin by the sounds.

'What was happening, Number One?' he queried. 'What signals were they? Have they sighted something?'

'No, sir, just the usual light chatter, otherwise all quiet.'

'I don't approve of these silly signals, Royce, they're quite unnecessary, and only encourage slackness. The only signals to be sent are those you put in the log. Do you understand?'

'Aye, aye, sir,' said Royce heavily, while Collins suddenly busied himself with the flag locker.

You absolute pig, he thought to himself, and turned his attention to the compass.

Kirby, who looked pale and drawn, stood fidgeting for some moments, his calm temporarily upset by all these unorthodox goings on, then giving Royce and the signalman another glare, he stalked from the bridge.

Collins's soft, tuneless whistle wafted quite clearly

above the rumble of the engines, "All the nice girls love a sailor——"

'Oh, for Christ's sake stow it, will you!' he barked, then realizing it useless to take it out on the unfortunate Bunts, 'See if you can get some kye laid on, it's getting a bit chilly now.'

'It certainly is, sir,' muttered Collins with heavy irony, and hurried off before he could receive another rebuke.

At the clamour of Action Stations, the hands poured up from below, and settled themselves once again around their weapons, muttering and cursing about what they considered to be an unnecessary precaution. Able Seaman Roote, who had relieved Parker as gunlayer on the pom-pom, while he was in hospital with his badly cut face, made no bones about voicing the opinion of the messdeck.

'It's ruddy daft, that's what! 'Oo does 'e think 'e is, I want to know? In this tub already I bin in twenty scraps, and nobody's ever asked me 'ow I was dressed before! But 'is bleedin' lordship up there says, "Hall thet his a-goin' to be quate different in the footure."' He mimicked in a high, falsetto voice.

"Lofty" Poole, his "oppo", showed his strong teeth through the gloom. 'Watch out Rooty, 'e'll 'ave you in cocked 'at and spurs afore long!'

The ex-milkman from Hackney laughed mirthlessly.

'You 'eard what old Bunts said? Poor old Jimmy-the-One was fair fumin'. Bunts reckoned 'e was goin' to poke the Old Man in the chops!'

'Yeh, old Jimmy's not a bad bloke for an officer; 'e was proper busted up about the Old Man catching it. The real skipper, I mean.'

They huddled together for extra warmth, and lapsed into a companionable silence born of long training.

Bunched abaft the squat bridge, the torpedo party too were going through their usual fumbling paces with their twin giants, their bodies rolling to the easy motion of the throbbing hull. The L.T.O., a small, unhappy-looking man from Cornwall, called Petroc, kicked one of the tubes savagely.

'You'm a big useless lump o' metal, that's what yew are!'

As the torpedo showed no sign of having heard this outburst, he continued. 'If yew don' sink summat this time, oi'll stuff the ol' man in yew, an' foire 'im instead! Recon yew won' loike that!'

Overhead the sky was a ceiling of black velvet, sprinkled with a million stars of every size and shape, which made their little ship seem unimportant and fragile. The short, stumpy mast revolved in a tight circle, pointing first at one group of stars, and then another, like a dark finger.

Royce thrust his head and shoulders beneath the waterproof blackout curtain covering the private world of the chart table, and with the aid of the dim light, he got to work with parallel rulers and dividers on the well-worn chart showing the approaches to the Hook of Holland.

The principle of inshore fighting is to creep among the treacherous sand-bars, where the convoys and their escorts cannot reach, and then pounce out at full speed, every man for himself. It usually worked.

Now at a dead slow crawl, the lithe shapes of the flotilla crept forward against the ebb tide. Station-keeping was no great difficulty on this occasion, as all the boats were leaving long phosphorescent trails astern, like fiery comets, but even so, carelessness, as they all knew from experience, could result in sudden, crippling damage, or the prospect of being left high and dry on a mud-bank for the enemy to collect at leisure.

Kirby stood very erect by the chart table, shrouded in his duffle coat, his eyes fixed on an invisible mark ahead. What schemes were passing through his thoughts Royce could only guess, but in his own mind the usual combination of cold excitement, and the tugging grip of fear, had already got to work. He shivered violently, and worked his shoulders vigorously, he wanted to stamp his feet too, but knew that this was probably the moment of decision, calling for complete watchfulness and silence. On the other hand, it would quite likely be just another empty patrol.

'Stop engines,' ordered Kirby curtly, and as the boats lapsed into silence, one after the other, the gentle slap, slap of the small waves against the mahogany sides sounded loud enough for even a dead German to hear.

Royce kept a careful eye on the compass, trying to determine their drift on the sluggish current, and the nearness of the other craft, and he jumped violently when Kirby suddenly jabbed him in the ribs.

'There,' he hissed, pointing over the port bow. 'D'you see?'

For the moment he could fix his eyes on nothing, and then for the tiniest instant, far away it seemed, he saw a minute flicker of light, then blackness. Yes, there it was, a faint beam of light, then it had gone again.

'What is it, sir?' asked Royce. 'It's no buoy, there are none about here. It was rather like a signal, but it was almost regular, wasn't it?'

Kirby raised his glasses again, and Royce heard him chuckle.

'I've seen that before on other slack ships. That was a loose deadlight over a port.'

He waited for the significance to sink in.

'Each time the ship rolls, the deadlight opens, and out shines the light. Probably some stupid officer in his cabin. Oh yes, Number One, there's a nice big ship on the end of that light. Stand by to engage with torpedoes!'

Royce flung himself down towards the torpedo party, hearing briefly as he did so, the click of a shaded Aldis lamp to the other boats. The engines purred to life, and they crept forward once more, this time in earnest.

Peering round the side of the wheelhouse, Royce saw the darkness ahead lose its silky smoothness, and slowly but surely a new, hard shape began to emerge. It was like a wild dream, it was so unreal and almost frightening, as this great ship moved silently across the water ahead of them. The range was still about a thousand yards, and yet the strange vessel rose like a factory, high above them.

'Phew, it must be the *Queen Mary*!' muttered Petroc.

The voice-pipe rattled, 'Stand by, tubes.'

They waited.

Still they cruised towards each other, on a course which could end in a collision if nothing happened. Surely the enemy captain must see them soon.

Petroc checked with his sighting bar. 'Three hundred yards, sir,' he whispered.

Then, quite clearly and crisply across the water, they heard the urgent clamour of a klaxon hooter, and a split second later there was a flat explosion from the bridge, as a snowflake rocket was sent on its journey over the surprised vessel. When it burst, in a gleaming, eye-searing glare, they saw before them, as if engraved on a black backcloth, a vast oil tanker of some twenty thousand tons, every detail clear and bright, from her tall, tapering derricks and lofty bridge, to the neat lifeboats stacked under their davits. In answer to the alarm, tiny figures scurried aft to a shrouded gun platform, while the great ship began to turn away from the attackers. A fresh, creamy froth rose from her stern, and she surged forward, the bow wave rising against the proud, raking stem. But in vain, even at the Tactical School at Portsmouth, no target could be better placed for a kill.

They all heard the harsh orders on the R-T, as Kirby flung his force to the assault. As their own bows lifted, and they swung on the new course, their engines screaming with hate, Kirby gave the signal to fire. With a cough of yellowish smoke, the great fish pounced from the gaping mouths of the tubes, ungainly and ugly, but as their sharp fins and propellers dug into their natural element, the sea, they shot forward remorselessly, gathering a fiendish speed. Instantly, the M.T.B. heeled over, lightened from her burden, scudding round and away, to leave the way clear for the next boat in the line.

They could clearly see the sharp bows of Emberson's boat cleaving rapidly on the same course as they had just taken, and when he fired his fish, it looked all the more impressive and terrible. The German gunners had been forgotten in the excitement, but now, above the noise of the engines, they heard the sharp bang of the twelve-pounder as they got the first shell away. Where it went they never knew, for at that instant, their torpedoes struck home, biting deep into the bowels of the engine room. They exploded as one, and the night was torn in two by the great roaring detonation. A tall column of water rose high above the masts, followed by a terrifying orange flash, more powerful than even the rocket had been, and before their shocked minds could readjust themselves, the centre of the main deck dissolved into a mass of writhing flames, the heat of which could be felt harsh on their faces. Another deafening bang heralded the arrival of one of Emberson's torpedoes, the other had apparently missed, and before their eyes, the vast bows dropped into the sea, as if sheered off by an invisible knife. Kirby signalled to break off the action, and withdrew from the new menace of the blazing oil which was pouring in thousands of gallons from the shattered tanks. It spread over the waves in a great fiery apron, stripping the paint from the ship's scorched sides, and causing the jagged plates to glow red, and to buckle into fantastic shapes. Slowly and majestically she dipped her head in submission to the savage onslaught, the great flames hissing and darting along the whole length of the decks, and above all other sounds could be heard the bellow of scalding steam, and more internal explosions, as her very entrails were torn to shreds. The propellers, now still, rose dripping and shining in the glare, whilst in a shower of sparks, the main derrick tore free from the tormenting fire and plunged over the side. More quickly now, the glowing carcass that had been a proud ship but a few moments before rose steeply, until it hung, apparently motionless, while the awful sounds of tearing metal and heavy equipment breaking through the length of the hull, ground across to the watchers. With a great sigh, and another sullen explosion as the boilers split asunder, she took the final plunge, pulling up with another jarring crash as she struck the bottom of the channel, and rolled over on to her side, to disappear in a flurry of foam and burning oil.

They watched in silence, as if in homage to the dying ship, the old hands with a hard feeling of satisfaction, the others, like Royce, in shocked wonderment. They cruised for a while around the creeping patch of flaming oil, knowing in their hearts that there would be nobody left to save from such a holocaust, but peering into the greasy water just in case. Only the pitiful oddments remained, a life-raft, a few pieces of smouldering deck planking, and a smoking bundle of charred rags and flesh, face down, a despairing shoulder turned against the desperate land of the living.

Kirby found it difficult to conceal his jubilation, and paced impatiently back and forth, until, with a hasty glance at his watch, he ordered his flotilla to reform, and continue north-east up the coast.

'That'll show them, Number One,' he said, rubbing his hands. 'Now we'll see what else we can find.'

Royce glanced at him in surprise.

'Surely we're not going to stay here, sir?' he asked. 'That ship must have been waiting for her escorts, and in any case, the local support groups will have been alerted by now, and they'll be down on us like a ton of hot bricks. It's happened before like that to this flotilla.'

The pale blob of Kirby's face turned towards him for some moments.

'Getting cold feet, Royce?'

'There's no need to go to panic stations yet, you know.'

Royce felt his face burning, and remembered his own foolish remarks to Leading Seaman Parker before that first patrol.

'Certainly not, sir, it's just that we've always pulled away from this coast after an attack; there's no room to manoeuvre.'

'I think I know this business better than you,' snapped Kirby. 'I would be very much obliged if, in this instance, the amateurs would stand fast, and try to learn something for a change.'

He jerked his head back in the direction of Emberson's boat.

'Take him for example. Wasted two torpedoes, mine would have been quite sufficient. And in any case, he missed altogether with one!'

'We might have missed with ours, sir, then it would have been very different.'

'Really, that's very interesting,' Kirby's voice was heavy with sarcasm. 'I'm not in the habit of wasting valuable equipment. I'm not in the Service just for a lark while there's a war going on; I'll trouble you to remember that!'

Royce choked back the hot fury that made his eyes swim with rage.

'Aye, aye, sir,' was all he dared allow himself to say.

As he lay against the side of the bridge, steadying his glasses, he found it difficult to believe that anyone could be so utterly callous and pompous, to be able to give a lecture about his career, quite calmly, after having just destroyed a valuable enemy ship. It was quite fantastic, all the more so, because he was so sure of himself, so self-reliant.

For two hours they cruised through the night, the dark coastline never far abeam, and then, quite suddenly, they saw the two trawlers coming straight towards them. Royce's heart sank. It seemed inevitable that they should meet again with the "floating forts", and that this would be another wall of destruction.

'They might be the flak-boats!' he shouted, above the increasing roar of the engines, 'Covered with guns and concrete!'

Kirby paid no heed, but headed straight for the nearest vessel.

Both trawlers were flashing lights wildly, and turning away from each other, their shapes lengthening, their stumpy funnels clearly visible.

'Open fire!' shouted Kirby, and the bridge rattled and vibrated as the tracer shells clawed towards the nearest dark shape. The Oerlikons joined in with their ear-shattering rattle, and at once a flurry of splashes churned the water around the trawler into a white frenzy, moving steadily, until a ripple of flashes tore along the decks, to hover, and then hold the high bridge in a deadly cross-fire. Pieces of wood flew in every direction, and faintly the sounds of breaking glass were heard, as the wheelhouse windows flew to fragments, carving the helmsman

73

to ribbons. She slewed round and stopped, steam pouring from her, and flames beginning to take hold of the superstructure, and as they turned round her stern, Deith's 1815 shot into view, his tracers swamping the other trawler with a deluge of fire, and like her sister, she began to settle down, a dense pall of smoke rolling over the sea towards them.

Kirby snatched the hand-set of the loud-hailer, his crisp voice carrying clearly above the crackle of burning woodwork and exploding ammunition.

'Get back in station,' he yelled, 'I can finish this one off.'

Deith's speeding boat turned in a creamy circle, and the whole flotilla must have heard his angry voice boom across the water.

'My bird, I think, sir!'

'Impudent young puppy,' fumed Kirby. 'We'll see about that!'

He flounced up and down the bridge, to the obvious delight of Collins, and then calmed himself with a supreme effort.

'Steer west-south-west, and take up course for base,' he snapped.

Then, as if to let off steam, 'So much for your "Floating Fortresses". It seems I've come along just at the right time!'

As the flotilla sped for home, and even until the horizon began to lighten, Royce stood silent and fuming beside his superior, not daring to speak, and conscious only of a helpless feeling of frustration at the unfairness of Kirby's remarks, and at the truthless way he was so obviously determined to capture as much of the limelight as possible for himself.

He mellowed a little at the sight of the glorious, glowing ball of the sun, rising in all her splendour over the horizon, and bringing life and colour to the flat glassy sea. It was a rare experience for them to sail in the sunlight, and as they felt the little early morning warmth fan their tired faces, they felt that the fangs of the night had been temporarily drawn.

'Aircraft, sir. Red nine-oh!'

The gunner's warning cry made heads turn skywards as one, and soon the glasses of the flotilla focussed on the minute black speck which had appeared from between the high, fleecy clouds.

'There's another, and another, by God, there's 'alf a dozen of 'em!' muttered Collins.

The hunt was on, and already these planes would be calling their base for reinforcements.

The six aircraft turned in a wide semi-circle, their wings glinting, until the sun was behind them, and then in a perfect line they screamed down to the attack.

Again the M.T.B.s' armament rattled into life, as every boat sent a barrage of shells and bullets to meet the attackers. Down, down, down they came, until the black crosses were clearly visible on their wings, and then the first in line, garishly painted in yellow stripes, opened fire with his battery of wing-mounted machine-guns, and a shower of woodwork and loose gear flew from one M.T.B.'s deck. But the concentrated barrage was too much for the others, and they pulled violently out of their dive, one with a light plume of smoke streaming behind it.

Marshalled by Yellow-Stripes, they reformed and headed for the clouds, and it was only then that they saw the five Spitfires zooming low over the water, rolling their wings in welcome.

'I'm going below now,' informed Kirby. 'Signal the Spitfires, "About time too",' and he stamped down the ladder.

Collins picked up his lamp, but Royce shook his head. 'Make "Pleased to see you",' he grinned. 'That sounds a bit better!'

The fighters streaked off after the Germans, and the sea became an empty glassy mirror of reflected morning glory.

'Signal from 3007, "That bugger has made a mess of my new deck",' repeated Collins with a broad smile.

Poor old Jock, but still it was a relief no one was hit. They had a big welcome back to the base, when they cruised slowly and carefully alongside the depot ship, the hands fallen in at their stations, and ensigns fluttering bravely. Kirby had made signals in every direction as they had crossed the boom, so that no doubt would be left in the minds of the naval staff as to whose victory it really was.

When the depot ship bugler was sounding "Sunset" that evening, they gathered together in the bar, where another piece of news was awaiting them.

Benjy Watson burst excitedly into their midst, his face beaming with pleasure.

'Guess what, old Artie's half-stripe has come through; the Little Admiral's got a rival now!'

Deith raised his glass, 'Good old lawyer, he's damned well earned it too!'

Emberson entered the wardroom at that moment, his face thoughtful, and in seconds his back was being thumped, and a large glass put in his hand.

Royce smiled, and called above the din, 'I'm very pleased, Artie, how does it feel?'

'Yes, what's it like Lootenant-Commander?' quipped Benjy.

Emberson looked sadly at each one in turn, before speaking, as if to memorise each friendly face.

'It's not as easy as all that, chaps. I'm being drafted to Harwich as Senior Officer of a flotilla of Fairmile M.T.B.s, so you see, this is the end of the road for us,' he ended quietly.

Their faces fell. It didn't seem right to break up the old crowd like this. Up to now, only death or disablement had parted them.

'Och, that's a raw deal.' Jock Murray was the first to speak. 'We'll miss you, lad.'

Emberson straightened up. 'I'm off tomorrow afternoon, so tonight let's have the mother and father of all parties!'

That was a cheering thought, especially as they knew that they were not required to go to sea for at least two more days.

'Right, but where'll we have it?' queried Lieutenant

Cameron. 'Can't have it aboard here, without Kirby and other outsiders horning in, with all due respect to your C.O.' he added with a grin, turning to Royce.

'No,' agreed Emberson. 'We'll have it aboard my boat, and Benjy's, as he's right alongside me.'

He turned to Benjy. 'Now you've got work to do. Get some Wren types laid on, tell them it's a farewell party, so they don't think we're up to anything. And you Jock, you're in charge of bonded stores. Scrounge all the booze you can. And get some beer as well from the White Hart. I think that just about covers everything.'

One hour later, the Quartermaster was treated to the happy spectacle of some sixteen officers threading their way along the catwalks to two of the M.T.B.s, each carrying an assortment of bottles, and hastily prepared snacks that the chief cook had been heavily bribed to prepare, whilst across the water floated feminine laughter, as the duty boat arrived from the signal tower. Benjy had made a good haul, somehow or other; not one presentable Wren officer now remained on duty in the port.

The atmosphere in Artie's tiny wardroom, which measured about eighteen by ten, was close, to say the least, but as the guests arrived it was evident that the cramped quarters would be a help rather than a hindrance.

Lieutenant Peter Page, Artie's Number One, had done well. In about half an hour he had folded up the bunks, put down a borrowed carpet, produced flowers, and still found time to fix up a kind of buffet, of which he was now in charge.

After the usual shouted introductions, which nobody heeded anyway, the party really got started, and very soon, with the aid of a battered gramophone, some sort of dancing was in progress, consisting mainly of swaying back and forth over the precious carpet, bumping heads on overhead pipes and treading on each other's feet. When exhausted, it was customary to take your partner on to the upper deck and sample the cool night air, before plunging back into the fray. It was in the latter position which Royce now found himself, with a ravishing blonde Third

Officer called Sylvia, who now persisted in calling him "old solemn-face".

Royce, who by this time was feeling slightly light-headed, proceeded to marshal his thoughts, and like all men who have had one too many, broached the question of Julia Harston, with what he fondly imagined was superb cunning, but what in fact sounded as if he was comparing the romantic Sylvia with one of many conquests.

'Really, darling,' she breathed, her expensive perfume mingling evenly with the scent of one of Benjy's gin-slings, 'don't tell me you're one of those awful men of the world that mother warned me about?'

Royce tried again, but it was quite useless, so after a somewhat wet kiss, he piloted his charge back to the party, where he passed her over to Cameron, who, being a Romeo of the first water, was quick to take advantage of the situation, and together they took a further stroll on deck.

Emberson shouldered his way through to him, with yet two more glasses.

'Enjoying yourself, Clive?'

'Yes, thanks, Artie. That damned girl Sylvia whatsit, I was trying to pump some information out of her, about a girl I want to find, John's sister. She was in the signals here, but went on draft, after——'

'Good heavens, I knew he had a sister, but I didn't know she was here,' Emberson was plainly amazed. 'Nice, is she?'

'She's wonderful,' sighed Royce. 'Hates me though.'

Emberson laughed until he shook from head to toe.

'It sounds fine. Please don't mind my laughter, old friend, it's just the way you come out with things.'

Royce smiled self-consciously. 'I know, but I can't get her out of my mind.'

'Leave it to me. I wish you'd asked me earlier, as I happen to know their drafting type, but she's on leave at the moment. Tell you what, I'll write to her next week, and get the gen for you, how's that?'

Royce's face showed plainly how it was.

'There's one other thing I wanted to tell you.' He

dropped his voice. 'I think we both get on well, and I've never known old John take to a chap as he did to you, so I'd like to have you with me at Harwich, as soon as you get a command. Don't laugh, it won't be long, in fact, I think it'll be when you pick up your second ring.'

Royce was touched. 'It'd be fine by me,' he said sincerely.

'I've spoken to old Wright, and he says he'll do what he can for you. I gave him a load of bull about you, of course. Seriously though, I'd ask for you now as Number One, but that'd foul your chances of an appointment. So remember, all you've got to do is pick up the stripe, don't fall foul of Kirby, whatever he does, and find Julia. I'll do the rest.'

After that, the world seemed a finer place to be in, and Royce's pent-up feelings burst forth with such enthusiasm and hitherto unsuspected gaiety that the already successful party was brought to a most happy and boisterous conclusion. In two's and three's, they ambled up to the darkened decks, and even the dismal wail of distant air-raid sirens failed to curb the full-throated, if unmelodious, singing. Having got the Wrens safely embarked upon their motor-boat, to the amused grins of the seaman on duty, they proceeded to march up the catwalks to the *Royston's* main deck, with Emberson perched shakily on their shoulders. The Officer-of-the-Day, already warned in advance, stood by the shaded police-light, at a solemn salute, as to the tune of "Don't Put Your Daughter On the Stage, Mrs. Worthnigton", the revellers voiced the famous Coastal Forces ditty, in honour of their comrade.

> 'Don't send my boat out to sea, Senior Officer,
>   Don't send my boat out to sea.
>   She's a bit of a roaring gash-boat
>   Of that we'll all admit,
>   Her boost is far too phoney,
>   The Captain's a bit of a Twit.'

For such a sad occasion, all of them had done their best to make the night a memorable one.

4

WHAT a short summer it seemed to Royce, so full of activity and not a little danger, that he did not have much
difficulty in avoiding Kirby, who, as autumn sent her icy
messengers scurrying through the rising winds of the
Channel and North Sea, became more and more wrapped
up in himself, rarely speaking to his crew, except in the
line of duty, and avoiding his officers in their spells ashore.
He walked like a man possessed of some weird driving
force, unable to trust his so-called amateur crews, he spent
every moment of his spare time poring over the flotilla
orders, and studying reports of other groups' activities.
It was well known that he was persistently badgering Commander Wright about their patrol areas, almost openly
accusing him of giving his flotilla the worst areas to cover.
This was mainly due to the fact that the record of suc-
cesses rarely seemed to come his way, and as he was quite
unable to see it was due to the fact that his method of
operations was far too fixed, and lacking in the necessary
reckless dash, he and the redoubtable Wright soon began
to get on each other's nerves.

Emberson had been true to his word with regard to
Julia Harston, but there success ended. She had been
drafted to Rosyth—it might have been Greenland for all
the use it was to Royce—and as he didn't wish to open
operations by writing to her, in case she stopped him dead
in his tracks, he spent hours of his watch-keeping time
dreaming and hoping for the chance to get leave, and make
the long pilgrimage to Scotland. When he confided these
matters to Deith, he nodded saguely, and merely said,
sadly, 'Must be love, old man.'

Around the world the tides of war ebbed and flowed,
and time after time the dark clouds of near destruction
seemed to hang over the British forces. While the armies
of the Commonwealth fought and died in the steaming

swamps, or the parched deserts, or trained and waited around the coasts of England, politicians wrangled and argued about expenditure and wastage almost as though the war was a private enjoyment of the forces, not to be encouraged unless from a political angle.

Fortunately, the majority of bomb-torn and rationed Britain faced the grim future with realism and fortitude, and found time to give a thumbs-up at any announcement of a hard-won victory, and should it be a reverse, they just shrugged, and hung grimly to the old supposition that we could always win the last battle.

The war at sea meant convoys, and still more convoys. Hard-pressed ships, many of which would have retired gracefully to the breakers' yards but for the war, battled every mile of ocean, bringing the life blood to the nation, and carrying men and material to a score of battle-fronts. Alongside the Royal Navy, the men of the merchant fleets carried on the grim struggle without complaint, the ultimate prey and target for every submarine, E-boat and bomber that the enemy could hurl against them, while the pitifully thin escorts hunted blindly around their helpless charges, shooting, depth-charging, and dying.

Unlike the army, they rarely saw their enemy. He was just another menace, like the howling gales which scattered the convoys' straight lines, and made navigation on a pitch-black night a screaming nightmare; or the hidden mine, lurking in the grey waters, inert and still, until touched by an unwary ship, with the terrible aftermath of the thunderous explosion, inrushing seas, and the pitiful cries of doomed sailors trapped within. No, to the men of the Navy, the enemy rarely had a personality. He was everywhere and nowhere, the constant menace, who made them think only of the next minute, of the next hour. Tomorrow was too improbable.

News from the other sea battle-grounds seemed bleak. In the Atlantic, the mounting fury of the U-boat assault was taking terrible toll. In one month, over a quarter of a million tons of allied shipping had been sent to the bottom, and while British yards were building more and more sorely needed escort vessels, corvettes, frigates and destroyers, so too the enemy pushed a stream of underwater killers across the sea routes. At night the Royal Air Force gamely endeavoured to bomb all sources of production, as well as the bases, but their efforts bore little fruit, for apart from the fact that all such places were strongly defended, the German war machine now had the choice of a vast coastline stretching from Norway in the north, to the Bay of Biscay. So, as usual, the brunt was falling on a handful of rust-streaked ships, held together by the determination of their crews, and driven by the fierceness of those who knew their backs were to the wall.

In the Mediterranean the story was the same, too few ships, too many of the enemy. And yet here, too, they were somehow holding their own. Fighting the convoys every mile of the way to beleaguered Malta, and covering and supplying the army in the desert, pausing only to pray, or die.

With increasing pressure by enemy heavy units in these spheres, it was obvious that it was just a matter of time before they tried a new method of attack in the restricted waters of the narrow seas. Intelligence reports had brought the disquietening news that many new E-boats and de-stroyers were being harboured in Ostend, Flushing and Calais, possibly with a view to making the movement of coastal convoys impossible, and thereby pave the way for an invasion. Already, by day and night, heavy guns fired at regular intervals across the Channel, causing casualties and destruction in and around Dover, and occasionally de-stroying a slow-moving coaster.

Fortunately, these grave matters rarely caused much concern amongst the seamen, whose duty it now befell to face all these fresh dangers, and their intimate worries usually proved more absorbing.

The 113th Flotilla was no exception, and as the winter broadened into a grim reality, Lieutenant-Commander Kirby fussed and grumbled, until the main worry—of the sailors at least—became that of keeping their kit clean and properly marked and worn, regardless of what opera-tion their boat might be engaged on, or the problems of drying damp clothing on the tiny, overcrowded mess-decks. As for the officers, they struggled on, bearing the main responsibility, and hoping that Kirby would drop dead.

On this cold autumn morning, the little wind-swept boats cruised bumpily over the steep, sand-flecked waves of the Belgian coast, although that unhappy country lay invisible just under the horizon. To make matters more uncomfortable, a fine, penetrating drizzle was blowing gustily in grey sheets, reducing the visibility to about two miles, and making watchkeeping a nightmare. As was his custom, Kirby refused to allow any man a break from his action station, with the result that everywhere Royce looked he saw his men crouched miserably by their guns, trying to take advantage of any scanty cover available.

His plight was probably the worst, for as he stood on the open bridge, bracing his legs against the boat's uneasy motion, he was a free target for anything the weather could throw at him. He shuddered, as he felt the first icy trickle penetrate his left boot, and his thick sock, recently received from his mother, was soon a soggy mass. About his neck a tightly wound towel was heavy and cold with rain and spray, and his glowing cheeks stung with the drizzle, which pattered across him like needles.

Kirby was perched on the stool in the corner, the hood of his oilskin suit shrouding his face, like a brooding monk, his sharp eyes darting ahead, and then back at the other boats, as they weaved forward into the grey seas.

Royce gently patted his face with the back of a glove, and peered at his watch. Eight-thirty, and they had been at sea for about ten hours. He smiled miserably at the thought of the warm glare of the bar in the White Hart, a hot meal, and bed, and then winced again as a steely needle of water penetrated his collar, and between his shoulder blades.

'Could I dismiss one watch, sir?' he asked. 'Could get some cocoa on the move and a bite to eat.'

The hunched figure appeared not to have heard, so he started again.

'Come over here, Number One. Look at that fool on the Port Oerlikon, what's his name?'

Royce leaned over, resigned to no cocoa. 'It's Weeks, sir, only joined two days ago. He's an Australian.'

'Yes, yes,' snapped Kirby testily, 'I remember. Well he's asleep!'

He bent over the voice-pipe.

'Cox'n, come to the bridge, and bring Weeks with you!'

The tinny voice rattled up the brass tube: 'Is he ill, sir?'

'No, you fool, he's bloody well asleep!'

There was a scraping of feet as the Coxswain handed over the wheel, and a minute later he appeared on the bridge, followed by Able Seaman Weeks. The latter was a tall, gangling individual, what the average person pictures as the typical Australian. His face, which now stared sulkily from beneath a woollen cap, was deep-lined and tanned, quite out of place in such a climate, and the wide grey eyes, which had once checked countless sheep on a Queensland farm, glowered rebelliously at the Captain.

Kirby didn't waste any time.

'Weeks, you were asleep on watch. That makes you useless to me, and a potential danger to this ship!'

The tall figure stiffened. 'That's a damn lie!' he retorted hotly. 'I was restin' me head on the blessed magazine!'

His lazy drawl struck an unnatural note in the tense scene.

Kirby went white.

'Silence!' he shouted. 'Don't be so impertinent. I know your type too well, in and out of the detention barracks, and proud of it I suppose!'

Royce felt sick.

'Excuse me, sir,' he pleaded, but Kirby spun on him.

'Attend to your duties, sir! Don't interrupt!'

Weeks took a step forward, and stuck out his craggy chin.

'I come umpteen thousand miles to fight the Jerries, and I'll damn well fight you an' all if it comes to that,' he said slowly. 'This is a crook ship, and fer your information, you are the worst god-damned Pommy bastard I've yet had the pleasure of meetin'!'

'That's enough of that!' barked the Coxswain, and stepped smartly forward.

For a moment there was complete silence, but for the steady patter of rain across the chart table, and the signalman's sharp intake of breath. The main figures of the drama stood facing each other, like actors who have forgotten their lines, Kirby, white-faced and quivering with rage, and Weeks, now relaxed and defiant. Royce and the Coxswain stared helplessly at both of them.

Kirby shook himself, as if unable to believe his ears. 'Get back to your station, Weeks.' His voice was almost inaudible.

'Coxswain, I'll see this man when we return to base.' 'Dismiss!'

He shouted the last order almost wildly, and Royce prayed that Weeks wouldn't start anything more.

Surprisingly, he saw the two figures shuffle from the bridge, Raikes in front, obviously shaken, and the Australian on his heels, his face expressionless.

Royce's discomfort at the weather was quite forgotten, and he peered hastily through his glasses, but his mind was so much of a whirl, that he saw nothing.

When he heard the voice again, it was flat and toneless. 'In all my service, I've never seen such an insolent, mutinous lout. Just wait until I've had time to deal with him!'

And that was all. Royce gave an inward sigh of relief.

The boats turned in a half circle and continued the eye-aching search for prey, the wind and rain now beating over the starboard quarter, and causing them to roll and twist uncomfortably.

'By the way, Number One, you'll be surprised to hear that your second stripe has been recommended,' remarked Kirby casually.

Royce jerked out of his reverie, startled.

'Gosh, this is a surprise, sir,' he gasped. 'Thank you very much.'

He hadn't thought a great deal about promotion, but now that it was so close, he found himself grinning like a schoolboy.

Kirby permitted himself to smile thinly.

'As flotilla leader, I think I should have a full lieutenant with me. Although I'm not saying you've earned it by any manner of means,' he added.

Even such a dampening remark was lost on Royce, and he hummed happily, waving to Watson's boat astern for no apparent reason.

Kirby shrugged, and shook his head.

'Really, Number One, perhaps I shouldn't have told you.'

Royce smiled, 'Sorry, sir,' and to himself he said, "It's taken you nearly a whole day to tell me anyway!"

'Aircraft, dead astern!' yelled the signalman, and they saw the warning lights flickering along the line of boats.

The deck throbbed as they increased speed, and the slim muzzles swung round to cover the approach of the plane, which could be seen vaguely through the scudding clouds.

A voice piped up from the waist.

'Sunderland, sir!'

And they relaxed, as the fat, friendly shape of the Coastal Command aircraft took on a sharper line through the driving rain. Having seen them and exchanged recognition signals, it began to circle, an Aldis lamp busy.

The signalman lowered his lamp.

'Three E-boats coming up astern fast,' he reported. 'About eight miles.'

They waited, while Kirby quickly pored over the chart.

'Hmm, they're making for Flushing, I don't doubt. Must have been in the Channel raiding our shipping. Hoist Flag Five. We'll attack in two groups as planned.'

Jock Murray's boat led three of the M.T.B.s away to the west, turning in line abreast in a flurry of foam, while the others worked up to full speed abreast of Kirby. On every boat the men tensed at the signal, flag five, "Attack with guns", and for most it would be a new experience to get to grips with E-boats in broad daylight. Usually they were but fleeting grey shadows, spitting death through the darkness.

Royce clambered down to the pom-pom, where the

well-greased shells lay inert and waiting. Leading Seaman Parker, back again from the hospital, his red face crisscrossed with small, white scars, grinned confidently.

'We'll give 'em what-for nah!'

'I don't expect they'll be thinking of anything but bed,' shouted Royce excitedly. 'Just as we do on our way home.'

Sure enough, three shapes could be seen approaching fast from the south-west, great bow-waves creaming away from the long, rakish bows, the silver-grey hulls low in the water, and hardly visible. The leading boat swung over to port, and a flat stream of green tracers cruised over the wave tops twoards them. The other two boats took up station in line abreast of the leader and also opened fire.

Again and again the pom-pom at Royce's side banged, and they saw the shells beat the sea into a savage froth around the second E-boat, while the machine guns got into a steady, screaming rattle. Twice he felt the hull shudder beneath him, and a smoke float aft was cut to ribbons. But the Germans had fallen into the trap, as Murray's quartet came roaring up from astern, every gun belching orange flames, and the E-boats were caught between a devastating cross-fire.

With a bang, the leading E-boat stopped dead and slowly capsized. The second one was ablaze from the bridge to the bow, and several tiny figures could be dimly seen through the sheets of rain, hurling themselves overboard.

For an instant the M.T.B.s slowed down to re-form, and seeing his chance, the remaining German captain dashed for the gap, his guns blazing fiercely. Royce saw that the torpedo tubes on the E-boat's decks were empty. Some British sailors had died during the night.

Benjy's loud-hailer boomed across the water, 'Tally-ho!' and with a roar of throttle they streaked in pursuit, the tracers knitting a deadly pattern between them.

Kirby shouted down from the bridge.

'Three more E-boats ahead, Green four-five! Range about a thousand yards. Look to it, Number One!'

He was looking savage.

The newcomers were obviously from the same flotilla as the others, and had apparently taken another route home.

Now the battle became fierce, the Germans fighting a delaying action back to base, no doubt praying for help to arrive.

It was then that it happened. Royce found himself lying on the slippery deck, his head and ears roaring. Shakily he scrambled to his feet, and stared round. He had heard and felt nothing, yet the boat had received a direct hit on the port bow, a stream of shells exploding the full length of the fo'c'sle. Parker was cursing, and struggling with the gun, it had jammed solid, while the loading number knelt at his side, wheezing and retching painfully.

Already the boat had a definite list, and as Royce ran to the bridge he saw smoke pouring from the after hatch. The bridge was untouched, and Kirby was dancing up and down with impatience, while the signalman called up the nearest M.T.B.

'Get below, and deal with the damage, then come back here!'

Royce dashed aft past the tubes, and reached the choking smoke cloud, where Petty Officer Moore and his mechanic were hard at work with the extinguishers.

'Nothin' bad, sir,' gasped Moore. 'It's the paint store. 'It with a tracer.'

Below it was a shambles, and as the lights flickered on, he saw jets of water pouring in through the shattered mahogany sides, the double skin of the sides bent inwards like brown teeth.

The Coxswain appeared on the scene with Weeks and two more hands, and with hammers and plugs they got to work, slipping and cursing in the icy water.

When he returned to the bridge he found the other M.T.B. coming alongside, Deith's red face peering anxiously over the screen at them.

'I'm continuing the fight aboard her,' snapped Kirby. 'I've got to bag those other Jerries before they get within range of the coast.'

Royce stood dazed and not understanding.

'You mean you're leaving us?' he stammered.

'Of course I am. You make for home as best you can, we'll catch you up.'

As he threw himself down towards the other boat, he turned, a smile on his face.

'See if you can earn that other stripe!'

With a roar, and a puzzled wave from Deith, the boat turned away in pursuit of the running battle, while Royce stood helplessly on the bridge, which suddenly became a lonely and terrible place.

For some moments he stood staring after the fast-moving boat, until its shape became obscure in the curtain of fine rain, still uncomprehending, and slightly shocked by the suddenness with which his boat had been reduced from a swift, living creature, to a heavy, listing hulk, in which he was now the captain.

His scattered thoughts were interrupted by the Coxswain, and Petty Officer Moore, who appeared at his shoulder.

'I've just finished me rounds,' announced Raikes calmly, 'and I've got all the bad leaks patched up, except for those more'n a foot or so above the waterline. I'm afraid the automatic pump 'as been sheared right off by a splinter or something. That'll be a dockyard job to put it right.'

'Yessir, but we've got the hand pumps goin' like a fiddler's elbow, so provided you can keep 'er down to about five or six knots, we might be all right,' added Moore.

Royce pulled himself together, and studied their competent faces with a feeling of new confidence, and inner warmth, but he knew that the responsibility, given to him by the thin wavy line on his sleeve, was his alone, and that they were waiting for his own deductions and orders. Unbeknown to them possibly, they had made his burden considerably lighter.

'The fact is,' he said with a rueful smile, 'we have to get the hell out of here before it gets too hot for us, and fast as we can with safety. We're very much alone, I'm afraid, and mustn't depend too much on the rest of the boys finding us again.'

He led them to the chart, and they stood politely watching while he outlined their approximate position. When he had finished, Moore pushed back his greasy cap and scratched his thinning hair with an oily finger.

'I dunno much about navigation an' all that lark, sir, but I must say there seems to be an awful lot 'er North Sea between us an' the old *Royston*!'

They laughed, and each felt relieved that the situation still allowed them such licence.

Raikes, a professional seaman, craned forward, and tapped the stained chart with a pencil.

'If you don't mind me saying so,' he said in his clipped and forthright manner, 'it'd be better if we forgot all about the others, who as you say'll probably miss us anyway, and took the plunge due west, straight across to Blighty, and hope to be picked up by a patrol.'

Royce saw the logic immediately. If they kept to their present course the enemy would probably pick them off as stragglers, whether they were with other M.T.B.s or not, whereas the lonely route would quite likely bring them into contact with a destroyer to cover their painful withdrawal.

So due west they went, slightly down by the head, and listing to port, the engines roaring and thudding as they pushed the hull along at a snail's pace, the uneven trim making their task doubly difficult. From either side came the monotonous clank, clank of the heavy pumps, as half the hands toiled to keep the bilges free, and the engine-room safe from the relentless waters, while the others, now fully alert, stood against the wind and rain, fingering their guns, and peering at each horizon.

Alone by the pom-pom, Parker laboured with his tools to get his clumsy charge unjammed and ready for firing again.

His assistant, who had been flung against the ammunition lockers by the force of the explosions, lay quietly behind the bridge, freed from the pain of his shattered ribs by the Coxswain's morphia, and wrapped carefully in two lifejackets. He slept the sleep of one who has already departed from the fears of battle. Old Petroc, resting for a moment from the pumps, shook his head dolefully, as he jammed a rolled pair of overalls under the injured man's head.

' 'Ee's a lucky un, 'ee is, recon he done it for the purpose. Loik e as not knew the bloody pumps'd fold up!'

Then, spitting on his blistered hands, he turned back to his job.

Royce, alone on the bridge, he had sent the signalman to help on deck, lay across the screen, the glasses gripped in his wet, chafed hands, while the icy trickles of water explored the only warm place in the small of his back. Already it seemed as if they had always sailed this sea alone, and that there was no foreseeable end to the voyage.

Clank, clank, clank, went the pumps, while Parker's hammer beat out a steady tattoo below him. His senses became dulled by the noises, while his shivering body seemed to cringe at the onslaught of the rain. He forced his tired eyes down to his watch, and marvelled at the fact that three hours had already passed since Kirby had gone off to search for fresh laurels.

An oilskinned figure, barely recognizable as Able Seaman Roote, appeared at his side, guarding something under his streaming coat. He peered uncertainly at Royce's face.

'Me an' the boys thought yer might like a bit of Chinese weddin' cake, sir,' his cockney twang sounded eager and somehow comforting. 'We nipped in the galley an' warmed it up a bit, an' thought you might like a bit an' all.'

His voice trailed away, as he whipped out a small basin of hot rice pudding. Royce vaguely remembered it from two days before, and he took the basin in his hands, revelling in its warmth.

'Thank you very much, Roote,' he said, touched. 'Just what I need.'

Roote grinned, his sharp, knowing face creased with pleasure, and as he hurried away he added, 'Beggin' yer pardon, sir, but we wouldn't er' done it fer someone 'oo shall be nameless!'

He was off before Royce could think of a suitable comment. Instead, he lifted the basin to his lips, there being no spoon, or any other instrument for that matter, and as he did so, he smelt and tasted the deep, rich fragrance of service rum. He laughed aloud, and gratefully swallowed the hot, glutinous substance. The old so-and-so's, he chuckled, they didn't miss a trick. He imagined Kirby saying, "Storing rum is a punishable offence, Number One!" or "A sober ship is a happy one!"

He pondered over his recent life in the game little ship that struggled along beneath him: of how the Coxswain who now shared his every confidence, had at first openly showed his contempt for him. Harston's death had drawn them closer together perhaps. Even a character like Roote, who, until he had volunteered for Coastal Forces, had been fighting a constant war with authority in general, and officers in particular, had shown him the meaning of loyalty, and the acceptance of leadership. It was funny, he had bullied them, punished them, and driven them beyond the barrier of comfort, yet, because of his fairness, which he was inclined to take for granted, they had accepted him as their own leader, and personal property.

Another hour passed, and the unpredictable weather of the North Sea changed again. The rain broke off with an angry flurry of gusty squalls, which made the wounded boat stagger in her stride, and the wind force became stronger, veering round astern, so that the waves became longer and heavier, their great, grey peaks, unbroken as yet by white horses, rolling menacingly up under the transom in long, even ranks, each crest lifting the box-like stern clear of the water, and causing the overworked screws to screech a protest as they whirred free into thin air. Then, with a heave, they would drop again into a trough, and the boat would shudder, and lurch forward, always fighting the man at the wheel, as he tried to stop the sagging bows from broaching the boat round into the broadside position of danger. The wind, laced with salt, found its way through the damp clothing, chilling the flesh, and making their faces raw, while the ensign at the gaff grew steadily more and more tattered, blowing straight forward like the banner of a departed warrior.

Even the spirits of the seamen began to flag, as they toiled at the pumps, or stood on watch, wet, cold, and hungry. The Coxswain scurried from one end of the boat to the other, issuing a rebuke here, and a word of encouragement there, and later, a tot of 'neaters' to all hands.

To reduce the rolling as much as possible, Royce had most of the unusable gear on deck heaved overboard. The smashed smoke-float, the motor dory, new but a month before, and now riddled with holes and damaged beyond repair, and countless articles which only made the boat struggle harder by their presence. The torpedoes were the main disadvantage, especially as they could no longer be fired with the bows at such an angle, but Royce decided against sending over four thousand pounds worth of machinery to the bottom.

It was about fifteen thirty when they saw a dark shape smudging the horizon on the starboard quarter, and anxiously they strained their eyes even harder to catch a glimpse of the stranger, while Royce gritted his teeth, and opened the throttles a little further, making the boat slightly steadier, but causing some of the makeshift plugs in the shot holes to weep and squirt water each time she bit into a wave.

The wind was still freshening, and the ugly, grey hills were now tinged with curved, angry white crests, and as they plunged into each trough, the boat shuddered and groaned, then shaking the salt froth from the streaming decks, she would stagger up on the next roller, while every man peered aft at the other vessel, which was growing rapidly larger. Royce jammed his glasses against the rattling signal locker, and wedged his aching shoulders into a sharp voice-pipe cover, while he endeavoured to get a good look at the ship which was obviously overhauling them. As he angrily dashed the salt from his streaming eyes, and wiped the lenses of the glasses on a piece of sodden tissue, he saw that the faces of his men were now turned up towards him, waiting for a verdict.

Slowly, gently, but firmly, he moved the powerful glasses along the top of the heaving locker, seeing the tumbling waves magnified to a horrible and larger distortion, then into his vision came the close-up picture of the newcomer. In the seconds that he held her, he saw a large, rakish trawler, of the ocean-going type used by the Norwegians before the war, now painted a dark grey, with a thin plume of smoke trailing from the squat funnel, lifting and plunging over the tumbling water towards him. The high, knife-like fo'c'sle rose at all times clear from the sharp bow-wave, and it was possible to see the powerful gun mounted high up, close to the stem head, in the manner of all converted trawlers.

Royce thought furiously and quickly, it was possible that the other ship had not seen them, as they were so low in the water, and should she be an enemy, and it was unlikely to find a lone British trawler this far from base, she might well be on a hurried mission to another part of the coast. It was worth a try, and shakily the little M.T.B. turned into a quarter sea, away from the trawler. Royce watched tensely, and his heart sank, as he saw the other ship's silhouette shorten as she turned bows-on again in their direction.

Having informed the engine room to expect a last minute dash, he called Petroc to the bridge.

'Get the remaining smoke float ready to lower,' he ordered. 'It won't be too wonderful in this wind, but it may help. And loosen the life-rafts, in case we have to ditch.'

Petroc turned his worn face to the angry waters, and shuddered.

'Like as not we'm needing 'em afore long,' he muttered.

A light winked across the water, and Royce snatched up the Aldis lamp, flashing the first letters that came to his mind. The trawler waited a moment, then repeated the challenge. Again Royce flashed a meaningless garble in reply. God, if only it would get darker, but even with the prevailing weather conditions and threatening clouds, they had another hour at least to dodge and elude their powerful adversary. As he watched, he saw a red ball mount to the trawler's gaff, and break out stiffly to the wind. The bold, red flag, with the black cross and swastika, which they knew so well.

At once there was a puff of smoke from her bows, blown immediately to nothing by the wind, and seconds later the flat, heavy boom echoed across to them. Even as they stared round, a tall, spindly column of water rose about a hundred feet ahead of them. Another bang, this time the shot was nearer, making their hull wince, as if struck a body-blow. Frantically Royce signalled aft, and the tub-shaped smoke float thudded into the water, the black, greasy vapour already pouring out in a steady stream, low across the wave tops. The wind plucked at the fringes of the pitiful smoke-screen, and tore the life from it, leaving only the core, and a fast-moving vaporous mist between them and the German.

'Open fire when your guns bear!' ordered Royce, and following on his words came the clatter of the starboard Oerlikon, as Able Seaman Poole sent a stream of tracer spinning through the smoke, the shells seeming to bounce across the waves as they groped for the enemy.

The next shell fell so close that a deluge of water cascaded into the bridge, making Royce splutter and cough, the salt water tinged with the stink of cordite.

Over went the wheel and the M.T.B. swung crazily to starboard, as another shell burst in the very spot where she would otherwise have been. Poole gave a wild whoop, as he saw his tracers spatter across the trawler's bridge, and they watched as she turned away, drawing out of range. Bang—and the awful scream passed close overhead, making them duck, and the ghostly waterspout rose a cable's length beyond them. If only the pom-pom would fire, cursed Royce, this was hopeless. Although the trawler had been hit, and had temporarily lost the range, it was just a matter of time.

The strength of the smoke-float was rapidly diminishing, and he decided that soon the time would arrive for him to decide how best he could use his engine power to try to make good an escape. The weather was steadily worsening, and the harsh sweep of the wind was approaching gale force, and the boat was beginning to get into real difficulties, which even without the appearance of the enemy, would have been critical enough.

He reeled to the engine-room voice-pipe, shouting hoarsely above the spasmodic bursts from the Oerlikons, which were now pointing straight astern, and the rising shriek of the wind, whose icy hand plucked the words from his mouth and flung them seawards.

'Chief!' he yelled, 'do all you can, I'm going to make a run for it!'

Moore's steady voice carried clearly up to his waiting ear.

'Good luck, sir!'

Royce snapped down the cover of the voice-pipe, and rang for half speed, and he felt an increasing rumble beneath him, as the boat thrust her stem into the grey and tempestuous seas. The bows, cracked and splintered, abetted by the mounting water in the flooded bilges, plunged heavily into every trough, throwing up great sheets of spray over the gun platform, and swamping the bridge. But still the revolutions mounted, and they thrust forward, the seamen on deck slithering and falling across the streaming salt spume, as they manfully fought with the pumps. Only the Oerlikon gunners, strapped in their guns by leather harnesses, remained firm in the onslaught, and Weeks at the port gun could faintly be heard cursing as he fumbled with freezing hands to fit a fresh magazine.

Another shell hissed into the sea off the port side without exploding, but it was very much closer than the last, so once more they lost valuable headway, as the boat clawed away from the tell-tale splash in an effort to elude the next shot.

It was obvious that the trawler was still overhauling them, and even with the poor visibility her shape was taking on a sharper outline, as she dipped and plunged in relentless pursuit.

Royce sent Parker below to report on the state of the repairs, as the pom-pom was now definitely classed as unserviceable, and when he reappeared, breathless and wild eyed, Royce guessed that the cards were stacked against him.

'S'no use, sir!' bawled Parker, snatching violently at the rail to stop himself from being pitched back down the ladder, 'The water's two feet over the mess-deck, an' still comin' up fast.'

He paused for breath, watching the officer's taut face anxiously.

'The sea is tearin' the outer skin right off the port bow, just under the tube!'

Royce could well visualize the scene. The havoc wrought by the savage cannon shells would soon be exploited by these heavy seas.

He reached across to the voice-pipe again.

'No good, Chief, slow her down, just give me steerage way!'

He toyed with the impossible idea of going full astern, to try to save the strain on the bows, and he lowered his head again to the brass bell mouth of the pipe. As he did so, he heard a sharp, abbreviated whistle of higher pitch than before, followed in the tiniest fraction of a second by a deafening crack behind him. Simultaneously, a blast of hot air struck him in the mouth. Dazed and incredulous, he realized that the voice-pipe was streaming smoke in his face.

He straightened, and stared aft, his stomach retching violently. Angry, red flames clawed along the stern, and a thick pall of black smoke rolled away on the wind.

It had been a direct hit on the boat's small quarter deck, the shell pitching down against the after bulkhead before exploding with sickening impact below, sending a stream of razor-sharp, white-hot splinters in every direction, and making the after flat a raging furnace.

With a sudden, almost fatalistic calmness, Royce gave his orders.

'Coxswain! Hand over the wheel, and come on deck. Get every extinguisher to work aft!'

Parker still stood at his side, his honest face white with shock.

'Come on Parker!' he snapped. 'Get all hands except the gunners down to that fire!'

Then urgently, he called the engine room.

'Chief! Moore! Can you hear me?'

A tired-sounding voice answered.

'Aye, sir, I'm here.'

A pause and a bout of violent coughing.

' 'Fraid I can't get you any more revs. The fire's in here now, and one of my lads has bought it!'

'Right, Chief, clear out! Bring the other chap on deck. We'll have to ditch!'

A longer pause.

'Aye, aye, sir, we'll do that!'

Overhead another shell screamed like a mad thing, but the German gunners were shooting wildly, their aim ruined by the M.T.B.s death pall.

Royce leaned over the side of the bridge, trying to get a glimpse of the trawler, but she was invisible through the smoke. He looked into the upturned face of Able Seaman Poole, who hung suspended in his gun harness, his arms swinging to the motion of the boat. His eyes were open wide with amazement. There was very little of him from the waist down. Royce sobbed, and was violently sick, his lungs aching and sour.

Raikes appeared below him, his face worried.

'Sir! The engine-room hatch is jammed solid. Pony can't get out! Can you come, sir?'

For the first time in a century, or so it seemed, Royce left the bridge, walking as if in a dream, stumbling across the splintered decks to where the hands hacked and slashed at the deck casing around the metal hatch of the engine room. Feathers of smoke streamed from every crack, and from the tiny, grill-like ventilator, where two of the hands were squatting. They moved away as Royce knelt down to the small, barred opening, and beneath it he could plainly see the dull red glow within.

As if out of the flames, a frantic, terrified voice, high-pitched and desperate, made Royce recoil with horror.

'God! Get me out of here! Please, will someone help me. Please, don't leave me!'

Then they heard Moore's harsh tones.

'It's all right, son, I'm here!'

There was an audible thud and the cries ceased. As the crackle of flames rose to an all-engulfing roar, they heard Moore coughing violently, then there was nothing.

Royce stood up, his nerves screaming, and he looked wildly at the white faces around him. Each one set in its own clear caste, but bonded together with their common suffering.

'All right lads, lower the rafts!'

He forced himself to say those fearful words.

'Abandon ship! And good luck!'

He noticed that one seaman was crying.

The knives flashed dully, as two seamen slashed at the rafts' lashings, and the cumbersome objects splashed alongside secured only by a thin line.

Some of the men went eagerly, and some gazed fearfully at the heaving waters, unwilling to leave the apparent security of the boat. But eventually they leapt down, shouting each other's names, and peering dazedly at the slanting deck. The boat was already much lower in the waves, but as the after part flooded, the trim was gradually corrected, as if in a final defiance.

Royce and the Coxswain stood side by side, holding grimly to the guard-rail, when a fantastic idea formed in Royce's racing brain.

'We're on even keel for a bit!' he shouted, his eyes smarting with the smoke. 'What are the settings on the torpedoes?'

'Ten feet, sir,' answered Raikes, puzzled.

'Right, just check they're both ready for firing, then over you go!'

Raikes, numbed by the loss of his friend, didn't seem to be able to grasp his meaning.

'What are you going to do?' he stammered.

'I'm going to blow that bloody trawler to hell! That's what!' yelled Royce wildly. 'She'll be up here in a minute to have a look round, and with luck, I'll be able to get both fish running even now.'

Raikes stiffened.

'I'll stop an' give you a hand,' he announced stolidly.

'Like hell you will, Coxswain! You look after the men and pick me up afterwards.'

They both knew there was little chance of that. Already the flames licked the deck near the fuel intakes, under which lay the high-octane spirit.

He pushed the Coxswain towards the tubes, and when he saw him checking the firing mechanism, he ran to the bridge, and threw the confidential books overboard in their weighted bag.

The Coxswain hovered by the rail, his face blackened and scratched.

'So long, sir, don't leave it too long!'

As he jumped into the nearest raft, they severed the line, and shoved off, staring silently back at the boat.

Royce waved and laughed crazily, 'Thank you, lads!' Now get clear!'

He staggered back into the choking clouds, stepping over the abandoned articles of clothing, and pathetic possessions, the boat dead already but for the crackling flames, and the rattle of loose gear and empty shell cases as she rolled heavily with a stricken stagger. Grimly he squatted by the sighting bar, forcing himself to concentrate on the small, dark patch of sea ahead, fenced off by a long, sullen bank of oily smoke. Frantically he shut his ears to the distant sound of paddles, as the rafts moved away, fighting the rising feeling of panic within him. Supposing the trawler had gone away, or came up too late, he would be fried alive for nothing. It was madness, terrifying madness, which held him in its grip. He lowered his sweating forehead against the ice-cold metal, and his body shook with a paroxysm of uncontrollable sobbing. It didn't matter any more. There was no Kirby to criticize him, no seaman to watch his weakness with contempt. Only Poole swinging gently at his gun, one of his arms now alight like a torch. Petty Officer Moore and his two mechanics burning below would no longer be interested, and Able Seaman Lake, the injured man, doped with morphia, had been cut to pieces while he slept, he too would shed no tears.

Desperately he turned his mind to home, and he imagined his mother getting the telegram. And Julia, he had not seen her again, to tell her, to tell her what? He lifted his head in his anguish, and there in front of him lay the trawler.

She was motionless, and barely half a mile away, her shiny sides reflecting and glistening with the white-capped waves, the menacing muzzle of the gun still trained on him, and several figures lining the decks. Gritting his teeth, and smearing the tears from his smarting eyes, he peered along the sights. Behind him, a sudden burst of machine-gun fire made him cry out, but it was only an ammunition belt burning. A great hissing roar came from below, as the seas poured in to quench the fires in the tiller-flat. There was a crack as the plate glass of the chart table succumbed to the heat, and the carefully folded charts were reduced to ashes. But slowly and remorselessly, the trawler drifted into the sights, the raking stem, the gun, with its vigilant and victorious crew, then the tall bridge, and the arrogant swastika flag, the emblem hated the length and breadth of enslaved Europe. His breath hissed, and with a silent prayer he squeezed the triggers. There was a puff of smoke, a dull thud, and the two slim shapes slid from the tubes, hardly making a splash, so close was the deck to the sea. Fascinated, he crouched, and watched the puffs of foam as the little propellers bit into the water, and the well-greased and intricate mechanism guided the two monsters down to the depth of ten feet. Suddenly there was a frantic flurry at the trawler's stern, as the engines roared into full speed; slowly she swung round, gaining speed, while Royce shouted curses to the winds.

Then it happened. One minute he saw her clearly ahead of him, escaping the M.T.B.'s final challenge, then there was a deafening roar, and a blinding flash, that sent great shock waves rolling towards him. A vast pillar of water rose two hundred feet in the air, and when it had settled, falling slowly like majestic white curtains, there was not one stick or spar to be seen. Shakily he staggered to the side, deafened and half blinded, his clumsy fingers fumbling with his lifejacket. He didn't remember jumping, only the great, icy, choking water closing over his head. Vaguely his spinning brain recorded the bitter taste of salt and petrol, and a terrible pressure on his lungs and stomach, as an underwater explosion tore the clothes from his body. Then a great, engulfing blackness swept over him, shutting out everything.

5

THE thriving naval base of Harwich lay cradled by the twin arms of the rivers Stour and Orwell, the great concourse of turbulent water, never still or easy at any time, now shimmered and heaved in the watery sun of the late afternoon. Whichever way you cast your eye, could be seen the vast numbers of lean, weathered grey shapes of destroyers, moored in twos and threes at their buoys; paunchy little corvettes in their breathtaking dazzle-paint; overworked minesweepers; and scores of tiny harbour craft scurrying about on their urgent business. At the far end of the anchorage lay the lithe hulls of the local submarine flotilla, watched over by the ugly hulk of their depot ship, whilst to the south, around Parkeston Quay, a light cruiser was enjoying an overdue boiler clean.

The pale glow glittered around the pierheads of the huge naval training establishment, H.M.S. *Ganges,* whose towering mast dominated the harbour. Around the piers, the heavy, clumsy cutters were pulled by their sweating young amateur crews, while leather-lunged Petty Officers strode up and down between the oarsmen, shouting, watching, and hoping for the best. These were the Navy's raw material, who now under the eyes of the main East Coast striking force, struggled manfully with the mysterious commands of 'Oars' and 'Give way together!' Carrying out these orders was even more of a mystery to most of them, at the moment.

Up and behind Landguard Point lay Felixstowe, its sheltered waters looking like a sheet of tarnished pewter, and here nestled the hornet's nest of the Coastal Forces Group: M.T.B.s, Motor Gunboats, and the Motor Launches, maids of all work. Most of them were painted in the popular bizarre stripes and waves of dazzle paint, while one flotilla sported black hulls, with red shark-like mouths and gleaming white teeth painted around their stems. Not "pusser" perhaps, but very effective by night.

From all these points and creeks of bustling activity, one landmark could always be seen with ease and clarity, the imposing red-brick buildings of the Royal Naval Hospital at Shotley. Once past the wrought-iron gates and the naval orderly in white gaiters and belt, and up the wide gravel drive flanked by the air-raid shelters, a feeling of great peace and business-like calm pervaded the very air.

The long wards, with their neat rows of iron beds stood like soldiers on a polished parquet parade ground. All seemed to be occupied. Some of the inmates lay quietly sleeping, or gazing at the ceilings, and some hobbled painfully along the floor on sticks or crutches, their pale blue jackets clashing with a variety of pyjamas. Behind screens at one bed, an Able Seaman lay in a coma, moaning very softly: two of his shipmates, conspicuous and uncomfortable in their blue uniforms and gold badges, sat quietly watching, waiting for him to die.

These, and many more, were the harvest of the unsung war at sea, who were now fighting their greatest battle.

Down yet another airy passage, identical to all the others, but for its numbering, where two young nurses sat sewing up a rent in a blackout curtain, to the small wards, where the post-operational cases were watched and treated, where a wounded man's slender life-line could be strengthened, or cut. The window of one of these rooms looked out across the harbour, and an elderly naval sister, her face lined and worn, stood idly watching a fussy frigate manœuvring towards her buoy, where the two half-frozen buoy-jumpers sat waiting to receive the picking-up rope. On the fo'c'sle, tiny figures in shiny oilskins waited stolidly, while upon the open bridge, her captain eased the ship forward against the treacherous and powerful tide. Behind the sister, in a darkened corner of the white-walled room, a still figure lay straight and stiff on the bed, his chin resting against the neatly turned sheet; his skin pale and transparent. Above the eyes, and covering the rest of his head, was a complicated criss-cross of bandages, whilst at waist level, the bed blossomed out in an ungainly bulge, where wire cages protected the motionless body from all contact. The sister shifted her weight to the other foot, and sighed deeply, and, as if in sympathy, the frigate hooted impatiently on her siren.

Noiselessly the door opened, and a tall Surgeon-Commander, with bushy black eyebrows and heavy jaw, strode purposefully to the bed, his stethoscope glinting in the fast fading light.

At his elbow the duty sister reached for the record card and chart from a shelf, and for some moments there was silence, but for the rustle of the papers, and the chink of bottles as the other sister tidied the small bedside table.

'Hmm, not much progress here, sister,' said the Commander at length, rubbing his chin with his thick, capable fingers.

'It's forty-eight hours now, sir, and Doctor Anderson said we should have seen some change, one way or another, by today.'

The gold and red braided sleeve reached under the sheet, and felt the pulse.

'Hmm,' he said again. 'Have his parents been sent for?'

'Yes, sir. Mr. and Mrs. Royce will be arriving some time this evening. The Wardmaster has just finished arranging transport at the station.'

The Commander sighed deeply; it was all conforming to the too-familiar pattern. Their torn, burned, shocked and shattered bodies came to him in a steady stream, but he was still unable to view the situation with the callous indifference often expected of his trade. This one, for instance, a mere boy, who had done heaven knows what deeds out there in the North Sea, now lay like a piece of stone before him, the mechanism of life ticking only feebly. He sighed heavily. He had just finished one surgery case, when the Matron had bustled in to his office in her usual brisk manner, with news of more survivors landed by a destroyer at the base. The usual pathetic procession had followed, led by the shock cases, their hair matted with oil, their shivering bodies covered by heavy blankets; then the stretcher cases, including this one, with his hastily bandaged body and blackened skin. He studied the chart again:

severe burns to arms and chest, head injuries, and an aftermath of shock. If there was to be an aftermath.

As if he had come to some decision, he straightened and glanced at his watch.

'I'm going for tea now. Call me at once if there's any change at all. Anything.'

And he strode out of the room. As he passed one of the wards, he heard the strident voice of one of the sisters, obviously rebuking someone.

'I don't care, do you hear?' she snapped. 'You just get back to bed while I get your tea. I'll jolly well report you if you don't behave!'

The Commander stepped into the ward, now brightly alight, the long curtains drawn.

Sister Adams smiled wearily.

'Good evening, sir. I wish you'd have a talk with Bed Five; he keeps wanting to go out. But he'll have to see the doctor in the forenoon tomorrow before I can let him move.'

He walked slowly across to the offender, who sat defiantly upright against his pillows.

'What's the trouble, my lad, and who are you anyway?'

'Petty Officer Raikes, sir, Coxswain of M.T.B. 1991. I just wanted to see my officer.'

He paused, his face creased with worry.

'Will you tell me, sir, is he going to be all right?'

The Commander was touched, and his frown faded.

'I've heard about you, Raikes,' he said, and squatted on the edge of the bed. 'You went back for him didn't you? The Captain of the destroyer told me all about it; how you took a raft through blazing petrol to save that officer's life.'

Raikes flushed and squirmed with embarrassment.

'Is he going to live, sir?' he persisted.

'You've done your part, and now we'll do ours. Try to rest for a bit, and leave the worrying to us.'

As he got up to leave, he turned: 'Raikes, I'm proud to have met you.'

Raikes lay back, heedless of Sister Adams, who clucked impatiently as she straightened his sheets and patted his pillows, and let his mind drift back to that moment of decision.

He shut his eyes tightly, and once more he felt the crazy rocking motion of the tiny raft. They had seen their boat drift away in a pall of flame and smoke, with the hunched, blackened figure alone on her deck, and they had forgotten their own suffering, even their will to survive, as with shocked eyes they watched the grim drama unfold before them. Suddenly the trawler had hove in sight, like another actor making an entrance, and they had seen the torpedoes streak on their errand of death. Hoarsely they cheered and cursed, as the explosion died, and then they had been shattered by the roar as their own little ship had burst asunder and plunged down. He forced his mind back, making sure of every detail, just as he had told the destroyer's officers. It was Able Seaman Weeks who had shouted: 'Jeez! Jimmy-the-One's back there! I saw his lifejacket!'

For Raikes that had been the moment of decision.

'What's it to be, lads?' he had croaked, as an angry wave smote him across the shoulders. For a brief instant they had peered across the heaving sea, at the blazing wall of petrol left by the dying M.T.B., but only for an instant.

Weeks had heaved himself up on his knees, causing the raft to rock dangerously.

'Too right we go back! Now gimme a ruddy paddle!'

Frantically they made the nightmare journey within feet of the licking flames, fighting every bit of the way. Somehow they found him, and pulled him across the raft. The half-naked body, torn and bleeding, and the fearful burns, swollen horribly by the salt water. And somehow they had got clear of the fire, huddling together for warmth and comfort, singing, cursing, and holding desperately on to life. Three hours later, the riveted side of the destroyer loomed like a wall beside them, the scrambling nets, the strong arms and helping hands, and the murmured words of encouragement. He remembered the feel of a soft towel dabbing at his tender skin, and the harsh fire of rum in his throat. The destroyer had circled the spot slowly, looking for the other raft. They found it an hour later, but only one figure lay tied to its pitching frame. The ship's doctor had tried to keep them away, but they had seen Leading Seaman Parker lifted tenderly aboard. He had smiled vaguely 'at them, and spoken in a strange voice. As they had watched, shocked to silence, Parker said, 'I'm home, Dad, I couldn't get in the cinema, so I come home early.' He started to laugh wildly, as they forced the needle into his arm.

Raikes breathed out hard, and opened his eyes. Poor old Parker, what a waste.

Faintly across the cold air drifted the plaintive note of a bugle, Sunset, and Raikes slept.

Out and across the uneasy stretch of swift-moving water, the light faded. The newly arrived frigate swung peacefully at her buoy, her engines still. On her quarter-deck, the duty signalman folded up the ensign, and made his way to the bridge, while the Officer-of-the-Day, having attended to the brief but permanent ceremony of Sunset, turned his mind to the string of details which awaited him, and every other Duty Officer in the harbour. Libertymen, Defaulters, Rounds, Darken Ship, Duty Watch, Working Parties, and all the rest. War or peace, it made no difference to his tight routine. On scores of other ships too, the vigilant Quartermasters paced their gangways, checked their moorings, and thought of home.

Threading her way in and out of the moored, darkened shapes, the destroyer's liberty tender panted her way towards Parkeston Quay, her small deck space overloaded with sailors, who were looking forward to a brief run ashore. As she grazed to a standstill alongside the slimy piles of the jetty, and long before the first lines were made fast, the noisy, jostling throng were scrambling up on to the concrete ramps, lighting cigarettes, and adjusting caps at a more rakish angle, and keeping an eye open for the Customs Officers, who might not take too kindly to the packs of duty-free tobacco stored in the useful respirator haversacks. One or two of them glanced curiously at the elderly couple who stood looking small and lost by the entrance to the railway station, and so utterly out of place, but in a very short while, the blue-clad throng had split and vanished, leaving these two alone.

But not for long. There was a splutter of a fast motorboat at the jetty stairs, and a Petty Officer's head, followed by a stocky, duffle-coated body, rapidly appeared over the edge.

He hurried over.

'Mr. and Mrs. Royce?' he queried, leaning forward.

Mr. Royce nodded. 'What a train journey we've had, haven't we, dear? Had to change three times.'

His wife smiled at him, but the Petty Officer, a pensioner, recalled to the Navy, saw that there was little mirth behind those anxious eyes.

'Well, follow me if you please. There's a nice supper laid on for you at the . . .' he faltered. 'At the hospital.'

Slowly they climbed down the slippery steps, guided by a torch, to where the sleek, blue launch throbbed and squeaked against her fenders. Once settled, the Petty Officer shouted, 'Let go! Shove off forrard!' And with a growl they slid into the darkness.

The passengers sat quietly in the tiny cockpit, shielded from the spray, and stared at the strange and alien surroundings of their son's world, hitherto but an unreal picture painted by the B.B.C. and Clive's regular letters.

Mrs. Royce turned her head, and could dimly make out the reassuring profile, always at her side.

'Do you think——' she started, for the hundredth time, and stopped helplessly.

'Don't worry, my dear, I told you before, they've asked us down just to help his recovery a bit.'

He squeezed her arm in the darkness.

As they stepped ashore at the smart, white-painted landing stage, flanked by the brass dolphins, another figure stepped forward to greet them, and following the steel-helmeted sentry, they entered the hospital grounds. The motor-boat swung away to her berth at the boats' pool, the old P.O. wondering sadly how long he was expected to make these heartbreaking journeys, backwards and forwards, with parents and wives and friends. He spat over the side of his boat, and turned his attention to the bow-man.

'Your turn to wet the tea when we've tied up, Nobby!'

The waiting-room where Mr. and Mrs. Royce found themselves five minutes later, was already occupied, and Mr. Royce gave an inward sigh of relief, knowing that further conversation at this stage would be impossible. As they sat on the well-worn sofa, he studied the two officers sprawled in the chairs by the radiator. One, a languid Lieutenant-Commander, with a keen but tired face, was idly glancing through an ancient magazine, while the other, a stocky, hard-faced Lieutenant, was scraping out his pipe with slow deliberation. The former suddenly looked up, his clear eyes questioning. Having apparently made up his mind, he nudged his companion, and stood up.

'Good evening. Have I the pleasure of addressing Mr. and Mrs. Royce?' His voice was a well-modulated drawl.

Mrs. Royce smiled, and nodded shyly.

'Well, bless my soul.' The Lieutenant stepped up to them with outstretched hand. 'I'm Murray, Jock to you both, if you will, and this is Lieutenant-Commander Emberson. We are great friends with your son.'

The ice was broken, for both names at least were familiar and often mentioned in Clive's letters.

Emberson drew up a chair. 'What a shame your having to come all that way by train—it's no joke in this part of the world.'

'No, it's one helluva journey, if you'll pardon the expression, ma'am,' added Murray.

Before Mr. Royce could make a similarly casual remark, he heard his wife's voice, with the merest quaver in it, and he steeled himself.

'Tell me quite truthfully,' she said quietly. 'Does it seem that we—that Clive——' She faltered and stopped.

Emberson and Murray exchanged quick glances.

'Now just you stop worrying.'

His assurances were halted by the sudden entrance of the Surgeon-Commander, and both the officers stood to attention.

'I'm Commander Lloyd, and I'm very glad you got here

all right,' he said gruffly. 'Now just come along and see your boy and then we'll fix you up with a real unrationed dinner.'

Without speaking, they hurried down the bare corridors to the private ward.

As the Commander reached for the handle, the door was wrenched open, and he nearly collided with the sister.

'Where are you going?' he hissed. 'What's happening?'

Mrs. Royce felt faint, and held her husband's arm, watching the sister's face, who was clearly put off her guard.

'It's all right, these are his parents,' barked Lloyd, trying to conceal his fears.

'It's the young officer, sir,' she stammered, glancing from one to the other. 'He spoke to me!'

'Good God! Did he?' and the bulky Commander pushed past her, closely followed by the others.

Mrs. Royce let out a soft cry as she saw the figure in the bed, but the doctor paid no heed to either of them, until he had finished his examination. Eventually he drew himself up, and let out a great sigh.

'Your son,' he said slowly, 'has done the impossible. He has, in fact, turned the corner quite safely.' He turned to the door.

'You may sit here for ten minutes; I'll arrange for your meal. Come with me, sister.' The door closed.

An ambulance drove noisily up the gravel approach to the hospital, and somewhere in the far distance sounded the wail of an air-raid siren, but in that small room, at that moment, there was complete peace.

When the sister returned, she found them still sitting there, and with a great smile she laid a tray of tea at the bedside.

'Thought you might like a nice cup of tea to be going on with.'

Mrs. Royce's eyes shone. 'Bless you for taking so much trouble. Could you please tell me what he said to you?'

The sister paused, puckering her brow.

'Well, I was just sitting there by the window, when I heard him move, so I went over. As I reached him, he opened his eyes and looked me straight in the face and said, "Are the others all right?" So I said, "Yes" or something, and he smiled at me, and sort of relaxed. You know the rest.'

'My poor Clive, his face looks so thin.'

'Don't you worry. Commander Lloyd says it's going to be just fine.'

'By the way,' Mr. Royce's voice was a little unsteady. 'What did happen to "the others"?'

The sister busied herself noisily with the cups.

'There were only eight survivors, I'm afraid.'

Reluctantly they had to go, and after an enormous meal, which they scarcely noticed, they were taken to a room in the annexe, where, for the first time since receiving the telegram, they slept.

The following morning was bright and crisp, with a keen, steady breeze sweeping the estuary into a million tiny white-caps. The sky was, for once, completely clear, a fine if rather hard blue. The vessels tugged impatiently at their cables, as if to jerk their crews awake for such a refreshing day, and already from countless galley funnels, faint wisps of smoke, and mixed aromas of frying bacon or utility sausages, blended invitingly with the more prevalent ship odours of oil and men. The Preparative flag mounted the gaff of the port signal tower, two minutes to Colours, and on the newly swept and scrubbed quarter-decks, the signalmen waited to hoist their ensigns, so that another naval day could be officially started. One minute later, Royce opened his eyes, and slowly, very slowly, his brain and senses battled to find some common understanding. At first he had the impression that he was suspended in space, a feeling of unreality and disembodied detachment deprived him of any sort of realization. There was only a bright haze surrounding him, no feeling yet of self-possession, or in fact, the will to bring himself back to his real world, so recently a world of torment.

Out on the vast parade ground of H.M.S. *Ganges,* an unknown boy bugler was to start the wheels turning once more, was to give Royce his cue, his reintroduction to the land of the living. The bugler raised his shining instrument, and moistened his lips. The Officer-of-the-Day roared hoarsely, 'Make it so!' and as the gleaming flag mounted the mast, the strident notes rang out round the sombre buildings, causing the dozing gulls to rise in squawking protest, and echoing and ebbing until they eventually penetrated the subconscious barrier of Royce's mind.

He squinted, closed his dry lips, and tried to move, and as the stab of pain lanced his back, he became, in that split second, fully aware of everything but his surroundings. At first, he was filled with fear, and then curiosity, as he painfully twisted his head towards the source of the light, where, sitting by the window with her head nodding, he saw a nurse. So he had made it. The very effort of trying to marshal his thoughts made him weak, but silently he struggled back over a period of blankness, until he saw with sudden clarity the enemy ship. It was so real that it seemed to shut out the light, to fill the room. He felt his body go clammy; it was the first time he had really noticed the presence of his limbs, and he tried to move his legs. He could not. Gritting his teeth, he tried again, holding his breath and contracting his stomach muscles with the effort. Little red and green dots jumped lightly before his eyes, and he lay back gasping, while in the back of his head a hammer began to pound mercilessly. So this was it, someone had rescued him, but for what? To be a helpless cripple? He shut his eyes tightly, and bit his lip to prevent a whimper of self-pity. Even his arms refused to rise above the sheets, and a surge of sudden panic made him fling his head from side to side on the pillow, each movement making the pain worse, until eventually he heard himself cry out, a sort of gurgle. Instantly, there was a patter of footsteps, and a cool hand pressed gently but firmly across his brow, and with it came a peculiar feeling of security. He stared up at the concerned grey eyes, and was dimly aware of a smell of soap, and the squeak of starch in the white uniform. He opened his lips, which felt like old leather, and tried again.

'Where am I?'

He halted, frightened, surely that wasn't his voice? It was too high, too cracked.

He cleared his throat, and felt the taste of petrol. Instantly, as if sparked by an explosion in his mind, the terrible memories came flooding back, tumbling over themselves, in wild and horrible confusion. Crackling flames, gunfire, and rushing water, tore round within his brain, like a symphony from hell, with a background of screams, some of which were his own.

How long this paroxysm lasted he didn't know; he only became dimly aware of strong hands holding him, and soothing voices, soft, yet persistent.

He lay limp and quiet, his mind dead once more, until one of the voices penetrated and held him in its grasp.

'Now come on, old fellow, wakey wakey, it's high time you sat up and took a little nourishment!'

Frantically Royce gathered himself together, and found himself looking into the heavy, confident face of the surgeon.

'Sorry, sir, everything went a bit rocky,' he stammered. 'But I feel a lot better now.'

As he said that, he really did feel a surge of life pulsate through him, and he tried to smile.

'Well now, since you've decided to stay with us, you'd better hear what's wrong with you.'

He raised one hand hastily, as Royce flinched.

'Now don't get worried, I promise you that you'll be all right and about again in a few weeks. Provided you're a good boy of course. Just the odd burn, and a scratch or two; you've been very lucky. Comparatively speaking that is,' he added with a broad smile.

The surgeon's matter-of-fact manner began to have the desired effect. All the perfectly normal service catch-phrases and casual slang made Royce feel more at ease, and he found himself thinking of things and happenings outside his own personal torment.

'Tell me, sir,' his voice was quiet and tense. 'How did I get here? Are the others safe?'

The big figure settled itself comfortably on the edge of the bed, and slowly and carefully the surgeon retold the story of Raikes's gallant rescue, of the destroyer's arrival on the scene just at the right moment, and lastly he came to the piece that he could personally vouch for, the survivors' arrival at the hospital.

Royce listened with amazement. It seemed impossible now that he had ever been involved in such happenings, let alone been the principal character. The other man's voice stopped, but Royce knew that he must have omitted much, just to spare him. He smiled grimly.

'And there were only eight of us left, you say? Are they getting on all right now?'

'Fine! Why you're the only one who's caused any panic so far, so you just think about getting better, and going on some leave! Besides, we need your bed!'

Royce lay back, and for the first time he felt relaxed, his worst fears had been dispelled. He had been tested, and he had made it.

In his opinion, the next three hours of his new-found life were the most difficult, when with his parents sitting by his side, he tried desperately to make light of all his experiences, and to prevent his mother from taking complete control from the sister, who smiled at some of her suggestions, which made Royce blush with embarrassment. Eventually they had to go, and he felt suddenly tired and weak, as his mother lingered by the bed, watching him anxiously.

'The doctor says you'll be able to come home soon,' she said, 'so look after yourself, my dear, and don't worry about not being able to write to us. We'll send you some things to replace the ones you have lost.'

Royce looked down at his heavily bandaged hands, the thought of not being able to do all the usual little jobs, writing, shaving, filling a pipe, or even opening a door, had not occurred to him.

Mr. Royce saw the look of dismay on his son's face.

'We'll be off now, Clive. It was grand to see you again. Your mother and I are proud of you.'

'Proud? I did what I had to do, Dad.' His voice too was getting weaker.

'Now you get some rest; we're off to get that train, and start getting the house ready for you.'

As they stood looking back from the open door, he cleared his throat.

'Yes, proud, that's what I said. We saw two of your officers this morning. They told us everything. Cheerio, son.'

The sister immediately took charge again, straightening the blankets, and making him comfortable, in the manner of nurses the world over, muttering dark threats, and grumbling at her patient. Unfortunately, it was not difficult for anyone to see she adored her latest patient, as the surgeon pointed out.

The days which followed were difficult for Royce, cut off from the life he knew and trusted, and constantly forced to endure the pain and discomfort of his injuries, and their treatment. He was not allowed any visitors, for fear that too much conversation would weaken him, but the letters and messages of good wishes and congratulations which had poured in from the *Royston* moved him beyond words.

The one exception to the rule was Raikes, who had been so persistent, and who had kept up his stream of inquiries to such a degree, that he was permitted to sit in the room for most of the afternoon, provided he didn't make Royce too excited. It worked beautifully, and most of the time the two men were quite content to sit and lie in silence, each sharing the richness of comradeship and achievement.

At the end of the first week, their little routine was interrupted by the sweeping entrance of the matron, in a high state of excitement, an unusual occurrence for that particular pillar of strength.

'Good Heavens alive!' she boomed, her starched cuffs waving. 'This place is a pigsty, it won't do at all!' She then proceeded to readjust every article in sight, until it seemed to be to her liking, although to everybody else the room looked just as usual, spotless.

Royce creaked his head round on the pillow, in the way he had now perfected.

"What's up, Matron? The Admiral coming?"

She shook her finger at him, frowning. 'Now, how did you know? I only knew myself ten minutes ago!'

Royce paled. 'You mean an admiral *really* is coming? To see me?'

118

'He certainly is,' she consulted a tiny watch on her plump wrist, 'and he should be here any minute.'

Raikes stood up, his eyes shining.

'Well, sir, I'm sorry to say this, but I'm desertin' you this time. Admirals aren't in my line!'

And with a wicked grin he vanished.

'Phew, what's gone wrong now, I wonder,' he muttered, staring hard at the ceiling. 'Surely they're not going to put me through it again.'

Vice-Admiral Sir John Marsh, Flag Officer in Charge of the base, was a small, unassuming figure, so that many persons had been shattered by his unexpectedly forthright, and often harsh, manner. And as he stepped lightly into the small room his sleeves ablaze with gold lace, his sharp eyes darting round, Royce could almost feel the energy given off by this miniature volcano. The Admiral wasted no time.

'My boy, I'm pleased to meet you,' he barked. 'I expect I'll be seeing more of you later, but right now I have to get on with the war.'

'Yes, sir,' agreed Royce lamely.

'However, I wanted to tell you personally, that I think you've done a grand job. A really fine piece of work.'

'But it was only a trawler, sir, I——'

'I know what happened, and I know what you did, exactly.'

'What the Admiral means,' Royce became aware that the Admiral's languid Flag Lieutenant, a very overworked young man, was hovering at the rear, 'is that some award——'

'Shut up, you fool,' snapped the other testily. 'What I mean is that you have been recommended for the Distinguished Service Cross. Suit you?'

Royce stuttered. 'Suit me, sir?' he gasped. 'I'm so, so . . .' He struggled for words. 'I just don't know how to thank you, sir.'

'I'm thanking *you*, Royce. Now I have to be off, but we shall meet again soon. Come, Roberts.'

The door swung behind them.

'Did you hear that, Matron, or am I dreaming?'

'Yes, but you don't deserve it. Look at your dressings; keep your head still!'

But before she bustled out she gave him a little hug.

So regular and efficiently planned is hospital life and routine, that even small things become highlights in the patient's life, and Royce found himself becoming more and more restless, as his strength increased, and he eagerly looked forward to any unusual happening, such as his somewhat dangerous shave, which an attractive, if inexperienced, V.A.D. gave him every other day. Or the re-making and changing of sheets, when the whole operation was completed without moving the patient. Quite an extraordinary feat. And finally, after the doctor's casual permission, the day when he was allowed to get up. Gingerly he eased his feet into his slippers, and lurched to an upright position, at least that was what he had planned. But for the ever-vigilant sister, he would have fallen. He was quite determined, however, and step by step, he wobbled to the window, his sore limbs and bandages giving him a weird top-heavy feeling.

If the journey was painful, the reward was great. As he stood, breathing jerkily, and leaning one shoulder against the wall, he saw the whole harbour laid out like a shimmering chart before him, and once more he felt at home, reassured. For a whole hour, despite the sister's threats, he stood eagerly drinking in every detail, and studying every vessel in sight, trying to follow the many activities of the bustling harbour craft, and the ponderous cranes lining the busy jetties. He felt more determined than ever to leave the hospital in record time, especially as all the others had already been released, and had gone on leave. Raikes had seemed almost reluctant to leave him, but he too had now left. Royce smiled inwardly. Good old Raikes, thank God he was going to get a D.S.M. for his selfless bravery.

He laughed aloud when he remembered his last letter from Benjy Watson, for even though it was a little exaggerated, and rather colourful, it seemed certain that Kirby was not just a little displeased by Royce's good fortune. But the mood passed, when he remembered the others who had been less fortunate.

Emberson visited him as often as his exacting duties permitted, and kept him fully informed of the local flotillas' activities and sorties against the enemy, and whenever possible he brought him brief items of news about his own boats, or of Benjy's latest episode.

'You got the other stripe, a D.S.C., and a reputation,' he drawled, his lined young face breaking into a warm smile, 'so I think you're booked for that command. Don't scoff, my lad, you wait and see.'

'Oh stop, Artie, you're driving me up the wall,' laughed Royce. 'Don't you know what it's like to be cooped up in here with all this'—he waved his arm towards the harbour —'going on just under my nose.'

Emberson regarded him thoughtfully for a while.

'Tell you what, Clive, come down to my boat next week; we'll have a wee party. Nothing vast, of course, your doc wouldn't like it.'

'Could I? Will they let me?'

'You leave it to me, old friend. It'd be a sort of recuperative holiday, a health-cure, in fact. After all, nothing's too good for a wounded hero!'

Royce almost danced. 'If you can fix that, *I'll* pay for the party!' he laughed gaily.

He could think of nothing else, and even when they removed his head bandages, and he saw the bare patches where his scalp had been neatly repaired, he merely remarked, 'It'll soon grow again.'

Eventually the day of the promised outing arrived, and as he stood by the Wardmaster's office, where that harassed individual struggled with the vast amount of paperwork required of a hospital at war, he felt rather like a small boy who, having recovered from mumps, is about to take his first glimpse of the outside world.

'I dunno what the Commander's thinking of, letting you go gallivanting off into the town like this. It'll be downright bad for morale, that it will!'

Royce looked at himself in the full-length mirror on the

wall, and smiled ruefully. He certainly was a weird sight, with his loose, blue hospital overall, and scuffed battle-dress trousers. Even if his new uniform had been ready for him, he would have been unable to encase his bandaged arms in the sleeves, while his healing body would certainly have taken unkindly to any sort of stiff jacket. He was even more appalled by his face. All youth seemed to have been drained from it, and left instead a haggard, almost shrunken imitation of its former self. The eyebrows had not yet fully grown, and his forehead still bore the angry marks of the fire's caress. The crudely clipped hair was disguised and held in place by a brand-new cap, with glittering badge, which he had purchased for the occasion, and now seemed to accentuate and magnify his wild appearance.

'Well, I'm going anyway,' he said firmly. 'I look dead already, and I will be if I stop here much longer.'

A taxi stood ticking over in the driveway, and the driver thrust his head out of the window.

' 'Ere y're, sir, Commander Emberson told me ter pick yer up and deliver yer safe to 'im.'

Royce grinned, and levered himself in to the back seat, and with a roar they were off.

Whether it was the jolting of the cab, or the excitement of being out again and still alive, or whether it was just the fact that he did not fully realize the inner extent of his injuries, he could not say, but after about ten minutes he was hanging on to the side-straps, and swallowing hard, to prevent himself from being violently sick. The aged driver had been watching him in the driving mirror and suddenly stopped the cab.

'I think I'd better be taking yer back. It don't do no good to kill yerself like this.'

Royce didn't trust his voice, but shook his head vigorously, and painfully scrambled out on to the pavement.

'I'll be okay, but I think I'll walk for a bit; you just follow me up, if you don't mind.'

'Lor' bless you, I don't mind, if you don't!'

So with the slim figure in the flapping blue coat, striding with great concentration down the pavement, and the old taxi growling along the kerb behind, they continued the journey.

Royce felt he could breathe better, and even the giddiness was a bit easier, although every so often he would pause as if to study a shop window, while the street swam in a mist around him. In this way he was able to fool the driver, and gather strength for the next stretch.

By the time they reached the wired gate of the Coastal Forces mooring area, he was shaking from head to foot, and desperately he manoeuvred his bandaged hands across his face, now shiny with sweat. A Petty Officer wearing a Naval Police armband stepped from a small hut, and saluted, his eyes wide with obvious amazement.

'Look *here* sir,' he sounded concerned. 'It's none of my business, but I think I should telephone the P.M.O.'

'No, it is none of your damned business!' snapped Royce. 'D'you think I've come this far to be held up by a lot of blasted red tape!'

The Petty Officer was unmoved.

'Very well, sir, then I shall take it upon myself to escort you to Commander Emberson's boat. Fortunately, it's not far.'

Royce relented, and smiled.

'Sorry, P.O., I think I must be getting a bit edgy.'

They reached the foot of the gangway without further incident, and Royce leaned against his escort, while he let his eye travel along the seemingly enormous length of the M.T.B. She was one of the new Fairmiles, and almost twice the size of those in his own flotilla. Vicious looking muzzles peeped from every direction, while the torpedo tubes visible from the jetty, pointed menacingly at the Fleet Mail Office. Her decks were suitably busy with overalled seamen, under the direction of a fresh-faced Sub-Lieutenant, smart in blue battledress and a gleaming white sweater. Very right and proper for the Senior Officer's boat he thought. Must be some of old Kirby's influence. He watched the young Sub moving purposefully about the deck, attending to his duties, and compared him with the image he had seen in the hospital mirror, half an hour or so previously. Was it possible that he had looked so full of youthful high spirits

123

when he had first reported to Harston? About the same age too, but only in years. His inner searchings were cut short, the Sub having stepped lightly to the jetty without his noticing. Must be losing my grip, he thought fiercely.

'Lieutenant Royce?'

He straightened automatically. It was the first time he had been addressed by his new rank, and it sounded strange, and rather formal.

'We weren't expecting you so soon, sir, this is very nice. The C.O.'ll be tickled pink. He's got some friends to celebrate your return, as it were.'

He paused, and peered at him, his face clouding. 'D'you feel all right, sir?'

Royce sucked in a lungful of salt air and nodded. 'Yes, lead on, it takes a bit of getting used to, that's all.'

'I see, sir,' but he obviously didn't.

'By the way, my name's Bird, with all the obvious disadvantages, and after I've finished on deck—we're just going to test our new Browning—I'll be in the wardroom drinking up the experiences of my betters!'

'Bitters, you mean!'

Emberson strode forward with hands outstretched.

'Clive, you crafty old devil, you made it then, and thwarted my reception committee.'

Royce held out his hand, and then they both looked at the shapeless bandages, Emberson with his hand half raised for the automatic handshake.

'Sorry, Artie, I forgot. We must bow to each other!'

The problem of getting him down the steep ladder to the wardroom had already been discussed, and two seamen stood below, guiding his feet, while the Coxswain and Emberson dealt with the top half. Royce didn't have to do a single thing for himself.

The wardroom was long for an M.T.B., and narrow, with all the usual varnished fittings, and pipes criss-crossing the deck-head. The sight of the rippling reflection of the quiet water on the rough anti-condensation paint, the gentle movement beneath his feet, and the accompanying shipboard smells and noises, were a welcome indeed.

A tall seaman in a tight white jacket was laying tea, and pulled up the most comfortable chair.

Royce sat on the edge gingerly, and grimaced.

'Nearly didn't make it, but it was worth the effort. I can't tell you what it's like to be back.'

'I know, I know, it's not much, but it's home.'

'Where are the others that your Subby was telling me about?'

'Don't fret, they'll be back. They've just gone over to the *Kitson* to look at this new radar gadget. All the new ships have got it in Harwich.'

The curtain was thrust aside from the door, and Benjy Watson, Jock Murray and three other officers entered.

'Here he is!' yelled Benjy. 'Who told me he had resigned?'

Royce looked from face to face, wondering what they thought of his crumpled appearance, and realizing just how much he had missed them.

'Too tough, that's me,' he grinned.

They enjoyed to the full the carefully prepared tea—goodness only knows where so much rationed stock had been filched, but it was marvellous. Then with pipes well alight, they talked and yarned until they were hoarse, and Royce felt again the creeping faintness and sudden giddy lapses, which caused him to speak quickly and nervously, as if afraid he would be forced to break off and leave.

The others knew full well what was happening, and several meaning looks were exchanged. Emberson would have sent for the taxi earlier, but his main surprise was still to come. He glanced at his watch anxiously.

'I'm very much afraid your probation is running out, Clive,' he said quietly. 'You have to be back in half an hour. That was the arrangement with the old Doc.'

Royce rose unsteadily, knowing that his reserve was beginning to fail. The faces around him blurred, and he blinked to clear his vision. He had been holding a cup between his muffled hands, as a dog will hold a bone, and the effort of setting it on the table was unbearable. He vaguely noticed that the others were silent. Even Benjy looked strange, and worried.

'Thank you for having me, gentlemen,' he forced a crooked smile. 'It's been just what I needed.'

It was at that moment that the Browning machine-gun on deck fired a practice burst, and although he had been forewarned, he was seemingly unprepared for its violence, and his own reaction. The wardroom, the officers, everything dissolved in front of him, all his racing brain could follow was the dreadful staccato rattle, that in a split second made his sick mind lurch, and with a gasp, he threw his body to the deck.

Even as they jumped to his aid, Emberson swearing horribly at the unseen gunners, the curtain by the door jerked aside once more, and the small figure of a Wren stepped hurriedly inside.

'I'm late, I'm afraid, sir, the bus——' she broke off, her eyes widening at the scene, her face suddenly white.

'What's happened? Is he all right?'

Emberson looked up, 'Blast, just too late,' he said. 'Quick, hold his head, and keep his shoulders off the deck!'

Royce lay on his side, only dimly aware that he was alive. Everything was dark, he heard a voice yelling, 'Coxswain, make a signal, urgent, send ambulance!'

Ambulance? At sea? Impossible. Weren't we in action? Yes, that was it, the guns, must keep them firing. He turned his body, but someone was holding him, stopping him. He struggled feebly, and tried to get his eyes in focus.

From far away he heard his voice protesting. It was at that instant he saw Julia looking down at him, close enough to touch, and then he felt content, the pain and urgency seemed to slowly disperse.

'Julia, my darling,' he whispered. 'You shouldn't be here, it's not safe . . .' his voice trailed away.

He was only dimly conscious of the white jackets, and the stretcher, but the vision of that face, with the tear-filled eyes, made him suddenly desperate, some hidden strength made him cry out, urgently, and as the mist closed over him, he heard that voice once more, just as it had been at the railway station, soft and sweet. 'It's all right, Clive, everything's going to be fine now.'

As the ambulance tore towards the hospital, its gong

sounding shrilly, he felt a great peace sweeping over him. The Cease Fire bell, that was it. Yes, everything was going to be fine now.

* * * * *

Royce sat by the window in his dressing-gown, the pale yellow glow of the afternoon sun lighting his face, and easing away the lines of strain. For once, he paid little heed to the activities of the harbour, and even yesterday's visit to the M.T.B., with the dreadful aftermath of delirium, and this morning's stern rebukes from both the doctor and the matron, had faded into insignificance, and all because of the letter, which he had read and re-read half a dozen times, and which now lay in his lap. When he had recovered from his drugged state of semi-collapse, he had been half fearful that the one bright spot, the one brief moment of pure happiness, had been but another dream, a figment of his tortured imagination, but the letter, hastily written on N.A.A.F.I. notepaper and handed to him by the nurse, had dispelled all his fears, and left him with a feeling of excitement, and a trembling anticipation. The letter was brief, and in her firm, neat hand Julia Harston had done her best to cram as much as she could into its construction, while apparently keeping one eye on an impatient railway clock. He started to read it again, smiling secretly to himself, and still unable to realize his good fortune.

She explained fully how Emberson had made a long-distance telephone call to her, and had in fact told her how Royce had been on the danger list, and had been asking for her in her moments of semi-consciousness, and he thought she might well be able to improve and encourage his recovery. A hurried explanation to an understanding Second Officer, a quick sub by one of the other girls at the signal station, a fast train south, and she had arrived in time to see his suffering, and to understand the pain and shock which he had endured so bravely. He found himself feeling rather pleased at that piece, for he knew in his own mind that if he looked ghastly when he had left the hospital, he must have been a gibbering wreck when she had made her

127

entrance. Altogether a bad impression to make under the circumstances. Reading this, he felt considerably better. She continued by telling him that she had had to hurry off back to Rosyth, but not before the hospital had informed her, rather coldly, that the patient was "as well as could be expected, in view of his escapades". He grinned, that was more or less what the matron had said to him. It was the end of the letter he really liked.

I'm so very sorry about the way I treated you when we last met, but I now know that we both understand. If you still want to see me, I shall be very happy, and I shall look forward to hearing from you. Please look after yourself, and give my thanks to Commander Emberson, who has told me so much about you.

Yours sincerely, Julia.

That was the piece that made him glow. And she had signed herself simply Julia. It was only a written word, on the cheap paper, but to him it was a breath of true intimacy. Once it had been only a dream, something to think about during the wearying hours of watch-keeping, but in a flash, or so it seemed, there had been a series of breath-taking and terrifying changes in his life, and the dream had changed to something real, and the future had been given life and hope. All the same, he mused, it would have to be handled extremely carefully, for up to now, the initiative had been in the hands of others, and if he wasn't going to make another mess of it, he would have to give the matter a great deal of thought. The first thing was to get his service life rearranged, and straightened out, and that meant he would have to get well clear from the hospital. He immediately got down to the latter problem, with his usual keen and methodical way, and the doctors and nurses, overworked though they were, were quick to notice his sudden interest in his treatment, and a new impatience at any delay or setback.

Within two weeks, he had discarded most of his outward signs of injury, and took pleasure in striding about the hospital grounds, and occasionally walking down to the

128

base to see Emberson, and on one otherwise dismal morning, he carefully put on his new uniform, said his farewells to the hospital staff, and headed for home, for three weeks' leave.

As usual, he enjoyed his leave to the full, and was pleased to be able to make his parents happy by being home again, but this time there was a difference, within himself he was a changed person. At first he ignored it, and tried to overlook something which might be only fancy, but as the days of enforced idleness wore on, he began to realize that Lieutenant Clive Royce, D.S.C., was a completely different being from the worried, but easy-going young officer who had once muddled and struggled through the early intricacies of life in an M.T.B. The harder he thought about it, the more baffling it became, he could not even place the exact time of the change. After all, he told himself repeatedly, he had not had an easy war so far, so it wasn't that, it was something far deeper.

He had written twice to Julia in Scotland, telling her of his progress, and how he hoped to be able to visit her as soon as possible. And he told her of his strange feeling, and fears. Her letters were, as always, witty yet soothing; friendly, but not showing a great deal of sympathy for his broodings. At first he felt rather hurt by her apparent sharpness, but as he strolled through the woods, ignoring the constant drizzle that seemed fated for his leave, reading her words over and over again, trying to find hidden meanings in every one, he realized that her approach was the right one. The past was history, but others would be looking to him from now on, relying upon his experience for their very existence. He knew then how he had changed. By responsibility to others. It was as if a curtain had been lifted, the way was now clear, and when the buff envelope was handed to him by his mother, four days before his leave was due to end, he felt in some way relieved.

'I have to report back to the *Royston*,' he announced simply. 'I don't quite understand it, I have to appear before a Board.'

His parents quietly helped him pack his newly bought kit, when Royce suddenly jerked up as if he had been shot.

'Good God!' he burst out. 'Surely they don't think I'm round the bend!'

So often, he had seen officers classified as unsuitable for Coastal Forces, and even for any seagoing duties; men who had once been hardened fighters, and seemingly indispensable, had suddenly become shattered wrecks, grey-faced ghosts, who shied from any decision, and jumped at every sound. Such was the price of danger.

'Oh no!' he groaned. 'They couldn't do that to me now. I must make them see that I'm all right now!'

It was a miserable journey back to the base, and seemed to take twice as long as usual, and even the first glimpse of the *Royston*'s ungainly bulk was no an anti-climax.

He hurried into the wardroom to pump his friends for information, only to find that the flotilla was at sea, covering a convoy, so there was nothing else to do but walk straight to the Commander's office, and get it over.

Commander Wright looked up with surprise, as a thin-lipped Royce was shown in.

'Good heavens, man, you're back early,' he roared jovially. 'It's damn good to see you again. Oh, and congratulations, me boy.'

Royce stood stiffly. 'I'd like to know if I may, sir,' he faltered. 'The Board tomorrow morning, can I appeal against it?'

'Appeal against it? Appeal against it?' Wright bellowed so loud that the Writer in the next office shuddered. 'What the devil d'you mean, sir? After all this trouble, don't you want a command? Damn and blast my breeches, explain yourself, sir!'

Poor Royce was past any explanation.

'Command?' he said weakly.

'Yes, don't you know anything about it?'

'No, sir. I thought it was the Old Crock's Rush they were giving me, you know, the Axe.'

Wright lay back in his chair, and laughed till his eyes were wet, looking rather like a newly boiled lobster.

'Oh, Royce, you'll be the death of me!' he wheezed. 'Here's me, pulling every damn string under the Old Pal's Act to get you fixed up with a command, and to be serious for a moment, we need experienced M.T.B. men badly, and you come in here nattering about being bomb-happy!'

He pulled a bottle and two glasses from a side drawer.

'Here, me boy, let's drink to it. I've done all I can, you just give Captain Marney the right idea tomorrow, and you'll be all set.'

Royce sat dazed in the chair, and scarcely noticed the neat gin, yet another phase was unfolding, seemingly beyond his control. A command, well.

As he left the office, walking on air, he could still hear Wright laughing.

6

CAPTAIN REGINALD MARNEY, D.S.O., Officer-in-Charge
Coastal Forces at the base, paced impatiently up and down
the spotless interior of his stateroom-cum-office. A Writer,
and the *Royston's* Yeoman of Signals stood discreetly at
one end, motionless, but for their eyes, which followed the
great man back and forth on his journey.

Captain Marney was an imposing man in his late forties,
his face brown and lined by years of service from Iceland
to Shanghai, and his short hair greying rapidly under the
weight of his many responsibilities.

'Well, that about covers it for this morning,' his voice
was clipped. 'Make another signal to F.O.I.C., Yeoman,
repeated "Staff Officer Operations and all Commanding
Officers".'

He paused, and let his keen blue eyes drift through the
well-polished scuttle, and finally rest on an M.T.B. which
was manœuvring alongside the Gun Wharf. Young fool, he
thought, too much rudder. The M.T.B. appeared to stop
rather suddenly, as it bounced off the rubber fenders of
the jetty, and the Captain felt vaguely satisfied that his
observations had not been mistaken. He cleared his throat,
and the Yeoman licked the point of his pencil.

'During the next month, maximum effort is to be made
against all enemy coastal shipping, in order to withdraw as
many of the German Forces as possible from our own
convoy routes. It will be appreciated if Base and Operations Staffs will co-operate with Commanding Officers
to the best of their ability during the next decisive period.
Send that off Restricted, as usual,' he ended.

He had been dictating letters and signals for two hours,
as was his usual custom each morning. As the other two
turned to leave, he added, 'And, Yeoman, make a signal
to M.T.B. 7784, er, "Suggest change of rudder at the

right time may prevent change of command at the wrong time".'

He smiled drily, these Wavy Navy chaps, ah well, it was all new to them. He sighed heavily.

His Chief Writer, a ferrety man called Slade, entered stealthily.

'Commander Wright and Commander Thirsk, for the Board, sir.'

'Very well, Slade, table, chairs, etc. The usual.'

He was a man of few words.

The "Board" assembled every so often, to arrange replacements for commanding officers, to fill the vacancies caused by death, promotion, new boats, and the many other nerveracking problems of supply and demand. At this moment, with ships being lost left and right, the demand was very great, and the supply was getting less and less experienced.

When Royce eventually sat down facing the grim-faced trio, he felt the first qualms of possible defeat, but he steeled himself, and took consolation from Wright's nod of encouragement.

Captain C-F came quickly to facts.

'Read your history, Royce. Quite like it, but I want you to tell me the story again. Right from when you first reported here.'

They listened in silence, studying the younger man's face, understanding the full impact of his words. When he finished, they sent him out of the room, to wait in maddening solitude. Not for long, and he studied their faces, especially that of the Captain.

'I think you'll be pleased to know that we're satisfied, and I am quite sure you'll do your best to make up in resourcefulness and courage, what you lack in training.'

He paused while Royce mumbled his thanks.

'Don't thank me, Royce, remember it's a great task you have before you. You must realize that you will be quite alone in your small way, just as I am here. There will be many difficulties which you must face without a pause, and without consultation with others. Your men will be mostly new to the trade, much more amateur than you ever were. And the reason I have selected you for the task, quite apart from your technical qualifications, which are obvious, is because you have not lost your sense of humanity, you have not allowed yourself to become hard. Remember, to become too hard, even in war, is to become too brittle.'

'I'll try to live up to that, sir.'

'Well, good luck. Now off you go, and get that well-needed drink. Commander Wright will give you all the details this afternoon.'

As the door closed behind him, the three regular officers relaxed, and looked at each other.

Commander Thirsk, a ruddy-faced destroyer captain, shook his head. 'Poor little beggars! In peace-time it'd have been years before we heard what that young man has just heard. Now they're expected to take a command when they can hardly salute properly.'

'Don't forget, Harry, it was harder to get killed then,' said Captain Marney soberly.

* * * * *

The somehow derelict-looking end of the port installations, known as the repair yards, was as usual a wild, carelessly distributed tangle of discarded machine parts, and uneven piles of rusting sheets of armour plate, while here and there, panting diesel generators chugged and roared, as they pumped power along the snaking cables, which wriggled away in every direction. Along the slipways, running with a potent mixture of green sea-slime, and oil, various small ships of war were suffering the many indignities of repair and destruction heaped upon them by the dockyard workers, who, in boiler suits and cast-off clothing, ambled from one job to the other, in a manner, which to the uninitiated, appeared to have neither planning nor reason.

It was difficult to connect the stripped or slimy hulls, which loomed uncomfortably on the trestles, their intimate parts strewn around the ramps in wild profusion, with the graceful grey shapes which rode at their moorings in the harbour. They were apparently lost, doomed to lie for ever amid chaos. The maintenance staff, however, took all despair and criticism in their stride, and in the manner of all dockyards, went their own peculiar way, and completed most of the work to schedule.

One particular boat caught Royce's eye as he and Commander Wright strode through the winding cobbled fairway, their chins tucked into greatcoat collars, to stop the penetrating north wind from undoing the good work of an excellent breakfast. She lay on the second slipway, her paint stripped from her sides, the mahogany planks sharp and bright, like a naked wound. Various wires and power cables trailed over her sides, and a small army of men hammered and scraped, sawed and painted, with workmanlike indifference. A lifebuoy lay on the ground by her side, the flaked gilt lettering still showing boldly, M.T.B. 1993, Emberson's old boat. The two men stopped for a while in silence, as if paying homage.

'Getting a well-deserved spruce up,' muttered Wright at length. 'Should have had it long ago.'

A harassed-looking Lieutenant, in dirty flannel trousers and battledress blouse, stepped out from behind a pile of oil-drums, his greasy hands clutching impressive bundles of official forms and lists. Wright returned a fumbled salute cheerily.

'Hallo there, Page how's the jolly old refit progressing?'

Page grimaced. 'Up the wall! That's what I'll be before long. I don't know when she's more trouble, in the water or out!'

As they left him, Wright glanced keenly at Royce who trudged purposefully at his side, his eyes peering ahead.

'That's what you'll be like after today, my lad. The grandeur of command. Oh, my hat!'

Royce nodded, but hadn't really heard, his mind, brain and soul were captivated and controlled by one thought, one swelling desire, to get to his new boat as soon as possible. He and Wright had pored over her facts and details, dimensions and builder's claims, until the early hours of this morning, and even then he had tossed and turned in bed, running over every last piece of available information about H.M. M.T.B. 9779. This was his greatest moment, or very soon would be, and he prayed silently that he would be equal to it. He had been vacantly munching his breakfast, when Wright had strolled in, and announced casually that the boat, fresh from the builder's yard, and her hurried trials, had just arrived at the repair yard, to have her final armament fitted. She was ready for him.

The crew had been drafted aboard her at Dover, the nominal list and other eagerly perused details lay in his greatcoat pocket within easy reach, and as he unwittingly quickened his pace, he felt like the new boy joining his first boarding-school.

'Here, slow down a bit!' puffed Wright. 'She won't disappear before you get there!'

He had been at the game too long not to recognize the symptoms, and he rested his hand on Royce's arm.

'Take a piece more of advice from an old hand, if you think it's worth anything. Remember one really important thing, and that is, the crew are much more worried about you, and what you're going to be like. And they are, for the most part, real amateurs, green as grass; you'll have to be really patient, and work for them, show them the way. And that goes for the officers too.'

Royce smiled gratefully. 'Thanks, sir, I was beginning to get in a flap, but what you said has helped more than you'll ever know.'

At that moment they turned the corner of the giant edifice of the machine shops, and the whole northern sweep of the headland came into view, and they shuddered at the vicious punch of the wind. Below them, pointing out into the stream like a rugged stone monument was the loading-wharf, along which trundled vans and cranes, trucks and wheelbarrows, packed with the essential materials for keeping a ship at sea, from rope fenders to toilet paper.

Most of the vessels were store ships, or tenders to larger vessels lying out at the deep anchorages, but Royce had eyes for only one craft, which shone in her new grey paint, gleaming and confident of her powerful beauty. She seemed aware of the bright splash of colour she made among the bustling shapes of the hard-worked launches and lighters, a slender, graceful creature, a living thing.

Royce stopped dead in his tracks, causing Wright to stagger backwards.

'Good God, what's up?'

'Oh, sorry, sir, I was a bit swamped by all this. She's a beauty!'

As they drew nearer, and lower down the sloping road, Royce began to realize how vast his new command was, compared to the rest of the flotilla. Like the boats he had seen at Harwich, she was one of the latest, powerful additions to the Mosquito Fleet, and to him at that moment she looked enormous. He forced his mind over the details again. She was nearly one hundred and fifteen feet long, and her engines generated over four thousand horse-power, giving her well over thirty knots. Although she only carried two torpedoes like her smaller sisters, she positively bristled with guns, ranging from a Bofors on the fo'c'sle, to heavy Brownings aft, while around the bridge pointed the familiar, slender snouts of two Oerlikons. A very tough customer, if properly handled. That thought made his mind turn to the crew, which, apart from the officers, consisted almost completely of Hostilities Only ratings. A sobering thought.

Of the officers, apart from their names, and brief service records, he knew nothing. Sub-Lieutenant John Carver, a twenty-one-year-old ex-professional photographer, was to be his Number One. He had been eleven months in the service, three months in an Atlantic destroyer, the rest under training of one sort or another. The other officer was an eighteen-year-old Midshipman, Colin Leach, who, nine months before, had still been at college.

They halted a discreet distance from the gangway, where a young seaman lounged, an enormous revolver hanging from his belt.

Royce smiled grimly. I'll have to do a "Kirby" on him, he thought.

'Well, Royce, this is as far as I go. I think it's important

138

for a new C.O. to have this moment all to himself. Cheerio!'
and before Royce could protest, he was gone.

He flicked open the collar of his coat, took a deep
breath, and walked slowly towards the boat.

Several things happened at once. First, the sentry jerked
to attention, and caught the lanyard of the revolver in the
gangway rail, causing him to wriggle awkwardly, and
prevented him from saluting at all. Royce gave him a
suitably cold stare. The next thing was the sudden appearance of an officer in immaculate uniform and white muffler at the guard-rail.

He saluted stiffly as Royce climbed to the deck, feeling
like an ancient mariner. This must be Carver. A tall, striking young man, with a long, handsome face and fair hair,
whose general appearance was only marred by rather
protruding eyes, which gave him a haughty, if not actually
arrogant look.

Returning the salute, Royce shook him by the hand, his
eyes darting quickly round the decks. Clean and neat, but
then, of course, it was a new boat. Too early to judge yet.

'So sorry we haven't finished loading stores,' Carver's
voice was surprisingly low and pleasant. 'I'm afraid I've
succeeded in upsetting the gentleman in the bowler hat
over there.'

Royce glanced at the gentleman in question, who
squatted grimly on his lorry by the boat's side, smoking his
pipe.

'He said his tea-break came first or something. The war
could, er, "bloody well wait!" '

Whether this was true or not, the joke was extremely
well timed, and Royce decided to allow himself to be
drawn slightly from his protective wall of authority. He
grinned, and clapped the other on the shoulder.

'He's setting us a good example, let's go below and
have a cup, that is if you've managed to get all that in-
stalled yet?'

The wardroom was long and slender like that on Emberson's boat, but there the similarity ended. The newly
varnished furniture, and clean white paint, gave it an
unlived-in atmosphere, bordering on discomfort.

'We'll have to get some gear in town, Number One, and make the place like home.'

A curly-haired seaman, in the conventional white jacket, clumped in with a tray of tea.

Royce studied the man's impassive face, as he laid the table. One of his crew.

'What's your name?' he queried pleasantly, and the man jumped.

'Er, Trevor, sir, Able Seaman.' The north-country burr was strong. 'Starboard Oerlikon gunner, sir.'

For a brief instant, Royce felt a chill run down his neck, as he saw again the mutilated body of A.-B. Poole hanging from the starboard Oerlikon, swinging gently in the flames.

He shuddered, then nodded. 'Thank you, Trevor, I hope you shoot as well as you handle a teapot!'

Carver was watching him closely, and when the seaman had departed behind the serving hatch, he coiled himself down in a shining new chair.

'What's it like, sir, going into action, in one of these boats, I mean. It's hard to visualize somehow.'

Royce looked at him hard. This was the first sign of Captain Marney's words coming true. He now had to show he was able to control his own emotions, and those of his men as well.

'Don't try, Number One. It's never so bad or good as you expect anyway. I'll keep you so busy that you'll probably not even notice.'

Carver smiled, and examined the toe of an elegant shoe.

'When I was training we were told about your last boat. I'm very glad to be learning under you.' He was quite sincere.

There was a scuffle, and a crash outside the door, and a youthful voice was raised in anguish.

'Blast the ladder! Ouch, my blessed leg!'

A new cap flew in the door, and landed neatly on a chair, and there were further sounds of heavy packages being put down.

'I say, Number One, has the Old Man blown in yet?' piped the voice.

Carver flushed, and rose awkwardly, but Royce silenced him with a wave.

'Lord, I've got so many Confidential Books to correct, I'll never be done,' and with a bang, Midshipman Leach burst in:

'I've just seen a boat all shot up on one of the slipways, I——' he stopped, his jaw dropping. 'Gosh, sir, I'm sorry, I didn't know . . .'

'As you see,' said Royce drily, 'the Old Man has arrived!'

At the same time he was thinking, how incredibly young, he makes me feel like a grandfather.

Leach certainly looked every inch a midshipman, but the uniform seemed to accentuate his youth. His round, pink face, blue eyes, now wide with horror, and unruly hair, gave him the appearance of a startled schoolboy.

Royce smiled. 'It's all right, Mid, have some tea, relax.'

'It'll probably be too strong for him,' said Carver severely.

As they chatted, and Royce fired questions concerning the crew, he knew that this was going to be a happy wardroom, and as they would not be living aboard the *Royston*, leaving her to the cramped crews of the little boats, it was just as well.

He spent the afternoon exploring the boat, and checking the lists with Carver who, although most willing, was lamentably uncertain of practically all the normal procedure. He would have to be led for some time. Leach's duties were confined at present to correcting A.F.O.s, charts, and all the other books and papers required of even this small warship, and this he did, with an enthusiasm which made Royce chuckle.

The Coxswain had not yet joined, and a Leading Seaman called Denton accompanied Royce on his rounds. He was a burly Londoner, a peacetime R.N.V.R., and a reliable influence on the mess-deck.

He piloted Royce into that long, homely space, now deserted while the hands worked on deck, and he saw with affection the neat lockers, with the garish pin-ups already in evidence. The built-in cupboards, the lines of damp dhobying, and rolled towels, gave the appearance of packed habitation, the discomfort borne by most sailors.

Next, Royce met the Chief, a P.O. Motor Mechanic from Derby, named Anderson. A lively young man, with a long face like a racehorse, he nevertheless impressed him by his knowledge and love of his giant charges.

'They make the boat fly, sir,' he rubbed his hands. 'You'll see, when we get out.'

Royce left him in the engine room, feeling confident of one other good man. But for the most part, the men he questioned were seamen by training, and not by experience. Gunners according to their badges, although they had shot at nothing but reliable and condescending targets towed by aircraft and trawlers. 'Give me time!' he muttered.

Eventually he found himself alone once more in the strange surroundings of his new cabin. He was amazed that so much could be jammed into such a minute space. From the neat bunk to the built-in bureau, it had an air of quiet efficiency. He unpacked his cases, which had been spirited aboard by some unseen hand, and changed slowly into his seagoing rig, listening while he did so, to the orderly chain of noises over his head, the full impact of his grim task of training and using the boat only dawning on him as his eye caught the brief sign on the open cabin door. It stated simply, "Commanding Officer". He sat heavily on the bunk, feeling suddenly deflated, staring at it for some moments, weighing up his chances of success, and the apparent possibilities of a horrible failure. There was now no one to give him guidance, no detached feeling that all he had to do was obey orders. He would be giving them. For once, he felt at a loss, and that he ought to be rushing on deck to see what his officers were doing. He restrained himself, and began to think slowly and deliberately, as he was to do many times in the future. Peering out of his small scuttle, he was able to see the *Royston,* and the Coastal Forces' moorings, about half a mile away. His orders stated that he was to take the M.T.B. alongside the *Royston* as soon as he had finished taking on stores, i.e. about 1200 hours. Such a narrow piece of water, comparatively clear of shipping, as most of the harbour craft had tied up ready for the midday meal, but to him, in a strange craft, with the prospect of going alongside under the eyes of the flotilla, it may well have been the North Atlantic. He was suddenly aware of a hush in the shipboard sounds, and as he stood with his head cocked, Carver clattered down the ladder to his door. He was now clad in a bright new duffle coat, and had his cap under his arm. He was obviously more than a little worried.

'All stores aboard, and ship ready to move,' he announced breathlessly. 'The Coxswain is waiting in the *Royston*. I've just had a signal,' he added.

"Blast!" thought Royce savagely. "Not even an experienced coxswain", but to Carver he said as evenly as he could manage, 'Stand by to slip.'

Pulling on his duffle, and slinging his glasses round his neck, he climbed to the bridge, where Leading Seaman Denton stood stolidly by the wheel. Unlike the other boats, this type had the steering position on the open bridge, and although it meant that the coxswain was more prone to injury in action, it had the advantage of allowing the captain to be able to direct operations with the minimum of wheel orders, which was so essential when a vessel of this nature was employed twisting and turning at high speed, and the captain was required to supervise and control the firing of torpedoes. He nodded to him briefly, and noted with satisfaction that the bridge was clean and sensibly laid out. A young signalman was fiddling with halyards behind him, and on the fo'c'sle he could see the hands taking the slack off the wires. He checked with the engine room, and rang down "stand by", and was startled by the immediate roar of the giant engines, which settled down to a steady confident rumble. The air was faintly tinged with exhaust fumes. Only when there was absolutely nothing more to do on the bridge, did Royce steel himself to begin the operation of actual movement.

'Let go forrard!' he bawled, and he saw a dockyard worker heave their bow rope into the water, and Carver seemed to be coping all right there.

He craned over the screen. 'Let go aft!'

Vaguely he saw Leach nod, his face anxious, and then

scurry right aft to watch the dripping wire snaking aboard.

When satisfied that there was no wire in the water to foul the screws, Royce rang down for "Slow ahead".

The strong current which was eddying round the end of the jetty had swung out the bows just nicely. Royce had allowed for it without conscious thought, and as the engines snapped into gear, the boat thrust purposefully out into the open.

'Steer straight for the depot ship,' he said, not wishing to complicate matters.

'Aye, aye, sir,' and Denton spun the wheel in his hard hands, his eyes squinting against the glare on the water.

Royce's heart had stopped pounding quite so horribly, and he felt instead a wild sensation of elation. He had actually started the ship himself, his own craft. He rubbed his hands.

Carver was looking up at him for instructions.

'Hands fall in fore and aft for entering harbour!'

Carver saluted, in a rather theatrical manner, and a second later Royce heard the twitter of the pipe, and the padding of feet on the wooden decks, as the hands fell in.

To the onlooker, she made a brave sight in her new paint and gleaming guns, with the white-jersied figures standing in two neat lines on deck. From beneath her cutaway stem, twin rolls of foam creamed away behind her, while from the gaff a starchy new ensign flapped in the slight breeze.

Carver stood in the eyes of the boat, staring ahead, and thinking goodness only knows, while little Leach stood aft, dwarfed by the seamen.

On down Fenton's Reach, to the destroyer flotilla leader, bearing the broad black band of Captain (D).

As they drew abeam, Royce yelled 'Pipe!' and again the shrill notes of the call echoed across the water.

They paid their respects to the Senior Officer. She, too, replied with a clear, trilling precision.

Royce beamed with pleasure, and wished he could confide with someone about his childish delight. At that moment the signalman shouted, and pointed over the port quarter.

'Ship closing, sir!'

Royce swung round, and saw with amazement the lumbering hulk of an ancient freighter, with black smoke gushing from her spindly stack, steering straight for him. She was still a good fifty yards away, and must have steamed round the point while they had been busy with salutes. Royce checked the marks, and found that he was in the correct channel, and had the right of way.

'Bloody fool,' he muttered, and Denton grinned.

The M.T.B. held her course for some moments, until in fact it became obvious to everyone on board that either Royce broke the rule of the road, or there would be an unpleasant collision.

'Hard a-starboard, and cut across her wake,' he snapped, and then switched on the loud hailer. He noted that the paint was hardly dry. He heard it squeak into life, and directed his attention to the towering, rusty bridge of the freighter.

'*Flying Lantern* Ahoy!' The harsh vibrations brought two little heads to the bridge rail, one wearing a battered, gold-braided cap, and the other a rakish trilby.

'Don't you know your regulations?' roared Royce, and waited.

The trilby vanished, then reappeared with a megaphone, which was handed to the captain.

'What's the matter?' Fraid we'll scratch your wee yacht?'

Some of the seamen tittered, and Royce flushed.

'No, we're scared you'll capsize in our wash!'

The captain called back an unprintable word, and went into his wheelhouse and slammed the door.

Royce felt better, and realized that he was practically up to the *Royston*'s buoys. More piping, then the delicate touch astern on the engines, as the heaving lines went to the waiting seamen on the pontoons. "Stop engines"; it was over.

As the boat shuddered into silence, and creaked against her fenders, he swung down to the fo'c'sle.

'I'm going aboard, Number One. Don't forget what I told me about Dress of the Day. Commander Kirby is probably watching even now. I see that the rest of the flotilla are now back. I'm going to find our new coxswain, P.O. Banks, or whatever his name is.'

'What shall I do now?' Carver sounded lost.

'Feed the brutes, and see that they get their tots,' grinned Royce, and started up the catwalk.

The first person he saw was the familiar, stocky figure of Raikes.

'Petty Officer Banks, reporting for Coxswain,' he said without a smile.

'What? Have you gone up the wall?'

Raikes smiled, and Royce felt a glow of friendship.

'Well, sir, this Banks chap did a silly thing. He found that some rotten perisher had mixed up the draft chit, an' he got 'imself sent to Scapa; cruel, ain't it, sir?'

Royce laughed loudly. 'Now I wonder what rotten perisher did that? It's good to have you back. Quite frankly, I need your services badly.'

'I watched you come alongside, sir, and quite frankly, I think the Navy's gettin' some very queer seamen nowadays. Still, we'll soon lick 'em into shape.'

Royce walked on air as he strode to the wardroom. He felt that now, at least, he had someone upon whom he could rely, to help the unkind process of training the crew to run more smoothly.

The very first person he saw in the wardroom was Kirby. Somehow he seemed smaller and older. He was leaning against the bar talking to Deith, who looked distinctly uncomfortable.

'Good grief!' said the latter, with a relieved smile. 'Here he is at long last,' and ignoring Kirby he shook him by the hand.

'Good afternoon, Number One; or rather I should say Lieutenant Royce now, shouldn't I?' Kirby's voice was flat. 'It's all working out for you, isn't it? Promotion, and a command. Well done.'

But his tone showed no warmth. As he turned and left the room, Deith shook his head.

'God, what a man. We've just been out on a practice run, and I missed the target. You'd think I'd tin-fished the *Nelson* for all the fuss he's making!'

The other familiar faces drifted in, tired and thirsty, and upon seeing Royce, they seemed to come to life. Benjy positively beamed.

'My boy, you're a hero, you're absolutely magnificent, you do credit to us all!' he thundered.

Royce grinned, for although he, too, was proud of the blue and white ribbon on his breast, he knew that at least six of the flotilla's officers already held that decoration, Benjy was one.

'I'm back all right,' he smiled, 'and I have a feeling that there is a party in the offing.'

There was indeed.

* * * * *

Viewed from the sea, the East Coast has probably less personality than any other part of the British shoreline, with its constant blue misty lowland, and the patchy fen district, a silhouette only broken here and there by the squat shapes of villages, church spires, and the occasional navigational aid. In winter, it becomes even more bleak, and the making of an exact landfall or fix becomes all the more difficult, especially when the compass binnacle is swinging through a jerky arc of eighty degrees or so.

Alone, on the angry, white-crested sullenness of the North Sea, with the half-hidden hump of land reaching away from the port beam, M.T.B. 9779 rose and fell uncomfortably, as she ploughed forward into the vicious little waves. Every so often, her sharp stem fell into an unsuspected trough, and there would be a flat smacking noise, and a sheet of salt spray would fling itself high over the tiny bridge, and make the decks stream and glisten. Up, down, up down, with a correspondingly sickening motion from side to side, until it seemed as if the whole world had always been built on this crazy pendulum.

In his cabin, Royce lay fully dressed on his bunk, one foot jammed against his bookshelves, to prevent a sudden passage to the deck, his hands were clasped behind his head, and he stared moodily at the blank face of the clock. He had been in command for exactly a week now, and every day, without exception, he had been forced to manoeuvre his beloved boat back and forth across the harbour, practising his crew at all the evolutions of seamanship, and trying to make them perform all the seemingly tiresome and unnecessary details of ship ceremonial, and all to Kirby's whims and desires. Only once had he been outside the boom-gate for a practice shoot, and that had been shortened by bad weather.

It must be impossible, he told himself, but all the same, it did seem as if Kirby was going out of his way to be awkward and unhelpful, as if he didn't want him to be part of his flotilla on patrol.

Commander Wright, in all his wisdom, had watched these happenings with anxiety and distaste, and at last, in desperation, he had approached Kirby on the matter. Kirby had stood complacently in his office, his neat hands inserted in the pockets of his monkey jacket, those piercing eyes cold and sceptical.

Wright had turned his eyes away, determined not to show his dislike.

'It's like this, Kirby, we've got to get these boats out on the job, every boat we can muster, provided it'll float.'

Kirby was unmoved.

'There's no point in putting an untrained crew to sea with the flotilla. They'd only be a liability.'

Wright turned, his eyes hard. 'Damn it, man, they're all untrained! We haven't got time, don't you see? This isn't peace time!'

'Some are more untrained than others.'

Was there a trace of a sneer on Kirby's face. Wright studied him thoughtfully, fully aware he was making little progress.

'As Senior Officer of the flotilla, I must take all the responsibility for my captains,' continued Kirby, speaking softly. 'And frankly, the reputation of the whole Group is being damaged by this influx of second-rate seamen.'

Like an ancient knight circling an adversary, Wright saw the small chink in the armour, and mercilessly he lunged.

'I've been as reasonable as I know how, but it seems to me that you're only interested in your own damned reputation,' he grated. 'These are good boys, all of 'em. I should know, I've been watching them die long enough. And, quite off the record, of course, if you can't make something of your flotilla, I'll bloody well see that we get someone who can!'

He sat down heavily, breathing fast, glaring at Kirby, who had paled.

'May I remind you, sir, that what you're suggesting constitutes a threat to me, personally?'

Wright smiled, but there was no mirth. 'Yes, I'm threatening you. What do you propose to do about it?'

Kirby stood stiff and shocked, like a man hearing sentence at a court martial, unwilling to yield, yet unable to find a way out of this unforeseen predicament.

Wright followed up the attack, by turning to his wall-chart, covered with coloured pins and numbered darts.

'Look here, there's a small convoy of three ships leaving Yarmouth tomorrow, they're stragglers of the last northbound. Young Royce can go as their escort. It'll give him time to break in his boat and crew, in his own way. All right?'

'Very well,' snapped Kirby, 'and I'll take him with me on the next sweep.'

He stood looking at Wright, his gaze now uncertain.

'All right, Kirby, carry on, and for goodness sake try to understand that it's harder for them than it is for you.'

'I hope I know my duty, sir!'

'I hope so, too,' answered Wright meaningly.

As the prompt result of that meeting, Royce was now at sea, his own master at last. With another glance at the clock, he heaved himself off the bunk, and adjusted his body to the uneven roll, then with a deep sigh he made his way to the bridge.

His head and mind were cleared in an instant by the keen air, and the sharp edge of the salt, and without speaking he checked the chart, while from the corner of his eye he saw Carver clinging to the voice-pipe, his face like death.

'Well, Number One,' he said eventually. 'How's it going?'

'I feel ghastly. And I've not picked out the ships yet.'

Royce swung his glasses shorewards. 'Hmm, where was your last fix?'

'Er, Lowestof lighthouse.'

'Well, that should be all right. Give them another ten minutes or so then we'll turn in a bit, and see if we can pick them up.'

It was like listening to another person, just to hear his own voice giving orders, making prophecies, with a calm, confident manner he had not believed possible. He chuckled to himself.

'How are the hands shaking down?'

'Fifty per cent are fighting sea-sickness, I'm afraid. So am I,' added Carver miserably.

'Right, go below, and have a warm. I'll hang on here for a bit.'

When the grateful Carver had departed, Royce leaned happily across the screen, humming to himself, completely disregarding the retching of the helmsman's stomach.

Sure enough, a few moments later, the signalman reported three ships closing from the north-east, so increasing speed the M.T.B. steered to intercept. To any seasoned captain they appeared the usual sweepings of the Convoy Pool, but to Royce, the three battered coasters represented his first personal convoy, and for the next quarter of an hour he weaved around them, jockeying them into a semblance of order, and generally getting them sorted out.

Then they steadied down on the starboard side of the little procession, and the awful motion started again. When Carver returned, still looking slightly green, Royce went below once more.

Half concentrating on the latest Admiralty Fleet Orders, and half on a corned beef and pickle sandwich, he sat in his solitary chair, wedged in one corner of the cabin, a feeling of contentment and confidence making his tired body relax. Eight bells, young Leach would be taking over his first watch at sea from the First Lieutenant. He cocked his head back, the sandwich poised in mid-air, imagining the scene. The hurried confidences, the whispered instructions, then the eighteen-year-old boy would take over command of the bridge, with the care and protection of the M.T.B. and three merchantmen in his hands alone. A frightening thought, although on this route, through the swept channel of the vast East Coast minefields, there was not a great deal of sudden danger. Too light for E-boats, too dangerous for submarines. Aircraft were the main worry. Royce shook his head when he remembered the shooting of his gunners. They would have to get in a lot more practice.

He jumped nearly out of his skin as the voice-pipe at his elbow whistled urgently.

Leach's voice was shrill: 'Sir, there's an object in the water. 'Bout a mile on the starboard bow!'

Royce didn't wait for a lengthy description; he flew up the ladder. Training his glasses round, while Leach fidgeted nervously at his elbow. It was a small, yellow shape, barely visible above the little waves. A rubber dinghy.

Lifting to the full throttle, the boat tore down to the fragile craft, the sailors momentarily forgetting their seasickness, and curiously gathering at the guard-rails. They slowed and circled warily.

The three airmen sat bunched in the pitching circular dinghy, their legs entwined in the centre, their heads jerking and nodding to the waves' cruel rhythm. Facing the M.T.B., one of the leather-clad figures stared blankly, his mouth hanging open.

A seaman shouted, his voice breaking the silence: ' 'Ere y'are mates, catch a line!'

The fools, thought Royce savagely, what a lot they've got to learn, then to Carver who had appeared hatless below him on the fo'c'sle: 'Get them aboard, quick as you can. Lay them out by the tubes!'

Leach caught his breath sharply. 'Are they . . . ?'

'Yes, dead as mutton,' said Royce shortly. 'Exposure.'

In shocked silence the seamen watched, while Raikes supervised the grisly task. Eventually they had finished, and with a roar the boat tore off in pursuit of the coasters. Royce sighted the bridge Lewis gun and squeezed the trigger angrily. The bobbing dinghy vanished in a cloud of spray and bullets. No trace remained of yet another small part of the nation's sacrifice.

He sighed, and looked at Leach, who was standing staring back across their creaming wake.

'All right?' he queried sharply.

'Yes, sir, it shook me a bit, that's all. I've never seen—I never realized they looked like that.'

Royce softened. 'Forget it, Mid. I'm afraid there'll be others, before we're finished.'

The hours dragged by, with little to take the hands' minds off that little drama. Two weary trawlers passed them, heading for the Channel, and in the far distance a corvette patrolled her allotted beat, otherwise the sea was theirs.

The three merchantmen kept in their steady, ponderous line, moving through the water at less than five knots, until eventually the novelty and tension of Royce's new authority began to sag, and he decided that the opportunity was ripe for getting through his impressive pile of ship's correspondence. Also, with him absent from the bridge, the other officers would be able to practice their capabilities as seamen.

He took a last look round the wintry scene.

'I'm leaving you in charge, Mid. Call me if there's any difficulty with navigation, or handling the boat'—he knew full well that he'd rather die first—'and I want to know about any strange aircraft, or ships. All right?'

'Oh yes, sir, I'll be all right now.' The young face was eager.

With a smile Royce clumped below, and as he spread the papers across his desk, he noted with relief that the violent motion of the boat had eased considerably, and there was now merely a heavy roll, and a slow-moving M.T.B. will roll on wet grass.

Every so often he heard the soft creak as the rudder was put hard over, and he smiled, knowing that Leach was cautiously practising altering course, just as he had once done, when standing his first watch alone.

'Captain, sir!' The voice-pipe rattled.

'Yes, what's the trouble?'

'Wind has dropped, and there's a bit of a mist coming up from the east.'

Royce digested this information carefully.

'Very bad is it?'

'Well, sir, I can't see *Bentaur*.'

'What!' Royce leapt for the door.

Bentaur was the leading ship of the line.

As soon as his head cleared the hatch, he saw the thick, yellow mist billowing like smoke across the water on their starboard bow. This was no mist, this was the real thing.

With five bounds he reached the bridge, and then as he scrambled up he steadied himself. No point in letting everyone see he was worried. Taking a deep breath, he strode to the front screen, where Leach's duffled figure peered anxiously forward.

By heaven, it was going to be a real pea-souper all right. He had seen it so often on this coast. One minute you have the damp, blustering wind, then a lull, and up comes the fog. The real enemy. He glanced at the other ships quickly, plodding along, confident and indifferent, but the leader had completely disappeared, wiped out by a sudden thick, swirling fence. What a dreadful business. He cursed inwardly. He could not tell the other two to anchor, and leave the *Bentaur* steaming on her own. In a couple of hours, his charges would be all over the place.

'Signalman!' he barked. 'Signal both ships to reduce speed, and stream fog buoys. Port lookout, fetch the Coxswain!'

As the Aldis clattered, he assembled his thoughts. There was just a chance he could catch the other ship, and shepherd her round to the rest of the flock, before darkness fell.

Raikes appeared, imperturbable as ever.

'Take over, 'Swain. I'm going straight up the line after the leader.'

'Aye, aye, sir.'

With a deep-throated roar, the boat surged forward into the gloom. In a second the fo'c'sle was hidden from

153

them in a thick, choking cloud and reluctantly they throttled down, edging forwards jerkily, every man training his ears and eyes.

Without warning, the deep-toned squawk of a fog-siren boomed out ahead, and Royce switched on the loud-hailer. Again, a bit nearer this time.

'That's queer, Raikes,' he muttered. 'He must be stopped, we're getting near to him so quickly.'

Raikes nodded, his keen eyes scanning the steep bank of yellow which surrounded them. The M.T.B. seemed to be suspended in space.

Then they heard it, the steady pulsating beat of engines, thud, thud, thud, getting louder and louder.

'Stop engines!' His throat was dry.

Gently rocking on an invisible sea, they waited, their eyes smarting in the thick vaporous clouds.

Royce saw it first, fortunately, an imperceptible darkening of the fog-bank ahead, then with awful suddenness, two anchors zoomed into view, about thirty feet above their heads, like two huge eyes peering down at them. As he jumped for the voice-pipe, he got a blurred impression of the high, rust-streaked stem aiming straight for them.

'Full ahead port, hard a-starboard!' His voice sounded strained.

The engines roared to life, and the slim hull tacked round, as the giant iron bulk of the *Bentaur* reared over them, her siren deafening them. Helplessly they watched the full length of her dull sides sheer past, missing by mere inches. Then she was gone.

Sweating inwardly, Royce remembered the loud-hailer, his voice boomed and re-echoed around them.

'*Bentaur,* ahoy! Stop your engines! Anchor immediately!'

As if in answer, there was a sickening, tearing crash, and the sound of screaming metal.

'God, she's hit one of the others,' hissed Raikes.

Carver had also appeared by this time, and stood awkwardly in the background, not quite sure of what was happening.

154

With Royce tense and full of foreboding, the boat crept back along her course. A dark shape loomed ahead.

The loud-hailer squeaked. 'Are you damaged?'

A hoarse voice floated down to them.

'Nay, but ah bluidy well will be if I stop here with all these bluidy lunatics!'

They pressed on until eventually, guided by bangs and frantic shouts, they discovered the two ships, locked together, with twenty feet of *Bentaur*'s stem firmly sliced into the other's fo'c'sle. Faintly they could hear the sounds of an anchor cable running out.

They scraped alongside.

'*Bentaur* ahoy! What the damage?'

There was a pause.

'Nothing much to us. But I'm afraid the other chap's lost a bit of weight!' came the cheery reply.

Royce fumed.

'Get aboard, Number One, and get them sorted out!'

Carver was relieved to be doing something, and went forward to await a rope ladder.

Royce paced up and down, deep in thought. Of all the damn fool things. It was obvious what had happened. The Officer-of-the-Watch on the *Bentaur*, seeing the fog, and realizing the others had vanished, had lost his head, and had come charging back to look for them.

Leach's face was at his elbow, almost imploring.

'It's all my fault, sir. I didn't know a fog could gather so quickly.'

'Well, you know now.' He didn't trust himself to go further, and Leach slumped miserably by the compass.

When Carver reappeared, breathless and rather grubby, Royce expected the worst.

'She's not making much water,' he announced, 'and the Captain says the fog's lifting already.'

It appeared to be as thick as ever.

Royce shrugged. 'I hope you've gained a bit of experience from all this, Number One?'

'Rather, I wouldn't have missed it for anything!'

Royce didn't know whether to laugh or swear.

'Dammit, you'll do, go back and keep an eye on things, before I lay you out with something heavy!'

He shook his head. What could you say to a man who thought a predicament like this was an interesting spectacle?

The merchant captain knew his weather lore, for within half an hour the fog began to move. It didn't lessen in density, it simply moved on, propelled by a languid breeze which obligingly wafted in from the north-east.

It was a sorry sight, like two jungle giants in a death struggle. *Bentaur* had come off best, but the other ship, an aged freighter with the strange name of *Madame Zest,* had a gap in her bows large enough to dry-dock the M.T.B.

The third ship had anchored of her own accord, and lay about a mile off, a cheerful spectator.

'Do you require a tug?'

Madame Zest considered for some moments.

'No thank you. We will be able to make about three knots. All damage above waterline.'

'I'm sorry it had to be you.'

'I'm not. We'll get a damn good refit out of this!'

Slowly and painfully they weighed anchor, and formed up in line, *Bentaur* slinking guiltily behind her wounded adversary.

Night fell, but it was clear enough to make stationkeeping easy, although at that speed it would be difficult to do much more damage.

Raikes was humming softly.

'With your permission, sir, I'll carry on below to check that the ship is properly darkened.'

It was a polite way of reminding Royce that he should not still be on the wheel.

Royce grinned, and as the Quartermaster took over the helm, he remembered Leach.

'Good God, Mid. You're quiet.'

Leach stammered: 'I thought I'd said enough, sir,' he faltered.

'Forget it. I have. And when you've been at it a bit longer you'll come to expect this sort of thing every day of the week!'

Leach's face filled with gratitude. 'Gosh, thank you for saying that, sir, you don't know what it means to me.'

'But that's just it, I do. Now go and rustle up some cocoa,' said Royce gruffly.

As the small figure scurried below, he chuckled.

'You're getting pompous already.'

'Pardon, sir?' queried the helmsman.

'Oh, er, I said keep an eye on the leading ship,' muttered Royce, flushing.

This was proving to be a better test for the ship's company than Commander Wright had visualized, apparently. Throughout the boat, there was a brittle air of jittery expectancy, as the seamen pondered and voted for what was going to happen next. Royce observed, with grim amusement, that few of his amatur crew would pass the port torpedo tube on their comings and goings, where, in the dim light, the dark canvas-covered bodies of the airmen lay lashed together, comrades to the bitter end. They will have to learn.

A pinpoint of light flickered ahead, the leading merchant man was making an announcement.

'Southbound convoy ahead, about two miles,' repeated the signalman.

'How the devil,' began Royce, then he remembered that from the freighter's lofty bridge, on such a comparatively calm sea, the dark shapes would be clearly discernible.

'Quick, make the challenge!' he snapped, but already the leading escort was creaming towards them, flashing menacingly.

As the lamps clattered, Royce reflected how different this type of procedure was to his normal round, where every ship seen in the night was an enemy.

Soon the silent, dark shapes had passed, and they had the sea to themselves again, and when dawn found them, cold and stiff, they were all longing to be rid of their heavy companions, who ambled so comfortably abeam of them.

Royce decided is was time to get a little sleep.

'Call me if anything happens, Mid, anything, you understand?'

157

It seemed as if the bunk had barely taken his weight, when the voice-pipe whistled again.

'Sorry, sir, but there's a destroyer coming up fast.' The voice was nervous.

Again he mounted the bridge. The sea was a dull grey, tinged with blue blotches, sullen and heavy, but in contrast, the sky had cleared and had been left drained of any colour whatever. The destroyer was approaching fast, and when only a cable clear, she slewed round, making an impressive wake, which made the M.T.B. roll heavily.

The metallic voice boomed across to them.

'Come alongside, I have fresh orders for you.'

Royce came to life, putting off tiredness like an old coat.

'Leading Seaman Denton, stand by to collect orders! Coxswain report to the bridge. Mid, Starboard Watch stand by with fenders, we're going alongside.

The orders fell from his lips automatically, it seemed, without thought.

With engines growling, Raikes steered the boat under the lee of the dark grey hull, while Royce hung anxiously over the screen, watching the gap of water narrow between them. One good bang and a lot of written reports would be called for.

At the destroyer's rail, a Sub-Lieutenant waited with a canvas bag, which he lobbed neatly at Royce's feet as he passed.

The voice of authority boomed once more.

'I am detaching one of my corvettes for your little brood; you proceed to Rosyth and refuel. I understand you've got to take the Press to sea on your return trip. Cheerio, we must get on with the war. It's still on, you know!'

Royce was at a loss for a witty answer. His mind was in a whirl. Rosyth, it was a miracle. Julia. A miracle! Feverishly he tore the envelop open. It stated baldly that he was to return to base after refuelling, and join the flotilla without delay. In order not to waste a journey, however, three war correspondents were to be given a ride down. To gain the right "atmosphere", no doubt.

Royce hummed gaily, as he bent over the chart, all his worries seemed unimportant now. Julia, at last.

'Steer north, forty-five west, half speed. Yes, what is it Mid? What's the matter?'

Leach was hopping. 'It's Number One, sir, he's still aboard the *Madame Zest*!'

Carver was still quivering when he swung aboard from a dangerous looking ladder.

'Strewth, I thought you were cross with me,' he laughed. 'Strewth! Didn't fancy stopping with those chaps. They're *real* sailors!'

* * * * *

With paintwork still gleaming, and the hands fallen in at their stations, the M.T.B. cruised easily alongside the oiling wharf, between a grubby corvette, and two M.L.s.

As the last rope snaked ashore, and the boat trembled to a half, Royce called his officers to the bridge, and informed them of his new orders.

'The point is, that we've got to get down to it. Drill them till they drop if necessary. You saw how they reacted to those airmen?' He could have added, "and you too." "I have a feeling that we'll be seeing quite a bit of action when we rejoin the flotilla, so get 'em down to it.'

'What time do the Press arrive, sir?' Carver's face was quite straight.

'Any time now, so you look after them till I get back. I'm just going up to the Signal Station.'

'Would you like me to go, sir?' Leach was eager.

'Er, no, this is something special.'

Was there a glimmer in Carver's eye? I'll stop that.

'Right, Number One, you can start now while you're waiting to fuel. Turn the hands to Damage Control Drill, and see if you can knock five minutes off the Fire Drill, too!'

'Aye, aye, sir!' But he still smiled.

In feverish haste, Royce shaved, and flung on a decent uniform, then hurried ashore, in search of the Signal Station.

After a somewhat agonizing route, between oil pipes, mountains of wooden crates, and a squad of Home Guard drilling, he eventually found the lofty, whitewashed building, overlooking the graceful sweep of the anchorage.

He was taken aback by the bustling efficiency of this vast establishment. In every direction messengers scurried, carrying important-looking signals, while from the various offices came the clatter of typewriters and teleprinters. He examined the doors carefully. The first stated, "Staff Officer, Communications, Please Enter". He gingerly opened it. Directly inside he saw a hatstand, upon which hung three caps, liberally covered with "scrambled egg". Quietly, he pulled the door to, and moved further along the passage. The next door had nothing on it, so he opened it hopefully. A Wren stood facing a wall-mirror, and turned as he appeared.

'The Officers' Heads are at the end of the passage!' she announced hotly.

Mumbling apologies, Royce withdrew.

'Can I help you, sir?'

Royce turned, blushing, to face another Wren, who stood smiling at his side. She was obviously bound for the forbidden room.

'Well, yes,' he answered thankfully. 'To be perfectly honest, I'm looking for Wren Harston. She's in the signals branch here.'

'That's right, she's in my watch. Just go up the stairs to the Tower, and ask the Second Officer. Her name's Mannering.'

Royce was overcome. 'Thanks very much; I've never been here before.'

She gave him an old-fashioned look. 'So I just gathered!'

The door swung behind her.

He started to climb the stairs, his heart heavy with excited and painful anticipation. This was to be an important moment, but his confidence had taken wings.

The S.D.O. and Signals Office presented to his anxious eyes a violent maelstrom of Wrens in white shirts and rolled sleeves, and millions of fluttering pieces of paper. The noise was overpowering, at least six of the girls were reading or repeating signals over an imposing battery of telephones, while others called mysterious numbers and references to each other. At an overladen desk, a buxom Second Officer was also using her telephone, it seemed for an argument, although she managed to drink a cup of tea at the same time. No one took any notice of him. He was invisible. He noticed that the back of the room was made of glass, and opened on to the signal "Veranda", where several girls, well wrapped up against the weather, were manipulating a ponderous signal projector. From another small door, a rosey faced Chief Yeoman emerged, puffing at a pipe. It was comforting to note that he at least was surprised to see another man in the room.

'Lost, sir?'

'I'm looking for——' He stopped, his glance travelling across the Chief's massive shoulder. She had just come in from the veranda, stripping off her oilskin and cap, shaking out the dark curls, and rubbing her cheek with a mittened hand. Quite clearly, he heard her say to another girl, 'There's an M.T.B. at the quay. What's she doing right up here?'

Blindly, he pushed past the astonished Yeoman, brushing a sheaf of signals from a desk, until he was right behind her.

'She's my boat. Care for a cruise?' he gulped.

She swung round, the large brown eyes wide with astonishment.

'Heavens! Clive! What on earth?' Her small hands fluttered about her grubby shirt, and patted her wind-blown curls. 'What a way to find a girl.'

'Only just got in. Got to leave in two hours. Can I see you somewhere?'

The words tumbled out of him.

'It's awfully nice to see you again. You're looking much better; a command suits you.'

She studied his face. 'It's difficult. But I'll see the Two-Oh.'

Dazedly, he saw her hurry to the desk, where the telephone argument was progressing well. The Wren Officer glanced in his direction, and said to the telephone, 'Hold on, Flags, but I still say you're mistaken!' and dropped the instrument heavily. It must have cracked "Flags'" eardrum.

'Don't be long, Lieutenant; you can have her for ten minutes. It's only because you're a stranger. Or are you?' The Wrens tittered.

Julia plucked his sleeve impatiently. 'Come on,' she whispered. 'I'll get you out of here while you're still safe!'

Outside, a thin drizzle had started, and they found themselves walking quickly away from the building, yet in no particular direction. Royce was torn by many emotions. He was happy beyond words to find himself in her company again, but worried and uncomfortable because it was not working out as he had planned it in dreams, so many times in the past. It was like saying good-bye to someone very dear on a railway station, a scene which is enacted every day of the year. The two persons wait, saying nothing, unless it is to remark on the weather, or some such triviality, although their hearts are bursting. Then, as the train begins to move, out comes the pent-up flood, the hopes and fears. Too late, the precious time has been wasted.

Desperately, he turned, 'Isn't there anywhere we can get a cup of tea or something? There's such a lot I want to say.'

'Only a canteen hut the dockyard maties use.' She pointed, 'Over there.'

The drizzle was getting heavier, and thankfully they pushed open the ill-fitting door of the little Nissen hut, and glanced round its spartan interior.

It was barely furnished with scrubbed tables, where the workmen could eat their sandwiches, and boasted a small canteen counter, and a pot-bellied stove which glowed warmly. Two men in overalls leaned against the counter, gossiping to the blowsy woman behind it. They all looked up in surprise, as the worried-looking young officer, and an attractive Wren in a rain-soaked oilskin, burst in on their private world.

Royce guided her to a bench by the stove, all the time drinking in every little detail about her. She took off her cap and shook it, hissing, over the fire, running her fingers through her hair.

162

'Phew, I'm afraid I'm not looking my best. I wasn't expecting company. I expect you're sorry you came?'

'Good Heavens, you look wonderful, really fine,' he burst out.

She looked at him, the little secret smile playing round her lips.

'I believe you mean it, too,' she said.

'I certainly do mean it, I——'

A harsh voice interrupted him.

'If you're wantin' anything t'eat, you'll 'ave to get it at the counter. We got no posh waiters 'ere!'

The two workmen grinned.

Royce fumbled in his pocket and banged down a six-pence.

'Two teas then.'

He hurried over to her, slopping most of the tea on the floor. He heard the awful woman say something about 'show 'em where they get off'. He didn't realize the reason for her hostility, or care.

Julia warmed her hands on the cup, her large brown eyes thoughtful.

'I would have liked to get a closer look at your boat. It's like old times to see an M.T.B. again,' she added wistfully.

She brightened suddenly, and for a brief instant he saw her brother's quick change of mood in her. 'Still, never mind, tell me all about yourself. How have you been getting on?'

Royce took a deep breath. The initiative had been passed to him.

'Never mind about me.' He leaned forward, looking into her eyes earnestly. 'It's you I'm worried about.'

No, that was no good. He tried again.

'I wanted to see you again, so much, you'll never know how much I've been thinking about you.'

He waited for a rebuke, none came. She was listening closely, her eyes lowered. He noticed the dark curve of her lashes.

'You see, I don't think it's right. You're right up here, and I'm stuck down at the other end of the line. I want to be able to see a lot more of you,' he ended lamely.

163

She smiled up at him, showing her even, white teeth. 'But you hardly know me.'

He suddenly seized her hand, desperately; this was it, now or never.

'Believe me when I tell you that I'd like to remedy that. I want to know you very much better, if you could put up with me.'

He was aware that she hadn't withdrawn her hand from his, nor had she raised any objection. He trembled, quite unaware that the three characters at the counter were watching closely.

'I'd like that,' she said softly, 'but what shall we do about it?'

Royce's heart gave a leap, his inside felt like rubber.

'Do about it?' His voice rose with excitement. 'You must come back to the old flotilla!'

'Shh!' she raised her finger. 'You must keep calm.'

He grinned sheepishly. 'Sorry, but I'm a bit in the air. I'm not used to being with a beautiful girl.'

'That's a good one. I'm in a mess at the moment!' But she was touched by his boyish sincerity.

He dragged his eyes to his watch.

'Lord, I'll have to be going,' he groaned.

Together they stood up, buttoning their coats, and with obvious reluctance went outside to the din of the dockyard.

The canteen manageress sniffed.

'Didn't even drink their blessed tea!'

They were back by the Signal Station again, and then stood sheltering in the deep doorway.

'You didn't mind my coming here to see you?' he asked.

'I'm very glad you did. Now what have we decided?'

'Well, look, it's Christmas soon; what are you doing? Have you any leave to come? Were you going home?'

She waved her hand, embracing the harbour. 'This is my home now,' she said flatly.

He could have bitten out his tongue. 'I'm a fool; I didn't mean that. Could you come down south?'

'To do what?' she questioned.

He laughed vaguely. 'I don't know. I don't even know if

I shall be out on Ops or not. But you could stay at the White Hart or something. Could you?' His voice was imploring. 'It would be wonderful.'

She wrinkled her nose. 'I'd like that very much. Leave it to me.'

She knew full well that if any other person had made such a suggestion it might have implied one thing only. But she knew that this anxious face was harbouring no such thoughts. Having decided that, she felt very much better, as if she had been given a new lease of life.

'I must be off now. My Number One is probably having fifty fits already.'

He held her hands in his, unwilling to leave.

'Think of us sometimes, won't you?'

She nodded, her eyes serious. 'Look after yourself, won't you?'

He released her, and stepped back, as if to sever the bond between them. Then he started to back away, while she still stood uncertainly in the doorway, her face wet with the rain.

He went suddenly hot, and he found himself clenching his fists. I must, he told himself, I'm not going without holding her just once. He squared his shoulders and marched back to her. She opened her mouth in an unspoken question. Taking her elbows in his hands, he gently pulled her towards him.

'Good-bye for now, Julia,' his voice was shaky. 'God bless you.'

And with that, he bent and kissed her quickly on the mouth. For one brief instant he felt the smoothness of her skin, and tasted a new compelling warmth. Then he turned and blundered away. He then realized that she had not spoken a word. Fearfully, he looked back, but she was still there, her face shadowed by the doorway. She waved to him slowly, then she was gone.

He found himself climbing aboard, without realizing he'd made the journey back through the yard. Vacantly he returned Carver's salute, and walked blindly to the bridge. He wanted desperately to be left alone.

Carver pattered after him, pouring out details in a steady stream. Fuel on board; boat ready for sea; war correspondents in wardroom swigging gin; etc.,etc.

He forced his mind to cope.

'Everybody on board, then? Right, make to Tower, "Request permission to proceed", then start engines.'

Thankfully he leaned against the chart table, his back to the signalman, who was busy flashing.

She didn't stop me, she didn't tell me I'm a fool, he repeated. 'Julia' he said deliberately. He glanced round quickly, but no one had noticed his weakness.

'From Tower, "Affirmative", sir.'

The little ship slid carefully from her moorings, and with her decks glinting in the rain, and a growing white froth at her rakish stem, she steered down the channel.

'Signal from Tower,' reported the signalman, surprise in his voice.

'They say, "Happy Christmas", sir.'

'What on earth do they mean? It's only November,' muttered Raikes, as he spun the spokes of the wheel.

But Royce plunged across the bridge, swinging up his glasses. In an instant he had found, and focused on the signals veranda. The small, gleaming figure stood by the searchlight, waving.

With his glasses raised, Royce waved, until the Tower was hidden finally by a towering cruiser.

He swung round, and even the seamen fumbling with the wires on deck seemed to him to be perfect.

'A very nice trip, Cox'n.'

Raikes sucked his teeth, and studied the line of buoys. 'All right for some, sir,' he grinned.

7

THE return trip was successful, in that it was quite un-eventful, for Royce at any rate. The crew still talked with misgivings about the first part of the trial run, the stiffened airmen, and the charging menace of the merchantmen in the fog, but Royce knew that it would change to a casual boast when they were ashore, in suitable company, and eventually it would warrant no comment at all. They would fall into the pattern and shape of the navy at war, provided they were allowed to live long enough.

He was thankful to be rid of the war correspondents, for to him they seemed somehow shallow and patronizing, with their ready flow of first-hand experiences, apparently from every battle-front but this one. They were ever ready to give full vent to such sentiments as, "you chaps are doing a magnificent job" and "nothing'll be too good for the boys in blue, when this lot's over". Of the merchant navy, too, "the heroes of the little silver badge". The last one made poor Raikes hurry from the bridge, pleading a stomach upset.

Royce had the impression that so many of these people, whose sole job it was to present the war news to the bewildered general public at home, did little to under-stand it themselves. He knew that this was a completely unfair assessment, it was just unfortunate that he had been blessed with such encounters as these. In addition, he wanted to be able to combine the running of his new ship, with thinking about Julia, and whereas at any other time, a new face, and a different viewpoint were more than welcome, these two great obsessions excluded all other possibilities.

He watched with anxious anticipation, as the seamen hooked on to their buoy astern of the *Royston*, keeping the engines ready to roar to the rescue should one of them develop a case of stage fright, and drop the lines in the water. The manoeuvre was successful, and thankfully, he shook hands with the "gentlemen of the Press", and saw them scramble into an immaculate pinnace which had been sent to collect them. Perhaps it was unfortunate that the cruise had been a blank, from their point of view, but no doubt imagination would rally to their support.

Within a quarter of an hour, he found himself aboard *Royston*, along with all the other C.O.s of the flotilla, assembled in the Operations Room. He was glad to see the old faces again, and to welcome the new. It was like doing something useful after being on the shelf. As he entered, Kirby, who stood by the wall charts, cleared his throat noisily.

'Ah, Royce, you're late. Your E.T.A. was thirty minutes ago. Was it not a straightforward run?'

The tired young faces turned towards him. He felt absurdly like a schoolboy, arriving after class had started.

'Had to drop my passengers, sir,' he said shortly.

'Well, well, first things first, I suppose.'

He turned his back, and stared at the charts, while Royce sank gratefully into a vacant chair.

'What ho, chum, how's the wee boat behaving?'

He glanced sideways into the wrinkled grin of Jock Murray.

'Fine, but I know now what a nitwit I must have been when I first started!'

'Who says you're not now?' Benjy hissed over his shoulder, grinning hugely.

'When you're settled, gentlemen?' Kirby's voice was sour.

He waited till they had given him what he considered to be suitably intelligent expressions, then continued. Royce thought he was looking much older.

'I think you're all fully conversant with this chart.' They noticed with interest that it showed the approaches of Ostend, with a riot of colours depicting minefields, patrol areas, and other local data. He really had their attention now.

'Intelligence reports that the fast minelayers which have been playing havoc in the Channel, and across all the local shipping lanes, are now based here. Tactics, as we know, are to dash out at high speed by night, get rid of the mines, and hurry back before dawn. What we didn't know was how they cleared our destroyer patrols.'

He paused, and dabbed his mouth with an immaculate handkerchief.

'We know now. Certain information is being wirelessed by agents here, in England, direct to France, concerning local convoys. Immediately the enemy receives this information, he dispatches minelaying aircraft to the Thames Estuary, or Southampton Approaches, or the south-west corner, "E-Boat Alley" as some of our newspapers deign to call it, or sometimes all three at once. Immediately, all commands concentrate the sweepers, plus escorts, to keep the ports open, while the patrols are needed to cover the convoys from attack while all this is going on.'

He surveyed them with a cold stare.

'It is at that moment, gentlemen, that the real menace slips from Ostend, and does its work.'

They exchanged meaning glances.

'As the sea-distances are so small, yet our patrol areas so large, it is obvious therefore, that we must destroy them as they leave the base. No other vessel can do it. No other vessel has the speed to get in and out before the enemy's air cover can be used. The task is ours.'

A babble of murmurs broke out, and Kirby raised his hand.

'If you please, I suggest you would do better to address your comments to me. Now.' He sat down.

Benjy scrambled to his feet, his jovial face slightly perplexed.

'How do we know when they are out, sir? I mean, they aren't going to drop us a wire, are they?'

There was a chuckle.

Kirby studied him pityingly.

'We will patrol in pairs, off this area, on every convoy departure night. Intelligence is giving us every support.'

169

There was a loud groan, and Murray rose hastily.

'Would it not be better to get them when they're well clear? We could perhaps bag all of them.'

'It would not.'

It was quite obvious that Kirby was running true to form. He was tight on all other information. It was his party, and that was all there was to it.

As they leaned against the bar, sipping their gins, they discussed the matter at some length. One thought was uppermost in their minds, "Just so long as it doesn't mess up Christmas!"

The following day, while Carver exercised all hands, Royce sat in his cabin composing a letter to Julia. He was so full of the prospect of seeing her again, and in the foreseeable future, that he found it difficult to put into words such details as the weather, the food, and the state of his health. Eventually, he took the plunge, and told her exactly how he had felt as he waved her good-bye, and almost guiltily he popped it into an envelope and dashed on deck to catch the postman. As the duty boat chugged away, he sighed, the letter was on its way, he had made a start.

He leaned for a while against the port tube, and listened to Raikes patiently instructing five seamen in the use of a scrambling net.

'It's like this. You sling it down over the side, and then you send two of the strongest lads down on it. One at each end. They 'elp to keep the net steady, an' they can yank the survivors outer the water. Any questions?'

A spindly youth, named Cleavely, whom Royce knew already, as he had been earmarked as a potential officer, stepped forward.

'But if they're badly injured, you're not supposed to handle them like that, surely?' His voice was shocked.

'Either you gets 'em up, or you leaves 'em!' Raikes was final.

'It seems a bit antiquated to me. Why not rig a davit, or something?'

' 'Cause you'll be too busy, I shouldn't wonder,' answered the Coxswain mildly.

Royce walked away, smiling. Raikes always had been one for understatement.

But altogether, as he made his tour, he found the hands very willing to learn their new trade, and were obviously much awed by the other battle-scarred boats which lay around them.

An M.T.B. swung away from the sweeping arms of the loading jetties, and crept carefully out into the stream, feeling its strength, then having made up her mind, she gathered way and headed for the *Royston*. As she turned her wet, shiny sides towards him, he read her large, white numbers quite clearly. It was Watson's boat. With her huge engines purring magnificently, she cruised gently past, too close as usual, her sweeping fo'c'sle barely five feet clear. Benjy's red face, rising from a peculiar yellow flying suit and red scarf, was a tonic, and made up for the day's lack of sunshine.

' 'Ow do, chum?' he bellowed. 'Coming up to the White Hart tonight?'

'Rather. Haven't been up there for ages.'

The M.T.B. coasted round, the seamen professionally standing by with wires and fenders, and Benjy raised his megaphone.

'Don't look so envious. We can't all have good crews!'

Royce shook his fist, laughing. It was good to be back.

The White Hart was crowded that night, and already the air was thick and friendly when Royce, Watson, Deith and Murray strolled in. They somehow found an empty table and sat surveying the scene, and their glasses.

'Who's going out first on this crazy patrol stunt?' asked Murray absently.

'Guess,' smiled Deith. 'The Guvnor himself of course, just to be sure that it's quite safe for us!'

Royce put down his empty tankard, and darted a quick glance at them.

'D'you think I can book a room here? Round about Christmas, for a friend, I mean.'

There was an ominous silence, then Murray leaned across with an air of assumed confidence.

'Is it a wee bit of fun you're contemplating, me boy?'

171

Royce grinned uncomfortably. 'No, it's nothing like that, you'll be sorry to hear. As a matter of fact I met a girl, but then you know her. What the devil am I trying to explain it to you for?' he exploded.

'Come, come, it's a Christmas wedding we'll be having!' Benjy was jubilant. 'Drinks all round!'

'Oh, for Pete's sake, you're like that Coxswain of mine. You can't tell him anything about personal matters without getting a peculiar look!'

It turned out, however, that the hotel boasted six rooms to be exact, and the landlord, after studying Royce carefully, said he would keep one vacant until further notice. That wasn't too difficult for him, as he rarely had any paying guests at all, but somehow he made it sound like a gracious favour. As he said later to his wife, it was most unusual for a sailor to book a room for one. Ah, well, things were changing all the time.

By the time Royce got back to his table, he found Benjy in earnest conversation with two well-painted, and somewhat middle-aged ladies, who were sipping large gins, and giggling loudly, flashing their eyes round the bar, as if to announce their new conquest to all and sundry.

'Blimey, dear, you are the bleedin' limit, you are!' cooed the first, whose make-up appeared to have been applied with a paint brush. 'What d'you take us for?'

Benjy shot a broad wink at the others, and patted her plump knee.

'Ah, here he is. I was just telling them you've been trying to find two bridesmaids for your wedding!'

Deith grinned wickedly. 'One of 'em was Miss Chatham of 1918 too!'

'Saucy little bugger, ain't he?' sniffed the second lady, who was definitely swaying a little.

But, like all women of their type, they took the rough humour like a kitten takes cream.

As they rolled happily back to the pier, Royce was still being ragged unmercifully, and was almost thankful to feel his own deck under his feet once more. He would have to protect his Julia from all that, he decided. She might get the wrong impression.

Early morning showed a trio of corvettes, and three Asdic trawlers, slipping their moorings, and making their way to the boom-gate. The local escort group were on the move, quite unaware that Intelligence had forecast their routine task as being the mainspring of the trap. Somewhere out across the grey, mist-shrouded horizon, perhaps even now, the fast minelayers were loading their deadly eggs in readiness. Royce watched them go, listening to the slap of their wakes against his boat, and then resumed his breakfast. We shall see, he mused.

The morning was uneventful, except that an air of eager readiness hung over the flotilla. All the boats were fully ammunitioned, stored, and had fuel tanks well topped up. Only essential work took any of the men ashore, and then only within the dockyard.

Royce and Carver stood side by side on the tiny quarterdeck, smoking their pipes, and watching the sea-gulls, swooping and screaming as the cook emptied his gashbucket over the side.

'What sort of photography did you do before you joined, Number One?'

'Oh, all sorts, free lance, dress models, anything really. If I could have done some of this stuff,' he waved towards the ships, 'I'd have made a packet.'

'I suppose you met plenty of women on that work?' Royce was casual.

'Oh Lord, yes, I've had my moments!' He laughed bitterly.

'Nice, were they?'

Carver turned towards him, his eyes glinting. 'Some of them. But if I may say so, none of them compared at all favourably with your Wren, from what I could see through my glasses!'

Royce looked astounded, and coughed hastily. 'Oh, er, yes.'

Carver grinned unhelpfully. 'The sun is over the yardarm, sir, allow me to buy you a gin!'

Leach was slumped in a chair reading yesterday's paper.

'Two pinks, Mid, and make it snappy. And have a lemonade yourself!' said Carver affably.

'Soon be time to get the wardroom decorated, chaps,' said Royce, making himself comfortable. 'I think we'll have a few guests aboard.'

They were discussing the possibilities, when the Quartermaster appeared at the door.

'General recall, sir. All boats to report when all hands on board.'

Royce put down his glass carefully, digesting this information.

'Very good. Have we anyone ashore?'

The Quartermaster, a raw youth from Plymouth, with the peculiar name of Sax, frowned. 'Only the postman, sir, an' he's due back now.'

So this was it; something more than rumour was on the wind.

One by one the boats reported "Ready for sea" to an impatient Kirby, and after a further exchange of signals they slipped quietly, and fell in line behind the Leader, making for the open sea.

Once clear of the boom, they opened up their throttles, and snarled away from the local traffic, making an impressive and much-resented wash.

On the bridge, Royce was making last-minute arrangements for all emergencies which might arise with his unblooded crew.

Carver was making a great show of station-keeping, and taking careful note of the other boats. As junior ship, they held the position of last in the line; quite satisfactory really, as it meant that at night you only had to keep station on the next ahead, without the additional panic of some ambitious skipper hitting you hard in the rear. Royce smiled to himself, as he knew from experience that Carver was watching his every action, so that when left in sole command of the bridge he would overlook nothing. So long as I don't forget anything as well, he mused.

Eight shining hulls, keeping perfect formation, they scudded along the choppy, grey surface, throwing back a dirty yellowish spume, which rose crisply from the sharp bows and rolled away on either beam, flattening and mingling with the uneasy waters. Kirby, in his newly arrived boat, 2002, led the flotilla, and Watson, as Second-in-Command, was fifth in the line. Royce levelled his glasses ahead, trying to catch a glimpse of Kirby's new First Lieutenant, a young, ginger-haired fellow called Crispin, but the small forest of stumpy masts and flickering ensigns obscured everything but an indistinct blob. Poor chap, he thought, not a very nice appointment for a new boy.

'It'll be dark in about an hour and a half,' he said, glancing round, 'I expect Kirby'll order "Test guns" soon.'

'D'you think we'll be all right if we meet this little lot?' Carver lowered his voice.

'Oh sure, we'll be all right. But you must impress on your gunners to hold their fire until they're quite sure of a target. Otherwise it's so damned confusing for the bods on the other boats.'

Kirby's lamp began to wink.

'Test guns, sir,' reported the signalman quickly.

Royce glanced at him sharply. This was Paynton, an undersized boy of about eighteen, his wide eyes nervous already. That wouldn't do, so much depended on him at all times. Royce made a mental note on future morale-boosting, and then nodded to Carver.

'Right ho, Number One, I want every gun to fire a short burst on a safe bearing, but until they get used to it, I want each gun to fire separately. Check 'em yourself.'

'Aye, aye, sir.'

For some reason he started with the heavy Browning machine-guns aft, probably to be out of vision from the bridge. After a pause they burst into life, a muffled and insistent rattle, like a million woodpeckers hard at work. Next the port Oerlikon. A bit wild here, the burst was much too long. That was A.-B. Rush, a big, pimply-faced man from Kent. Rather a sullen type he appeared to Royce. Trevor, on the starboard Oerlikon, behaved like a concert pianist. He caressed his well-greased gun like a delicate instrument, then with a final pat, he fired a short, steady burst, the tracers whistling smokily away towards the horizon. A cool enough gunner there, all right. Leading Seaman Denton performed comparatively well too on the big Bofors cannon on the fo'c'sle. It was an intriguing weapon, which had its ammunition inserted in clips like a giant rifle, and fired in a sharp, remorseless series of ear-splitting cracks. Denton would be all right anywhere. A little old for Coastal Forces perhaps, but very dependable. His crew, an A.-B. named Manners, who looked for all the world like a jovial hippopotamus, especially now, in his shiny oilskin, and Larkin, a little Ordinary Seaman from Ireland, also seemed happy enough, and had already neatly christened the gun "Vera" with bold, imposing lettering.

Carver came back smiling.

'All right, were they? I thought they were quite good really.'

'Bloody awful!' answered Royce cheerfully. 'Now you take over the con, I'm going to have a word with the torpedo crew.'

And relishing the open-mouthed expression of dismay on Carver's face, he lowered himself to the deck.

The L.T.O., Currie, saluted. 'Tubes correct, sir.' He was a ruddy-faced young man, with the easy confidence of the mechanically-minded. His two assistants, Barlow and Ash, both very new and very young, stood silently watching their Captain, as his quick glance took in the long, slender tubes poking out from either side of the bridge, their intricate mechanism coyly shrouded with little canvas spray hoods.

'Very good. I just wanted to impress on you that, although the guns do a helluva lot, you are the chaps I want to carry right up to the Jerry's front door, where you can get rid of your babies.'

He let his words sink in. He remembered the trawler crossing his sights, the noise and the pain. God preserve these three from all that.

'Where d'you come from, Ash?' he asked suddenly.

The short figure in the Ursula suit stiffened.

'From Surrey, sir,' he faltered.

'Oh, what part?'

'Dorking, sir. I was a delivery boy at the big butcher's there, sir.'

'I'm a Surrey man, too,' said Royce pleasantly. 'And what about you, Barlow?'

'I was a runner, sir,' he grinned apologetically.

'A what?'

' 'E means a bookie's runner, sir,' explained the L.T.O. 'A good skive before the war.'

Royce returned to the bridge. What a delightful occupation, a bookie's runner, but what would be shown at the labour exchange, I wonder?

Leach had joined Carver, and they both turned to greet him.

'It's getting awfully cold,' observed Leach, wrinkling his freckled nose distastefully. 'I wonder if I could arrange some kye?'

'Yes, and fix it for all hands, on and off watch, while you're at it,' added Carver.

Royce nodded approvingly. The lessons were being learned.

Leach scurried below to organize the glutinous mixture beloved by all British sailors, and Royce stood by the screen, narrowly watching the next ahead, 2003, another new Fairmile, commanded by a hatchet-faced Lieutenant named Mossbury. He had been transferred from Harwich, and was already showing signs of strain. A bit "bomb-happy" they said. He saw with interest that his crew were exercising at the smoke floats or something. Didn't believe in slackness anyway.

Whatever lay ahead, on the sullen horizon, the boat felt good, growling away beneath him, making all the bridge fittings chatter in harmony. Sax, the Quartermaster, gripping the wheel in gauntletted hands, whistled softly through his teeth, his mind elsewhere, while Paynton was clumsily splicing a new flag halyard, apparently engrossed.

'Going to be a clear night, Number One,' he announced at length. He looked at his watch. 'We'll split into pairs at sixteen-thirty. Kirby and Page are going in first, to smell out the ground.'

Carver rubbed his hands vigorously. 'Let's hope something starts soon then.'

More cocoa, more signals, and they found themselves beginning to lose sight of details on the next ahead: the ominous signs of a sudden nightfall were making themselves apparent.

At the prearranged time the boats split up and, like the tentacles of an octopus, they moved from a central pivot, reducing speed, and coasting smoothly over their allotted areas. Their own companion was to be Deith, in 1815, and as the others faded like shadows into the deepening gloom, the latter swung his boat parallel and hailed them.

'We'll keep about two cables apart! If anything happens it'll come from the south-east.'

That was now on their port quarter.

'Just the night for them, too!' shouted Royce. 'Three local convoys out, no moon, but nice and clear!'

With a few more comments, they drew apart, and settled down on their lonely patrol. Somewhere behind them, Kirby would be manœuvring into position to get behind any enemy vessel which ventured into this area of the Channel.

'If they come out, won't they be heavily escorted?' Carver's face was a dark shadow by his side.

'No, they depend on speed. If they're spotted they beat it without dropping a thing. They don't want half the sweepers in the Home Fleet up here undoing all the good work.'

Leach appeared. 'Well, how far in do they expect to get?'

'Oh, they've managed to get pretty close to the coast before now I understand. It's not so much the number of ships they sink, in actual fact, it hasn't been many, but they tie up every blessed thing while the poor sweepers are going over the whole blessed area.'

'Hmm, what a waste,' observed the thoughtful Carver. 'I suppose if we catch them, they'll send out some more?'

'Maybe.' Royce sucked on an unlit pipe. 'But if we don't catch 'em, well, it might mean that the Mid here'll miss his Christmas in harbour!'

'And my C.O.' said the Midshipman quickly. They laughed.

'Split up, and check all the guns. I know it's been done, but I want to be sure that the loading numbers keep a steady flow of ammo, if required, that is.'

Having got rid of them, he turned his attention to the signalman.

'How d'you feel, Bunts? Bit different from the Signal School, eh?'

'Yes, sir, but I think this is just fine. It's just that actually being on active service is rather queer, I mean, sir, it's so unlike any other sort of feeling, isn't it?'

Royce could sense the boy staring at him through the gloom.

'Yes, indeed. You should be quoted in the House of Commons, my lad. I can just hear the Honourable Member for Somewhere-or-Other saying, "Active service is rather queer!" Yes, I think it would go down very well.' He laughed.

'Oh, I'll be okay when I'm doing something,' said Paynton earnestly, 'I've got to be.'

' 'Course you will, Bunts,' said Royce casually. 'I'll have the hide off you if you run up a dirty ensign, or something!'

He turned to the dim compass. He'll be all right. I don't wonder at his being jumpy, he thought. You feel so naked and unprotected on an open bridge.

'Aircraft about somewhere,' muttered Sax, glancing overhead at the vast ceiling of stars.

'Not much good, even if it's a Hun,' observed Royce. 'We can't fire at anything but our special target, I'm afraid.'

'Glad they don't know that too,' said the Quartermaster dourly.

A brisk breeze had arisen, whipping the black, heaving carpet around them into uncomfortable, hard little waves, whilst above them the velvety sky was sprinkled with millions of pale stars, which seemed higher and smaller than usual. Not even a puff of cloud was to be seen, and no moon pointed her finger across the dark surface to guide them. It was perfect for aircraft, but a naval game of hide-and-seek would be extremely chancy. As he ran a gloved hand along the port screen, Royce felt a crunchy crispness under his palm. A sea-frost was forming early, in readiness to make the gunners lose their feet, no doubt. Those gunners, would they keep their heads? he mused. It was comforting to see the brief wake of Deith's boat in company.

Overhead, the aircraft droned hollowly, as if lost, and then slowly faded away. There was a flurry of foam, as Deith's boat moved closer again.

'We'll drift a bit, I think!' he shouted. 'We're most likely to hear something than see any blasted ship in this blackout!'

The motors died away, and they jogged up and down, the silence only broken by the slap of the waves against the hulls, and the rattle of loose equipment on the invisible decks.

Carver had taken up his station on the fo'c'sle, and on both boats the hands were closed up at first degree of readiness. Raikes, who had taken over the wheel, drove one fist into the other, and said nothing. Paynton, his face an oval blob, leaned purposefully over his locker, focusing his glasses astern. Occasionally there would be a cough, or a nervous laugh from the deck beneath them, followed by a quick rebuke from some equally well-hidden authority, then there would be only the sea noises once more. A large fish jumped violently out of the water close to the boat, and fell with a heavy plop, before any comment could be made. The flag halyards shook and rattled in the keen breeze, and a pencil rolled off the chart table with the clatter of a tree falling. Royce's taut stomach began to settle. It looked as if it was to be a fruitless business after all. In a way, he felt vaguely relieved. Royce dived his head under the apron of the chart table, and switched on the feeble light. Here, shielded from the cold spray, and the electric air of taut vigilance, with the familiar and homely figures, and pencilled lines, a few inches from his nose, he felt the private security and comfort of an ostrich with its head in the sand. The absurdity of this comparison made him relax slightly, and even smile, and picking up his dividers he began to measure up the narrow distances from the enemy coast. Was it possible that, just a few miles away, Belgian people lay in their beds, or plotted against their invaders, or even stood looking out to sea, hoping for freedom? It was a strange thought.

He shifted his glance up across the grubby chart, chafed by wet oilskins and disfigured by mugs of cocoa, until he found the familiar names of the English coast: Ramsgate, Newhaven, and poor Dover, which daily shook to the thunder of the German cross-channel artillery. So many little people, all trying to live, and make the feeble strands of life spin out just a bit longer. He straddled his legs wider, to steady himself, and he felt a cold draught penetrate up the rear of his oilskin and explore his nether regions. He started again to examine his pencilled marks, and again his mind wandered happily away. What of Julia? What would she be doing now? The reality of seeing her had already drifted into a dream-like mist of a fairy tale. He sighed, and rubbed his cheek, already sore from the salt.

'Oh sir! Sir! There it is!' Paynton positively squeaked. 'The signal!'

Royce came back to the present with a jerk, and cracked his head on the side of the table. Cursing, he swung his glasses to his eyes, but they were unnecessary. Away to the south-east, four stars were falling slowly and gracefully from the heavens. Two red over two green, the signal. Somewhere between these flares and his own ship lay the enemy. His mind raced, and his ear dimly recorded Raikes saying gruffly, 'You just remember to report properly next time, Bunts. This ain't no fireworks display.'

A shaded light winked across the water, as Deith excitedly prepared for the chase, then, with a steadying rumble, the engines took control of the resting craft, and pushed them gently forward, with just enough force to raise a small bow-wave, and start the hull quivering with life and power.

The trap was sprung, as somewhere around the black wastes of the Ostend approaches, eight M.T.B.s converged, like the mouth of a poacher's bag, secure in the knowledge that a fast force of Motor Gunboats would by now be hovering on the horizon, in case support would be required.

As they crawled slowly forward, like hunters after game, every eye, ear and muscle was strained, until the very nerves cried out in protest. Men swallowed hard, their throats suddenly dry, others fought off waves of sickness, or cursed helplessly at the black wall ahead of them. It was almost a relief when the horizon lit up in a savage, white glare, which made their eyes jerk in their sockets, and, seconds later, a dull roar boomed hollowly around the cave of night. The glare died slowly into a flicker, which left a red carpet draped across the horizon, getting smaller and smaller. In that mere tick of time, before the light completely died, Royce's powerful lenses caught the briefest hardening of the shape in the dull red glow, almost as if someone was standing in front of him, half blocking his view. He blinked, and lowered his glasses. Nothing, not even the glow any more to guide him.

Below him, he could hear Carver chattering excitedly with his gunners.

'Silence!' he grated savagely, and darted a quick look at the compass, his brain working furiously.

He raised his glasses again, but the ebony seas mocked him.

'There was something peculiar about that,' he muttered. 'There must have been something just about to cross in front of the fire. If only the glare had held a bit longer!'

Suddenly, he took a deep breath, his mind made up. There had been something, there was a ship out there, slinking stealthily back home, hoping that the confusion of the fire would take all attention from her. It was now or never.

'Bunts, signal to Lieutenant Deith, "I am going to engage", got that? Coxswain, full speed, steer south-forty-five east!'

It seemed an age, but in fact seven seconds passed and then, with a vast, ear-shattering snarl, the torpedo boat leapt forward, the beast unleashed. Royce grabbed wildly at a support, as the bows rose up in front of him, sending two great banks of solid white foam roaring away on either beam. Aft, the narrow stern buried itself deeply, as the whirling screws bit down deeper, and harder, until the rushing waters cascaded past and over it like walls of solid snow, gleaming starkly against the black nothingness beyond.

Deith's boat fanned out to run parallel with them, and a brief glance showed Royce that the boat's keel was visible as far back as her bridge. His own boat must be like that too, he marvelled, meaning that every so often, as she bounded over the waves, he and the bridge were suspended in space. It was incredible.

'Stand by tubes!' he barked, his voice harsh and unnatural, and to Carver he bellowed, 'Open fire as soon as your guns bear!'

Heaven only knows what Leach is thinking about down on the bucking stern, with his machine-guns, he thought, probably trusting to luck, and the ability of his skipper, as he had once done.

A fine thing it would be if his eyes had played him false, and they were tearing down on nothing, or another British boat. There could be no second chance. Their engines would already have warned any ship within miles of their attack.

On and on, blindly, with teeth gritted, and eyes smarting. Perhaps the bearing had been wrong, perhaps they had overshot the target, perhaps—God! What was that? The M.T.B. bucked and reared like a mad thing, recovered, and thundered on. He lurched to the rail and peered away across the port beam. Just briefly, before their wake surged down and obliterated everything, he saw a white-crested bank of water roll away astern. What the—then, like a shaft of light, his brain cleared. 'They had just crossed the wake of another vessel, moving fast!'

'Hard aport!' he yelled, and the boat reeled round,

engines screaming, the blurred shape of Deith's boat following suit.

They straightened up and scudded after the invisible ship.

Still they saw nothing but their own glittering cascades of foam, heard nothing but the eager bellow of power beneath them, which mingled with their own heartbeats, and own silent prayers, and shouted curses.

They were quite unprepared for the next move, which was to be made by the enemy.

Without warning, a sharp, pale blue beam of light sprang out of the darkness, wavered, and then fixed on to Deith's boat. One minute there was nothing, and the next instant, this terrible searchlight had sprung across the water, pinioning the startled M.T.B. in its eye-searing glare. Although the little boat twisted and turned desperately to shake it off, the light held them pitilessly, until to Royce it looked as if the boat was held stationary on the end of a pillar.

'Quick, Carver! Open fire! Get that light!'

Desperately he pressed the bell switch by his waist, and heard the tinkle echo round the boat.

Instantly the Bofors came to life, and the rapid crack-crack made his head sing. The port Oerlikon and Browning quickly followed, and Royce almost wept with rage and helplessness, as he saw the lazy tracers climbing wildly clear of the target.

Deith's gunners, mesmerized and blinded by the great, unblinking blue eye, fired but a few shots, no one knew where they fell, and when the German eventually decided that the drama was being prolonged unnecessarily, he too opened fire, making a red and white triangle of fire, the apex of which centred upon the M.T.B.'s bridge. Royce saw the pieces of woodwork whipped into the air by a hail of bullets, and a tattered sheet of armour plate rose like a spectre in the harsh light, and vanished over the side. He saw, too, the tiny figures fall from the guns, one running wildly, flapping at the air, before pitching through the rail into the boiling waters.

'Hard over, Raikes, round on her other beam. I'm going to engage with torpedoes!'

Moving with the grace of a bounding leopard, they swung in a semi-circle, Royce speaking carefully and slowly to the torpedomen, ignoring the spasmodic fire of the guns, and concentrating every fibre in his body, shutting out the horror of the other boat in its death-agony. Once on the ship's disengaged side, he saw her clearly silhouetted by her own gunfire, more like a small destroyer than a minelayer. But as they tore towards her, the great searchlight began to swing round, seeking them out, and as it crossed her own deck, he saw the dull gleam of the mines in their trestles aft. This was the target, their goal.

'Fire!'

And even as the beam deluged them with light, Royce knew within his heart the torpedoes would run true. Automatically, his brain sorted out details, discarding the unnecessary.

'Hard a-port, drop smoke floats.' That was it, just like the instruction books, just like he'd heard Harston and Kirby say so many times before.

The dense smoke rose from the float, and hung ghost-like over the searchlight's beam, making the scene un-earthly, which it indeed was. Raikes hadn't moved except with his hands, as he manoeuvred the boat towards safety. Paynton beat the screen with his fists, and shouted wildly, 'Why don't they hit? Please make them hit!' His prayer was answered, as the gleaming fish struck home into the entrails of the minelayer.

Surprisingly enough, the noise seemed deadened. It was more like a vast, hot breath, which engulfed the whole boat, making their throats retch and choke, their faces sear. Already blinded by the searchlight, they missed the vast, red column of water which towered over the stricken ship, and as the light was suddenly extinguished, so too the ship was removed from their vision, blasted into oblivion. For a shocked period of several minutes they kept moving, while the sea hissed and splashed with flying and

185

falling fragments, then when all was still, Royce swung the boat and headed back at maximum speed, making for the tiny, flickering beacon in the far distance.

Deith's boat was well down by the stern, and blazing fiercely. They could quite clearly hear the roar and crackle of woodwork, and the sharp bang of exploding ammunition, as they speeded desperately to help. Within a hundred yards of their sister, it happened, a billowing yellow cloud of flame, a crackling roar, and the hiss of steam, as the cold waters hungrily engulfed the shattered hulk.

Royce stared dully, numb.

'Stop engines. Stand by scrambling nets!'

His voice was far away. He knew he would never see Deith again, never hear the gay laugh, or feel the warmth of companionship. The pattern was still falling into place.

A shout from the fo'c'sle.

'Two men in the water! Port bow!'

Clumsily, they scrambled aboard, two of Deith's seamen. Bleeding, coughing out the raw fuel, and whimpering softly. Royce saw Leach's set face, as he guided them gently below. There were no others.

'Another explosion, dead astern!' yelled a voice, and they saw a queer glow, shaped like a pine tree, rising higher and higher, until its power finally faded, and it was wiped away for ever.

The three minelayers had been removed, as ordered.

Royce forced himself to concentrate his full attention to the boat, and shut out all personal feelings, and he listened with an almost detached air, as Carver and Leach reported to the bridge.

'I can't understand it,' muttered Carver shakily. 'Not one casualty, not one blessed man! Just three small holes aft, one through the transom, and the others on the starboard quarter. All above the waterline.'

'What about you, Mid?'

'No damage, sir,' Leach's voice was trembling. 'Gosh, you were wonderful, if I may say so, sir, I thought we'd had it!'

Raikes coughed. 'Another signal, sir. "Re-form".' He pointed over to the flashing light.

Royce stretched, feeling suddenly cold and stiff.

'See what I meant about gunnery, Number One?' But he was no longer angry; he knew that after this they would shoot straight. For their own sakes, and for him.

'Yes, I feel badly about that. But they tried, sir; it wasn't their fault.'

'I know.' Royce forced a tired smile. 'We were lucky really.'

Carver swayed slightly to the boat's motion. 'It wasn't luck. You pulled it off on your own.'

'Don't be such an arse!' said Royce crossly. 'Get some hot fluid sent round. We're getting out of here fast!'

The stormy dawn found them streaking rapidly for home. Kirby led his flotilla, and several of the boats bore signs of battle, but apart from Deith and his men, the casualties had been very few. To the great men at Whitehall, it would appear to be a clean-cut operation, and the public might not even hear about it.

Kirby's boat turned, and wallowed heavily down the weaving grey line of boats, his loud-hailer calling loudly for reports of damage and casualties. As he drew level, Royce strained his aching eyes across the narrow gap, and tried to ascertain the extent of Kirby's operations. He noted that both his torpedoes had been fired too, and part of the boat's side was marked in long claw-like scars. He was not left in doubt for long.

'Been busy, Royce? I hear you bagged the second ship?'

'Yes, sir.' A pause. 'Deith bought it, I'm afraid.'

He cursed himself and the unreality of this life which forced him to speak with studied indifference of a true friend, butchered before his eyes.

'They come and they go, and I'm sure he would have preferred it this way. I got the first minelayer, and Mossbury took the other. Quite a good show, really.'

Royce fumed. Had the man no feelings? As if any breathing, sane, or intelligent being would choose to be fried alive! He choked back the hot words. Instead, he merely lifted one glove in acknowledgement. As far as Kirby was concerned anyway, the incident was closed.

Kirby turned away, and increased his speed towards the lead of the line, while Royce watched him go with smouldering eyes. What this war is doing to us, he thought bitterly.

Although dawn should have made its full appearance, a heavy, wet mist, mingled with a soaking drizzle, kept the visibility down, and darkened the skys with a fast-moving blanket of grey vapour. It was very depressing, but typical.

With the first light, came a visible change too in his command. Instead of an air of woolly indecision, the hands grouped silently by their guns, matured and woven together as a crew overnight.

The only openly cheerful face was that of Paynton, who had taken part in, and recovered from, his first action like a nervous patient after a difficult operation. He was, literally, glad to be alive. Even as Royce slumped moodily against the port screen, he could hear the boy's soft humming, as he busied himself, oiling his Aldis lamp. He had taken to the "trade", but as Kirby had put it, "They come, and they go." Royce laughed aloud, and Raikes twisted his head sharply, his eyes shrewd.

'Told yer they'd learn, didn't I, sir?'

'You did, 'Swain. I thank the high heavens we had the chance.'

'Aircraft dead astern!' yelled Paynton suddenly.

As the signal rippled up the line of boats, the men forgot their chilled bodies, and numb fingers, and reached for the tools of their new profession. As he raised his misted glasses, Royce heard Denton's gruff voice from the Bofors.

'Nah then, *proper* shootin', this time!'

There it was, a black beetle, whose shape expanded and contracted as it felt its way through the gaps in the cloud.

'What do you make of her, Number One?' he called.

In his bright new duffle coat, and gleaming cap, with the fair hair curling from under the peak, Carver looked every inch the film star, about to make a momentous action or statement, which would bring an empire crashing.

Instead, after a long look, he said lamely, 'I think it's a Wellington. But then again, I——'

'She's divin'!' snapped Raikes suddenly, and pulled himself protectively against the wheel.

Out from the cloudbank now, gathering body and menace, the plane skimmed lower.

Royce sighed. "Take your time, gunners, then open fire!'

The plane was pointing straight at him, its twin propellers making silver circles on either side of the bullet nose. Then a throaty rattle filled the air, and a hail of cannon shells changed the oily waters into a frenzied dance of flying spume. Then it was gone, darkening their decks for a brief instant with bat-like wings, the black crosses directly over the masthead.

With a roar of engines the pilot pulled out of his dive, and turned for the safety of the clouds.

Crack-crack-crack! went the Bofors, and in jealous haste the Oerlikon joined in, sending a spray of shells after the intruder. Above the thunder of their own power, they could still hear the more resonant note of the German circling, apparently dissatisfied with his first efforts.

'*That* wasn't no Wellington, sir!' shouted Trevor, from behind his gun. 'Gave me quite a turn!'

There was a snigger, and Carver turned to the bridge for support. 'Rather like one though, don't you think?' He was never at a loss.

'I think she's coming back!'

The aircraft zoomed into view, this time from the port quarter, her guns spitting as she dived at them. The rattle was so sharp, that it deprived their brains of power or motion.

Brownings first this time, then the others, and from the wreaths of smoke around Cameron's boat, it was plain to see they were being well supported.

'Two aircraft, bearing red four-five!'

Lower than the first plane, the twins swept in barely a hundred feet off the sea, their wing-edges afire with yellow, spitting flames. For God's sake, Kirby, do something, he cursed.

'Ninety degree turn to starboard!' yapped Paynton.

Thank heavens, Kirby was bringing his boats into line abreast, giving maximum fire-power to the aircraft. There would be no unhappy straggler to be picked off at leisure. They surged round, working up to full speed, the air splitting with their full-throated snarls, the water burst asunder with a vast wall of twisted bow-waves and rolling wakes. Every boat came to life, the professional and the amateurs, old hands, and the new. Butchers' boys, clerks, bus conductors, and fishermen, with eyes narrowed, teeth gritted, and stomach muscles pulled in tight. Royce pulled the stripped Lewis into his shoulder, and squinted into the sights. It was all blurred. The grey background, the dark bottom-edge of torn water, and then into line the speeding, wafer-thin silhouette. He squeezed the trigger, and felt the ancient weapon pummel his shoulder. The first plane swung wildly away from the mounting cone of destruction, but the twin held his course. Something thudded into the bridge deck, and a chorus of shouts broke out from aft, and the plane was over them, revealing the shark-like underbelly. Twisting and turning, she swung away, but lacking the support of the other, she was done, for as she passed free of the boats, a savage line of bursts rippled her from nose to tail, making her stagger. Then, with a forlorn cough, one engine died, and a thin plume of black smoke billowed out of her cabin. Lower and lower, and the drizzle almost blotted her out, when at the point where sea met sky, she struck, bounced, and pancaked heavily, in a shower of spray, and vanished.

Of the other two planes there was no sign. There was only the flotilla, now needlessly speeding in their determined little line.

'Detach from group, and pick up survivors, if any,' read Paynton.

'Blast!' He's done this deliberately, he thought furiously. Probably thinks I'll go off my head, because of Deith.

'Acknowledge!' he snapped.

It was lonely being away from the others so soon, and

with the throttles down, they pushed back into the teeth of the weather. He called the officers to the bridge again.

'What was all that damn shouting aft, Mid?'

Leach smiled nervously, his pink face pinched and haggard.

'Sorry about that, sir. The Brownings were running short of ammo, and the loader, Cleavely, didn't arrive. Both my chaps reckoned they could have finished that Jerry, if they could have given him the whole magazine-full.'

'Well, have a word with him. I won't have anybody going chicken in the middle of a stunt like that!'

Was that me talking? The harsh captain? What price nervousness now?

He turned quickly to Carver, lowering his eyes.

'Well?'

'Oh, jolly good, sir. I said this is a lucky ship. Just a few more holes for the Chippy, and that's the lot! I'll get the Jerry airmen to clean the boat up, if we find them!' He laughed.

'I can manage without your humour, thank you!' he snapped. He saw Carver's face stiffen. 'And I'll trouble you to brush up your aircraft recognition. Make yourself useful!'

He stalked to the front of the bridge, furious with Carver, and more so with himself. They think I'm jumpy, too hidebound, that's what it is. He looked quickly at Raikes, but the Coxswain's face was quite expressionless. He was aware that Leach had gone forward to supervise the scrambling nets, and noted with childish satisfaction that he looked extremely miserable.

Raikes glanced over his shoulder. 'Go and fetch the new ensign, Bunts, you'll find it in my cabin.'

Captain and Coxswain stood alone, side by side, as they had on the sinking M.T.B., Royce thin-lipped and strained, and Raikes steady-eyed and thoughtful.

'You remember that time we shot up the oil-tanker, off the Bight, sir?'

'I remember. I hadn't been aboard very long at the time.'

'That's right, sir. I recall the C.O. saying afterwards that he thought you'd make a very good officer. You know why, sir?'

'You tell me.'

Raikes looked steadfastly ahead, at the small white horses. His face was grimly determined.

'Beggin' your pardon, sir, but he said it was because you'd managed to joke about it, although you'd been through a private hell of your own.'

Royce felt a lump in his throat.

'That was quite the politest telling-off I've ever had! Blast you, Raikes!'

'Aye, aye, sir.'

'And thanks very much, too.'

'S'all right, sir. I've served long enough to know that whatever ship you're in, gashboat or flagship, the junior officers always think their C.O.'s past it! You'll never change the Andrew.'

Royce felt fresh and clean, and forgot his inner pain, and when the signalman returned to say he couldn't find the ensign, he was very tempted to say that he had only been sent out of the room while his captain got a fatherly "bottle". Instead, he said, 'Well, get some cocoa then!'

They eventually found the airmen floating in their brightly-coloured life jackets, their faces turned up towards the boat in a trio of shivering, coughing wretchedness.

The scrambling net splashed down, and two seamen, Jenkins and Archer, climbed down until their legs were lapped by the icy water. Denton kept a watchful eye from the rail, while Carver and Leach made up the reception committee. Royce noted with great satisfaction that the gunners maintained a vigilant watch on the skies while the boat lay motionless, although their curiosity must have driven them frantic. Yet another lesson learned.

The three airmen stood dripping on the deck, gazing round in ill-concealed astonishment. They must have thought it unlikely they were going to be found.

One of them, a small, pudding-faced youth, held his

shattered hand inside his tunic, his features twisted in agony.

The tall one, fair-haired and tight-lipped, snapped at him angrily, and then drew himself very straight, as Royce stepped down from the bridge.

'I shut be greatfull ef you gould attend to mein unter-officer, Captain. He is slightly vounded!" he said stiffly.

Royce nodded, and Leach stepped forward with the first-aid satchel.

The other German, a hard-faced brute of a man, with a shock of dark curls, snarled angrily.

'It's a pity ve dedn't get you first!' he snapped. His accent was slightly American.

The officer rattled a string of obvious harsh comments, and the airman stood stiffly to attention, looking rather ridiculous.

The officer bowed slightly. 'The man is a fool, Captain. Ignore him. He has not learned to, er, how do you say, play the game?' He smiled briefly.

'Take them below, Mid, with an armed guard.'

As the strangers were led below, Royce shook his head and sighed.

'I don't know, Number One. I thought they'd look different somehow. You know, the Master Race and all that. They're very like us to look at, aren't they?'

'If I may say so, the comparison ends there. Cocky little bastards!'

Leach came back panting. 'All tucked up nicely. Two survivors and three Jerries. In the wardroom and P.O.s' mess respectively.'

Royce climbed the bridge ladder, then stopped, his foot poised halfway, and looked down into their expectant faces.

'By the way, I think you both did very well. Oh, and Number One, I'm sorry I bit your ears off. It was completely unjustified, so forget it.'

Carver beamed. 'I'm sure I deserved it, sir!'

'No, I forgot something. But I was reminded of it just in time,' he said quietly, and hurried up the ladder.

They had an inspiring welcome at the base, complete with sirens, and witty signals from every direction.

Not the least of Royce's pleasures was to see that as the three captured Germans were being escorted ashore, one of the war correspondents of his Rosyth trip was standing open-mouthed on the jetty, and looking suitably impressed.

He joined the other two in the wardroom as soon as they had snugged down.

'Won't worry you now, blokes, but there's just one little bit of advice I can give you to save any embarrassment in the future. If you get yarning with the other officers, never mention those who've "had it". No matter how much they meant to you.'

He felt suddenly tired and heavy, and looked dully from Carver to Leach, trying to fathom out their reactions to his words, which to him already seemed meaningless and pointless.

Carver was holding out one slim hand, studying it thoughtfully.

'Look at that, shaking like a jelly!' he mused, and for a moment, Royce imagined he had not heard.

'I think that idea you've just mentioned is a damn good one. When a chap has been through what you've put up with in the past, I think it must be extremely necessary to sever all strings, and especially when you've lost a friend or two.'

He nodded several times, like an old man, his fair hair flopping over his high brow.

Leach looked up defiantly.

'I wasn't a bit scared! I couldn't see a blessed thing from down aft! But that M.T.B. burning like that . . . I kept thinking, it might have been us!'

Royce shrugged heavily.

'Anyway, it wasn't us. And by God it never will be if I can do anything about it!' he said savagely.

Carver stood up slowly, unwinding himself like a cat, and stretched himself languidly, wringing from his tall frame all the discomforts of cold, tiredness and anxiety.

'It's my humble opinion, sir, that we've nothing to

worry about, so long as we have a professional for a C.O.'

Royce looked glassily at him, trying to think of an answer, trying, too, to fight off the fear that he was letting the strain of command crush his will power. He felt so very, very tired.

There was a tap on the door, and Paynton stepped in. 'Signal from Senior Officer, sir. "All First Lieutenants to exercise hands at Fire Fighting at eight bells".'

'Very good,' smiled Royce. 'Acknowledge.'

Carver fell back into his chair, like a deflated balloon, his face crimson.

'Well, damn me!' he exploded. 'I mean to say, that really is a bit too much, sir! Doesn't he think we need a bit of rest?'

Leach stood up, yawning.

'Well, I'm for forty winks. Don't let the Fire Brigade make too much noise, will you, Number One?'

'Oh Hell! What shall I do?' Carver was desperate.

'When I was a First Lieutenant, I used to ask that very question,' grinned Royce, feeling slightly better. 'Call me if you need inspiration.'

Carver flung his slippers across the wardroom at the departing Midshipman, who turned and eyed him sadly.

'*Quos deus vult perdere prius dementat,*' he quoted solemnly.

'Come again?' gurgled Carver.

'A rough translation is, "Those whom the gods wish to destroy, they first send mad!" ' And he ducked quickly away round the door.

As Royce lay back in his bunk, he smiled contentedly to himself. With a crew like this he had to be all right. They were too precious to be sacrificed without a battle. He closed his eyes.

8

ROYCE sat comfortably at the wardroom table, a cup of tea at his elbow, methodically checking and re-reading the impressive piles of ship's correspondence, and demand-notes. He leaned back, and started to fill his pipe, noticing as he did so, the bowed head of Leach on the opposite side of the table, apparently engrossed in correcting the Admiralty Fleet Orders.

Outside the warm shell of the low cabin, he could hear the steady swish of icy rain against the wooden hull, and the squelchy thud of the Quartermaster's measured tread above his head. Every so often, a powerful squall would rake the harbour reaches, lashing the sheltering vessels, and he would hear the mooring wires groan a protest, as the boat jerked back sharply. He tried to shelve the problem that had been gnawing at his mind since they had returned to base. He glanced again at the bulkhead calender. Ten days to Christmas. That was it. Julia's present. The great problem. It had to be something special, but what? He frowned.

'Something wrong, sir?'

'Er, no, Mid, I was just thinking about Christmas,' he said, truthfully.

Leach dropped his scissors and glue brush.

'Yes, it'll be my first in the Navy,' he said excitedly. 'Will we have a party?'

'We will indeed. We'll ask everyone if necessary. Just to please you. Commander Wright has stated that the flotilla will be in harbour for Christmas. Unless there's a flap on, of course.'

Carver entered, and hurried to the stove.

'God, it's parky on deck,' he shivered, 'Just got the last of the stores stowed away. I've sent the hands to tea.'

Royce nodded, 'Ah, Mid, I want you to go to the Coxswain, and ask him about getting some turkeys for the lads. See if he's got it in hand.'

'Aye, aye, sir.'

'Look, Number One,' he said, when Leach had left them, 'I want your help rather badly.'

'Oh sure,' answered Carver airily, 'Anything you name. Except Fire Fighting, of course!'

'Ass! No, this is rather serious.'

He paused, searching for words, while Carver studied him, his face expressionless.

'My, er, Christmas guest. Well, she, that is—— Oh damn it! What I mean is, I want to give her a decent present, and really I haven't a clue about these matters.'

The other man eyed him shrewdly.

'And as a loose-living sort of character, I might be able to advise you, eh?' he laughed.

'Good heavens, I didn't mean that! But you did say you'd had quite a bit of experience in this field.'

'You haven't anything in mind, I suppose?'

Royce coloured slightly, 'Well, I did think of a night-dress. You know, something special,' he mumbled.

'Leave it to me. I know a chap in London who can get just the thing. Black Market of course, but as money is no object,' he lowered one eyelid dramatically, 'I dare say it will be something special all right!'

'You don't think that she'll get the wrong idea, do you?' Royce was anxious, and no longer cared if it showed, 'I mean, you know how it is.'

'Well, I think I know how it is. But you shouldn't have to worry too much. Much better a present like that, than a set of knitting needles or something!'

'Phew, what a relief! You really are a pal. When can you go?'

'I'll 'phone the bloke tomorrow morning, and fix it up. I've no doubt he'll post it to me. We've done quite a bit of business in the past.'

He smiled wickedly.

'How will you know her size?' queried Royce suddenly. 'I don't know myself.'

'Not to worry. It doesn't matter a lot, and I got quite

198

a good look at her. Of course, I may want her to come over for a fitting!'

'You blighter, that'll cost you a large pink gin,' shouted Royce, 'But thanks, anyway, and I give you full control of my purse.'

Leach came back, shivering.

'Raikes said you'd already got the turkeys fixed up with the N.A.A.F.I. manager,' he said peevishly, 'I got all wet for nothing!'

'Oh, er, yes, Mid, I forgot. Captain's privilege, you know.'

He and Carver exchanged a quick glance of mutual understanding. The manœuvre had been completed with success.

Ordinary Seaman Jenkins poked his head round the door, the light reflecting from his gleaming oilskin.

'Air-raid warning's just gorn ashore, sir,' he croaked, his eyes darting round the warm comfort of the wardroom. 'Wind's rising from the nor'-east, an' the rain's gettin' worse,' he added gloomily.

Royce desperately wanted to say, have a drink to warm your inside, but custom and discipline prevailed.

'Very good. Tell the Coxswain to close up the gunners as soon as it's a Red warning.'

It was customary for the flotilla to assist the town's anti-aircraft guns when the enemy came too near to the port.

Shortly after the Quartermaster's announcement, *Royston* signalled, "Air-Raid Red", and Carver mustered his guns' crews around the dripping weapons. Away across the town could be heard the rumble of ack-ack fire, and on the dark, storm-wracked mantle of the horizon, they saw the red flashes of their exploding shells. Tiny pin-pricks of light.

Then steadily, above all other sounds, above the slap of water, the moan of the wind, and the pattering of rain, rose the uneven beat of powerful engines. The too-familiar, Berrum-Berrum-Berrum, that night after night heralded the approach of death and destruction to men, women and children. It was peculiar to think that thousands of feet above them, on this bitter evening, dozens of human beings squatted on little stools, and peered at complicated instruments, solely intent upon this one devilish purpose.

There was a dull roar from the town, and a bright flash, followed by an echoing rumble of falling masonry. The first bomb had fallen. Another and then another, and dimly across the dark anchorage they heard the clamour of fire bells. Slowly the bombers faded away, out of reach of the probing guns, and the *Royston* signalled, "Stand Down".

'Too high for us, anyway,' mused Royce, as he squinted upwards against the driving rain. 'I think the party's over for tonight. They were probably on their way back home, and had a few bombs to get rid of.'

As the hands clattered thankfully back to the warmth of the messdecks, the three officers stood watching the flickering fires ashore.

'Not much of a raid, anyway,' muttered Leach. 'The A.R.P. seem to have it all under control.'

'Yes, I think I'll take the First Lieutenant ashore for a pint,' said Royce suddenly. 'We're not wanted tonight, and it'll do us good to stretch our legs.'

'Hmm, yes, and I could make an important 'phone call, I suppose,' answered Carver drily.

'What, leave me out here at the buoy alone?' squeaked Leach.

'Never mind, Daddy won't be long. . . .'

As Carver remarked, as they sped swiftly across the dark waters of the harbour in the motor dory, Leach was really tickled pink at the idea of playing Captain for a while.

While the confident Carver made his way to a telephone box, to make the all-important arrangements, Royce wandered around the squalid, little streets which backed the dockyard in an uneven semi-circle. In one, there was an unusual disturbance, as firemen, air-raid wardens and police, hacked and pulled at the shattered remains of one small house, the front of which lay scattered across the roadway. In the poor light of shaded hand-lamps and torches, he saw the pathetic, broken furniture, stripped wallpaper, and a picture hanging at a peculiar angle, whilst the air was thick with the smell of recently extinguished fires. Even as he watched, he saw two uniformed figures carry a small, limp bundle into the lamplight, and as they laid it carefully down on the pavement, he saw the old lady's silver hair moving faintly in the breeze. It was he knew, the only movement she would ever make again. He turned away bitterly, and strode back to the yard gates, where Carver was just leaving the booth.

'All set,' he grinned, 'He'll send the loot as soon as he can. But in any case, he promises to have it for you in time for Christmas.'

Royce shook himself, and felt suddenly cold, 'Thanks a lot, let's go and get that drink.'

'Have you by any chance noticed, Number One, how the Jerries have been stepping up their raids in this area?' he asked, as they crunched blindly over some broken glass.

'Well, I had got the idea that it's been worse since the time I came here,' confessed Carver thoughtfully. 'Any reason, d'you suppose?'

'The way I see it is, that we've been doing so well over the other side in the last few months, and Jerry's determined to cut us off at the roots, so to speak. The dockyard, oil tanks, and I suppose they'll also be after the poor old *Royston!*'

They pushed open the doors of the White Hart, and Carver paused, 'So long as they don't get any more accurate, I don't care!'

Royce thought of the little figure, with the silver hair, it was likely that a lot of people would be better off if the bombers had found their real objectives.

The hit-and-run raids on the East Coast by day and night, did little to slow up the mounting offensive by Coastal Forces against enemy shipping, however, and even four days before Christmas, after a long patrol, which necessitated the flotilla's refuelling at Harwich, with a taut Kirby in the lead, they had sent a German destroyer to the bottom. The flotilla's biggest warship kill so far. While the other officers celebrated the victory aboard the *Royston,* Royce paced impatiently up and down his cabin, six paces either way, as he waited for Carver's return from shore. Disaster was staring him in the face. The promised gift for Julia had not arrived from London, and Carver had dashed ashore to get to the bottom of the delay. After an age had passed, he heard the splutter of a motor-boat alongside, and he forced himself to sit staring at the door.

Carver's face, however, was cheerful.

'He gave me a terrific line about the hold-up. Said it was his partner's fault. But he promises definitely it'll be here tomorrow evening.'

Royce sighed deeply.

'Thank the Lord for that!'

'He's not a bad chap, really, he won't let me down. Never has yet, anyway.'

'Hmm, it would appear that you're a pretty fast lot!' said Royce gravely.

'Yes, as a matter of fact, I had thought seriously of writing a book about my experiences. Complete with photographs, of course. "How to Be Happy Though Married" might make a good title!'

As they were not intending to put to sea during the Christmas period, unless 'so required by a given emergency', all the youthful captains got down to cleaning and decorating their boats, in order that the entertaining of guests might be all the more satisfactory. As Royce, followed anxiously by Leach, poked and pried into messdeck and engine room alike, he felt satisfied that his own boat had never looked better. Brass gleamed, and grey paint shone brightly, while the gay contrast of paper chains and coloured home-made lanterns brought gaiety and humanity to both the crew's quarters and the wardroom. He laughed aloud, when he saw an open cookery book, displaying a sizzling turkey, lying in the galley. He turned to Petty Officer Raikes, who was hovering in the rear.

'D'you know, I've never seen such a thing in a galley before, Cox'n.'

'An' neither 'ave I, sir. We must be makin' naval history!'

In the wardroom he congratulated his exhausted First Lieutenant, who lay limply in his chair.

'Thank you,' he groaned, 'I feel as if I'd done the perishing boat on my own.'

'That'll be the day,' muttered Leach.

'I thought we'd get all the routine over tomorrow, Christmas Eve,' interrupted Royce hastily, 'We'll do the whole thing ourselves, we'll even have a pukka Divisions, on the fo'c'sle, if it's fine, and on the mess-deck, if it's wet. Then Christmas, we'll have a very gentle routine, Number One, with heaps of food for the lads. How does it strike you?'

'Fine,' answered Carver, brightening, 'I'll get the gramophone working again, and we'll get a couple of hymn records from the Base Padre. By the way, sir, what time does your guest arrive?'

'Oh, er, about twelve hundred. She'll go to the hotel first, and then I'll bring her straight aboard for a drink. See that the Gin Pennant is flying. We might as well have a few characters here for her to see.'

'And to give you a little support?' queried Carver innocently.

'Hah, a fat lot of support that'd be!'

'And what about Christmas Day, are we having any guests then?'

Leach was already making mental calculations.

'Oh sure, the flotilla and *Royston* will hold Open House all day, I believe. So you'll be all right, Mid. She can come.'

The boy blushed to his eyebrows, and Royce thought, "I'm a fine one to talk".

That evening they arranged their cards around the wardroom. From other ships, from parents, distant relatives, and friends. It was a pointed fact that Leading Seaman Denton, and Campbell the Telegraphist, were the only married men out of the whole ship's company, and as Royce carefully pinned Julia's neat card over the boat's photograph, he reflected that he would like to be the third.

Voices sounded outside, and the Quartermaster peered in.

'Officers' mail, sir, an' one parcel for the First Lieutenant. Registered.'

A silence fell in the wardroom as the seaman left, and all eyes were on the package in Carver's hands.

'Well, here it is. Open it, sir,' grinned Carver, and thrust it towards him.

Royce took it awkwardly, and turned it over and over in his grasp. Leach produced a knife, and he found himself tearing off the wrappings. He never knew quite what he had expected, but the article which suddenly came to light, left him speechless.

'Good God!' he gasped, 'Look!' he sounded helpless, which he was, 'I can't give her this. There's nothing of it!'

It lay on the polished table, across an open copy of Admiralty Fleet Orders. It was black, a thing of beauty, but almost transparent. In fact, as the round-eyed Leach leaned forward, he gasped, 'Gosh, I can read the new A.F.O.'s about fire buckets right through both sides of it!'

Carver was a little shaken, but did his best not to show it.

'Well, that's it,' he said defiantly, 'It happens to be the best that cash can procure. I didn't know the old blighter was sending me quite such a passionate outfit, but now that he has, believe me, any girl'd give her eyes for it!'

'Blast your eyes, this isn't any girl!' spluttered Royce. 'She'll get the wrong idea completely. And now the shops are all shut till after Christmas! What have you done!'

He sat down heavily, staring at the nightdress, while the others stood uncertainly by the table. Carver, as usual, rose to the occasion.

'I think some very excellent pink gins are called for. And a great deal of thought.'

'Make mine a very large one,' said Royce weakly.

'What are you going to do?' Leach was hopping with excitement.

Royce reached for the glass, 'God only knows!'

'I can't imagine what you're worried about,' said Carver evenly, 'After all, she won't be expecting a present at all, so you can say you got it in Ireland, that you won it, or something.'

'But I've never been to Ireland, and in any case, you don't just win things like this!'

He reached out cautiously, and touched it. It was beautiful. In fact, the thought of Julia actually wearing it made his head swim.

'Blast it!' he croaked, 'I'll have to think of something.'

Funnily enough, it was Leach who settled the matter, when Royce had practically acknowledged defeat.

'Why not tell her the truth? Tell her what really happened.'

The other two stared at him, and slowly their faces relaxed. It was a solution. Not quite what Royce was looking for, but a solution. The decision was made, the box and wrapping produced, and the contract was sealed.

The rest was up to him.

* * * * *

The morning of Christmas Eve was a memorable one, both for the weather, and for the spirit of friendly comradeship which hung over the boat. Normally, the idea of Divisions, and a church service, with all the necessary business of changing into best uniforms, and other forms of regimentation, is repellent to sailors serving in small craft, but today, as they fell in by watches on the long fo'c'sle, Royce sensed a feeling of oneness with these men, whom he led, and who trusted him. Curiously enough, he had never seen them all together on his own boat before for such a ceremony, as normally in harbour, Church Parties went to the Depot Ship, which boasted all the facilities, and he felt pride and affection, as he saw the Petty Officers, and Leading Seamen, reporting their men to Carver. Even Leach, immaculate in his new uniform, looked a different person from the tousle-headed boy he normally saw about his duties.

Carver had mustered the hands, and called them to attention. He turned smartly about and saluted.

'Divisions mustered for Church, sir,' he snapped.

Royce returned the salute, and for a brief moment they stood eye to eye. Carver alert, and waiting for the next order, and Royce wondering what it was that the Navy had, what tradition or quality made these men, who had been raw amateurs like he had been, into part of the Service. Had made them a team, proud and jealous of their heritage, although if questioned, all would have denied it. He could not find the answer. Instead, he said, 'Carry on.'

Carver turned, and carried on.

As the order 'Off caps' was given, the Church Pennant broke out smartly from the yard, and a silence fell over the boat. Tucking his cap under his arm, Royce stepped forward, his eye taking in the scene as if it was a picture.

The seamen stood in their straight lines, rolling gently to the slight harbour-swell. Here and there, a blue collar flapped in the crisp air, and a lock of hair moved. Overhead, a high-flying gull screamed angrily, and somewhere, in the far distance, there was a rumble of cable, as a frigate dropped anchor.

His clear, steady voice gave strength and realism to the prayers, in which sailors have joined for many generations. He lifted his eyes from the book, as he came to the lines which he knew by heart, and looked at the lowered heads, and the proudly curling ensign.

'. . . be pleased to receive into Thy Almighty and most gracious protection, the persons of us Thy servants, and the Fleet in which we serve. Preserve us from the dangers of the sea, and from the violence of the enemy. . . .' It was all there.

After the short service, he carried out his inspection, speaking to every man, and trying to fathom the mysteries of each moulded face. Raikes, the calm professional, compact and steady as a rock, and in the line behind him, Manners, looking more like a hippopotamus than ever with his bulging stomach. Ash, the ex-butcher's boy, Archer, the Newfoundlander, with his permanent grin, and Petty Officer Anderson, looking quite out of place without his overalls and grease-gun.

Finally it was over, and the hands were dismissed, with a Christmas greeting, to go for their rum.

Royce stood in his cabin, eyeing his reflection in the

glass. It was nearly time to leave for the station, and he could feel the excitemenet rising within him.

He gave his jacket a final brush, and went on deck, where his two officers waited by the ladder.

'Motor-boat just put off from the railway jetty to collect you, sir,' announced Leach.

'Good luck,' smiled Carver, 'Bring her back safely.'

'I'm going to need all the boat's share of luck, that you're always talking about,' said Royce, eyeing the distant railway. 'Still, thanks all the same.'

The station was practically deserted, as all the people with Christmas leave had long since departed for their homes, and as Royce strode up and down the grimy platform, with nervous impatience, he wondered what stroke of fate had decided that he and Julia should have met on this very place, such a short time ago.

He stamped into the unheated waiting-room, with its smell of carefully preserved dirt, and looked unseeingly at the security posters. "Careless talk costs lives" announced one, and "A loose lip means a lost ship" said another. He frowned and looked at his watch, for the twentieth time. I wonder if—he pondered, and then he heard it, the distant, shrill whistle of the engine. He wrenched open the door, and watched the little train wheeze into the station, and stop with a final shudder. Porters shouted hoarsely, doors opened and banged, and several passengers alighted. A few workmen from the aircraft factory outside the port, some marines, several sailors, and then, when his heart was beginning to sink, he saw her step down from the end carriage, and stand quite still on the platform. For a full moment, he stood rooted to the ground, watching her, once again thrilled by her nearness, and filled with the desire to protect her from everything, and everybody. The next thing he knew, his legs were hurrying him towards her. She turned, and recognition forced the frown from her face. Instead, she smiled, and Royce, remembering their last good-bye, was, for a moment, completely flustered.

'Why, hello, Clive, I thought you'd forgotten, and I'd be left here stranded,' she laughed.

'I may forget a lot of things, but I'm not likely to do that,' said Royce softly.

'You look very well, Clive. It's nice of you to ask me down like this, although I'm quite sure I'm wrong to accept.'

Then seeing the look of consternation on his face, she smiled up at him.

'I'm only joking, I'm jolly glad I came. Really.'

He seized her by the arm, and picking up her case, steered her to the waiting taxi, the words falling over themselves, as he told her of the ship, the hotel, the fact that he wanted her to go aboard for lunch at once, and a hundred other things.

She was touched, he was so obviously pleased to see her, and so eager to make her happy. She had not known much happiness since the death of both her parents, and then her brother, but now, as she sat beside this taut, young officer, with the worried eyes, she felt in her heart, that a real, warm happiness was returning.

'Here we are. The White Hart,' announced Royce, bundling out of the cab, 'How long will it take you to get ready?'

'Give me ten minutes,' she laughed, 'After all, a girl needs about that, after coming all the way from Scotland!'

He watched her being taken up the wide staircase to her room, unable to take his eyes from her, drinking in the easy grace of her body, as she stepped up the worn carpet, leaving the aged porter breathless. The landlord came out of his little office, and nodded a greeting.

'So she's arrived, has she?' he cracked his lined face into what to him meant a smile, 'I hope you're going to behave yourself, although I wouldn't blame you if you didn't.'

Royce met his watery gaze, 'Don't worry, I'm afraid you'll probably see more of her than I will. Look after her, won't you? I don't care what it costs.'

'Oh, the real thing, is it, young feller?'

'I sincerely hope so,' said Royce fervently.

The old man put his hand on his shoulders.

'Thank you for saying that. You've done quite a bit to restore my faith in human nature. Come and have a whisky while you're waiting. She'll be half an hour, if she says ten minutes.'

Royce knew that it was a rare event for the landlord to "push the boat out", and he knew too that he was now officially out of the mere "customer" status.

The whisky was as genuine as the old man's good wishes, and he leaned against the bar, feeling the spirit warming his inside.

An army Lieutenant suddenly looked up sharply, and sucked in his breath, and the soldier, even as Royce was looking at him, put down his glass, nudged his companion, and said quite audibly, 'Gosh, Tom, what a lovely girl!'

Royce turned his head casually, and froze. Julia stood uncertainly at the foot of the stairs, one small hand resting on the rail, looking round the large room. But a new, different Julia. He had never seen her in civilian clothes before, and had never really considered the matter. She had changed into a close-fitting green tweed costume, with a sort of yellow scarf about her throat. Her black hair shone and reflected the many bright lights in the room, and as her eyes found his, they lit up with such beauty, that he heard his own heart pounding.

She walked quickly towards him, her whole body seeming to revel in the freedom from uniform. No one spoke, but Royce knew that every eye was upon them, admiring her, and envying him.

'There, fifteen minutes exactly. Well, twenty, anyway. I hope you didn't mind my changing?'

'Mind? Good heavens, no, you look marvellous,' said Royce loudly.

Colour rose in her cheeks, and her eyes softened.

'Shh, Clive, you're as bad as you were at Rosyth, except that this time we're not drinking tea!'

'Shall we go, Julia?' he said her name carefully, like a jeweller handling a precious gem, 'I'd like you to meet my friends.'

As they left the bar, the landlord refilled his glass, and drank it straight down. Then, refilling it yet again, he raised it to the swinging doors, 'Happy Christmas to you both,' he said huskily.

The harbour made a brave sight in the watery sunshine, as they reached the jetty, and Royce was surprised to find the motor-boat already waiting for him. Carver was to be congratulated. As they swept up the line of mooring buoys, he pointed gaily to the M.T.B. which swung easily at her wires.

'There she is!'

'Oh, very tiddley, she looks quite big from here.'

They motored alongside, and the bowman hooked on. Royce guided her carefully up the ladder, and on to the deck. His own deck. Another surprise awaited him there, for Carver and the Quartermaster, both in their best uniforms, stood at the salute, while Leach and Raikes stood a little farther inboard, at attention. Obviously Carver was putting on a good show.

He now stepped forward, bowing slightly to the girl who stood at the gangway, an amused smile on her lips.

'Welcome aboard,' he said solemnly, 'May I, on behalf of 9779, bid you greeting, and wish you a Happy Christmas, in advance.'

'This is my dreadful assistant,' grinned Royce, and waving the others forward, 'And this is Colin Leach, the Third Hand.'

They shook hands warmly, and then Julia turned to Raikes.

'You, I know, don't I?' she said softly, 'It's just like old times, isn't it?'

Raikes took her hand in his large paw, and studied her carefully.

'It's good to see you again, Miss Harston,' his voice was gruff, 'It'll be better'n old times now.'

'If I may make a suggestion, sir,' there was a slight edge in Carver's suave manner, 'Could the Mid take your guest round the boat? The cox'n can be Chief Guide.'

'Well, I thought that was to be my privilege,' Royce was puzzled.

'Ah yes, sir,' said Carver smoothly, 'But there is a small

210

service matter which now requires your attention. I think you will be able to clear it up soon, and then I'll get the cocktail shaker out.'

'Er, very good,' answered Royce, 'Would you care for a quick tour, Julia? I'm afraid I've got some little job to do.'

'Ah, the weight of command,' she smiled, 'All right, but I warn you, I might hear some awful things about you!'

As she was ushered away by her attentive escort, Royce turned in bewilderment.

'What the devil's gone wrong now?. We haven't got a flap on, have we?'

Carver looked uncomfortable.

'Well, no, sir.'

'Come on, spit it out!'

'The S.O.'s on board. In the wardroom.'

'What, Kirby? That's a bit unusual, but what the hell, nothing's gone wrong lately, has it?'

'I think you'd better see him yourself, sir, if you don't mind.'

Royce strode impatiently to the hatch, and as he swung down the gleaming ladder, he swore hotly to himself. If Kirby thought he was going to mess up his biggest moment, he'd get a shock, why, it was unthinkable—he jerked aside the curtain, and stamped in. Kirby was sitting awkwardly in one of the big chairs, and for a moment, Royce couldn't think what was different about him. His uniform was as impeccable as usual, and his head just as well groomed, but when he tried to rise to his feet, it became all too obvious. He was completely drunk. Royce was so aghast, that he just stared. It was unbelievable. It was as if he had discovered a curate in a disorderly house.

Carver was breathing heavily behind him.

'You see, I didn't know what to do with him,' he hissed.

'What the blazes are you two gabbling about?' Kirby swayed sideways, and clutched at the scuttle for support. His eyes were no longer piercing, in fact they were glazed, and he seemed to have the greatest difficulty in focusing them.

211

"I jush wanted to, wanted to———' He stopped, and fell back against the side, his hair flopping over one eye, while his mouth opened and shut noiselessly.

Royce snapped into action.

'Quick, get the coffee to work, before the others come,' and to Kirby, 'Very nice of you to take the trouble, sir, I'm sure. Please take a seat.'

It was like a dream, it seemed impossible that this could be the perfect, self-contained superman, that they had come to loath. He was fumbling inside his jacket, and mumbling.

'Saw you bring a, hic, bring a young lady aboard,' he paused, and looked up at him glassily, 'Thought you might like to shee a picture of my wife?' He wrenched out his wallet.

Royce fumed impatiently for the coffee. For once he felt quite at a loss. The Commander was waving a faded photograph towards him, and he got a blurred impression of a frail looking lady standing on a beach, squinting into the sun, and waving at the camera. Royce had no idea what had brought the man out to the boat, but he suddenly felt terribly sorry for him.

'Very nice, sir,' he said at length, 'I hope we shall have the pleasure of meeting her one day.'

Kirby didn't appear to hear, but carefully poked the picture back into the wallet.

'Well, thash all, Royce!' and he stood up with a jerk, knocking an ashtray to the deck. 'I jush wanted you to know,' and he leaned heavily on Royce's arm, 'That I've made something of thish flotilla, an' I'm bloody well proud of it.' His stomach bubbled menacingly. 'And whash more, I'm bloody well proud of all of you. Thash all!'

And grabbing his cap from the peg, he lurched to the door, where he wheeled round colliding with Julia and Leach, to whom he bowed.

Leach went white, and Julia looked from one to the other in amazement.

'Oh, this is Lieutenant-Commander Kirby, our Senior Officer.' Somehow the explanation seemed unsatisfactory, and Royce hurried on.

'Is his boat alongside?'

'There was a motor-boat approaching,' said Leach, his eyes fixed to Kirby, as if mesmerized. 'Shall I help the Commander on deck?'

'No, I'll see him over the side,' said Royce hurriedly, and guided Kirby to the ladder, where, with Carver's assistance, he struggled on deck. Commander Wright's red face beamed up at them from the motor-boat.

'So there he is, the rascal! Led me a proper dance he has!'

And he reached up to assist a safe descent into the boat. As Kirby slumped into the cockpit, Wright craned up to the M.T.B.'s deck.

'This is your friend Watson's doing. Slipped him a Micky Fin! All the same, he did mean to give you all a Christmas Greeting, you know.'

'Yes, sir, I know he did. And if I may say so, I think he'll be respected for this lapse, rather than criticized.'

'Hah, we've not finished yet, there's still two more boats to go!' roared Wright, and with a wave, the boat sped away.

Royce rejoined the others, and accepted a glass shakily.

'Phew, I never thought I'd ever see a thing like that. Poor old Kirby!'

Carver raised his glass. 'Here's to our guest. I might tell you, you're the first of the fair sex ever to set foot on these sacred decks.'

'I'm honoured,' answered Julia. 'Why is that?'

Carver smiled at Royce. 'Our Captain wanted you to be the first.'

Royce felt himself colouring.

'That, plus the fact I didn't hear anything horrible about you during my tour of inspection, makes you quite the nicest captain in the Fleet.' She raised her glass to him, her eyes warm.

'Thank you for being the first,' mumbled Royce, and drained his drink, without noticing any taste.

He was, in fact, completely happy, and was content to leave the lunchtime conversation to Leach and Carver, while he sat and simply devoured her with his eyes.

'We're having the big eats tomorrow at fourteen hundred, or thereabouts,' Carver was saying. 'After the lads have had theirs. That gives us time to serve them with their grub for a change. Very democratic ship this. When will you be coming?'

Julia laughed, 'I haven't been asked yet!'

'You must come just as soon as you can,' blurted Royce. 'I've made arrangements with the N.A.A.F.I. boat to run you over whenever you arrive.'

'I'd love it anyway. Will there be many others?'

'Oh, just a few,' Carver was vague. 'And now you've christened the boat, Mid'll be able to bring his young lady too!'

How quickly the hands of the wardroom clock flew round, and soon it was time to think about Julia's transport arrangements. As he helped her down into the motor dory, the anchorage was in darkness, the stars hidden by scudding banks of cloud.

The engine coughed into life, and the helmsman steered the boat skilfully between the moored vessels, A keen, icy breeze whipped the water into angry little whitecaps, and Julia shivered.

Royce sensed rather than saw the movement, and without further thought he stood in the swaying boat, and stripped off his greatcoat, calling to her above the clamour of the engine.

'Here, put this on, or you'll end up on the sick list!'

She nodded thankfully, and slipped her arms into the coat, drawing its thick folds around her body.

'Thank you, that was very sweet of you,' she called. 'But what about you?'

He laughed happily. 'Not to worry, I've got sort of used to this sort of thing.'

'Oh, have you? I thought I was the first female visitor you'd had aboard?'

'Gosh, I didn't mean it that way!' he stammered hastily.

She found his arm, and squeezed it gently. 'It's all right, I'm only teasing again.'

The boat squeaked against the jetty, and together they ran quickly up the slippery stairs.

'Shan't be long, Cox'n! Go and get a cup of tea at the Guardhouse, I'll call for you in about ten minutes.'

The muffled figure at the tiller nodded, 'Aye, aye, sir.'

As they walked briskly along the cold, deserted streets, towards the hotel, Royce slipped his arm through hers, conscious of her nearness.

'I like the way you always think of your men,' she said suddenly.

'No more than anyone else. After all, they don't get a lot of luxuries, do they?'

'It's a lot more than some officers I could mention. There's one who calls in at the Signal Station sometimes, he's always boasting that he never speaks to anybody below a Petty Officer!'

'I'll bet his men just love him!' said Royce, for some reason feeling a pang of jealousy.

How could he possibly hope to win her affection, when they were to be separated by the length of the whole country, and she would be back at the vast naval base, surrounded by dashing and eligible officers, many of whom were shore-based, and had apparently little else to do, but pay visits to the Signal Station.

'Penny for them?'

'Oh nothing,' he answered mournfully. 'I was just thinking how very quickly this Christmas leave is slipping away.'

They turned into the High Street, only a hundred yards to go now. A searchlight cut half-heartedly into the night sky, swung in a small arc, and then went out. Two policemen passed them, pushing their bicycles, their chins tucked down into their capes.

Royce stopped suddenly, pulling Julia up short. He looked round searchingly, but was confronted by the blind eyes of the darkened windows.

'What's the matter?'

'Sorry, but d'you know, I've been looking forward to seeing you again so much, and I've hardly had a moment alone with you since you arrived. And now there's nowhere to go.'

He looked down at her upturned face.

'I know, it's just one of those things. Never mind, perhaps we'll manage tomorrow.'

Royce groaned inwardly, he knew what his boat would be like on Christmas Day.

'Look, there's something I must say, even at the risk of upsetting you, and I wouldn't willingly do that for the world,' he said quickly, 'You might have guessed that I'm more than just fond of you.'

She started to speak, but he hurried on desperately.

'No, let me finish, I've got to get it off my chest. The fact is, and believe me, I've thought about it a lot, I knew when I first saw you on that dreadful station, that there could never be anyone else, never be another girl who would make me feel as I did then, and as I have been feeling ever since. You see, Julia, I love you.'

For a moment, there was silence, then she took his arm, and together, they walked on, slowly. At length she spoke, and her voice was so low that he had to bend his head to hear.

'What can I say, Clive? Of course, I'm not upset. How could I be? I'm very flattered. But you have known me such a short time. Why, I may be quite different from what you expect.'

His heart plunged, and the night became darker. He realized then that they had stopped outside the White Hart, and at that moment he hated the sight of it.

'But,' she went on, her voice serious, 'there's another reason.'·

Further and further, his soul spiralled into the bottomless abyss.

'Do you really think it's wise to talk of this so seriously, when any day or hour, one or both of us may be taken, like John was?'

The side door of the hotel opened slightly, and the porter poked out his head.

'Ah, thought I 'eard you, miss. I've got yer key ready.'

She nodded to him, and turned to Royce, who stood back limply.

'Please, Clive,' she whispered, 'I'm tired, it was so unexpected, I must think. You do understand?'

'Yes,' he answered miserably. But he didn't.

'Do you still want to see me tomorrow?'

'More than anything in this life. I'm grateful that you didn't just box my ears for being impertinent,' he said, trying to smile.

She took his hands in hers. 'I'll be there. Now take your greatcoat, before you freeze.'

He took the coat dumbly, and struggled into it.

'Well, good night, Julia.'

He couldn't tell what expression the darkness was concealing, he could only see the pale outline of her face. Without warning she reached up, and he felt her warm, soft hands on his neck.

'Dear Clive,' she said softly, and kissed him lightly on the cheek. Then she was gone.

He walked across the road, and looked up at the hotel's darkened windows. How long he stood there he didn't know, but eventually he moved off towards the harbour, kicking blindly at a paper bag which blew along the pavement.

What else had he expected, he asked himself. What could she see in him anyway? Damn and blast, he swore, she was just letting him down gently. Still, she hadn't actually said no. And she had kissed him. If only there was more time.

He found the boat's crew waiting by the jetty, and clambered into the tiny cockpit.

'All right, sir?' questioned the coxswain.

'No, all bloody wrong!' snapped Royce. Then relenting, 'Sorry, Cox'n you know how it is.'

'Yes, I know, sir.'

The others were waiting up for him, sleepy and rosy-faced. There was a strong scent of gin in the air.

'All right?' asked Carver brightly.

'No, all bl——' he checked himself, and smiled half-heartedly.

'I'm afraid our side didn't do too well,' he confessed. 'Perhaps our second innings tomorrow will be better.'

'Yes,' piped up Leach. 'You wait until she sees her present.'

'God! The present!' gasped Royce, his jaw dropping, and his eyes met Carver's. 'I think I'll have to call that off.'

'Check the moorings, Mid,' said Carver distantly.

Leach smiled, 'Aye, aye, I get it.'

When he had gone, Carver tapped out his pipe, and looked thoughtful.

'You're wrong, you know. About her, I mean.'

'How the hell do you know?' said Royce irritably.

Carver shrugged. 'Call it my intuition, if you like, but look at it this way. She's a very lovely girl, and a very intelligent one too. It stands out a mile that she could get any man she wanted.' He grinned crookedly. 'She could get me any time. Yet she comes all the way down here, to put up at an hotel, and to spend Christmas in acute discomfort with us on this boat, which, although we love it, is no yacht. And all this at your suggestion and bidding. Do you want me to go on?'

Royce nodded, and Carver poured himself a large gin from a bottle which stood at his elbow, two-thirds empty. He took a long sip, and grimaced.

'Well then, in my opinion, she's not exactly indifferent to you.'

'Mind you,' interrupted Royce, 'she used to be stationed here when her brother was my C.O. She wanted to look round, and to see the boat,' he ended lamely.

'If I may say so, at the risk of being court-martialled or something, you're talking bloody rubbish!' His eyes were beginning to look glassy.

Royce said nothing, a faint shaft of hope was penetrating his heart.

Carver drained his glass, and stood up, unsteadily.

' 'Sides which, you'd be good for each other.'

'Thanks, Number One, you've been a big help. It's good to have a Father Confessor aboard.'

' 'S'all right, Skipper, any time. She's a wonderful creature. And, again if I may make so bold, you're a bloody wonderful chap yourself, so there!' He finished defiantly. 'Now I'm going to bed, and when I awake, I'm going to have a very merry Christmas!' And he wobbled out of the wardoom.

Royce relaxed, and lay back in the chair. He felt as if he had been put back together again.

9

CHRISTMAS morning was one mad rush. And by the time the crew had been served with their monstrous dinner, and the officers had sampled the puddings, and had "sippers" on the mess-deck, and in the P.O.s' Mess, they were feeling more in the seasonal mood themselves.

Royce changed into his best uniform, and entered the wardroom. His two officers were already fussing around the table's cramped seating arrangements, and consulting the steward.

Suddenly, a red-faced Raikes and Able Seaman Sax appeared at the door. Raikes was obviously full of the unlawfully bottled rum from the P.O.s' Mess, and was looking very solemn.

'Yes, Coxswain,' said Royce, surprised that they should leave their own respective celebrations.

Raikes pushed Sax forward roughly, and for an awful moment Royce thought the bluff seaman had been up to something.

'Come on, me boy, spit it out!' barked Raikes, grinning.

The other officers drew aside—they had obviously been expecting this—and Sax drew a deep breath.

'Sir, I 'ave been selected by the ship's company,' he began carefully, 'to be the one to present you wiv' this little gift.' He held out a small parcel in a large hand. 'An' we want you ter know that we 'ope you like it.' He stopped.

'Go on,' prompted Raikes.

'Oh yes, an' what's more, we want you ter know too, that we've got the best skipper in the 'ole blasted Andrew!' He finished breathlessly.

Royce took the parcel, and eventually a thin box came to light. He opened it shakily, and took out a pipe. Not an ordinary pipe, but one produced by a leading London firm. It had cost them plenty.

Able Seaman Manners piped up from the back: 'If you don't like it, we can change it for you, sir?'

Royce looked up at the circle of rough, anxious faces.

'Like it?' He held it carefully in his hands. 'Like it? I'll take great care of it. Thank you very much, lads.' He cleared his throat. 'Thank you very much,' he said again.

'Come on lads,' said Raikes roughly, 'back to yer debauchery!' And the laughing, noisy throng clattered away to the fo'c'sle.

'Well, what do you think of that?' said Royce quietly.

'Bribery, that's what it is!' laughed Carver. 'There's been more trouble getting the right sort of pipe than I had getting the nightdress!'

Royce walked out on to the deck, into the keen north wind, and stood at the rail, just looking at the new, shining pipe.

The Quartermaster, Ordinary Seaman Elton, stamped his feet, and cleared his throat noisily.

'All right, annit, sir?' he said cheerfully. He was still looking forward to his Christmas dinner, which would be waiting for him as soon as he was relieved. 'Recon yer won't be wantin' to drop that in the 'oggin?'

Royce smiled. He was too overcome by the crew's unexpected kindness, to voice much comment, and merely assented quietly.

The Quartermaster's red-rimmed eyes suddenly sharpened.

'Allo, 'ere comes the "Fisherman" agin!'

The Fisherman, as it was known, was the R.A.F. Air-Sea Rescue launch, stationed at the base, and commanded by a jovial little Yorkshire Fying Officer, who was renowned for his success at finding his colleagues, floating in their rubber dinghies and Mae Wests, or just holding on to their shattered aircraft, wherever they might be. At this moment, the graceful black and yellow hull was just swinging out into the fairway, away from her moorings, and after a noisy gear-change, she threw up a sheet of foam from her raked stem, and steered purposefully for the boom-gate.

As she drew abeam, the skipper, dressed as usual in his

battered grey cap and kapok jacket, raised his megaphone.

'Just like the blessed navy! You lie stinking in harbour, while we go out on the job!'

Royce cupped his hands. 'Nuts! What the hell are you going out for? I didn't think there had been much local flying lately, because of the weather.'

'Nah! But Coastal Command have reported an empty dinghy floating off the Mullion Flats, so Joe Soap here has got to investigate. Christmas Day, too. I ask you!' His other remarks were drowned by the increased roar of engines, as the boom-defence vessel dropped her flag, to announce that the front door was open.

Royce waved cheerfully after him, and shivered in the sudden squall which ruffled the water.

'Bit of a blow coming up, I think, Elton.'

'Aye, sir. Signal Tower report gale warning in the channel for tonight.'

Their attention was taken by the blunt shape of the N.A.A.F.I. boat, puffing manfully round the bend, her decks crammed with unlawful passengers, who were cadging lifts from one vessel to another. She was heading straight for the M.T.B. moorings.

'Ah, some of the guests. Stand by to help them on board, Q.M., and tell the hands below, there's a free lift to the *Royston* going, if they want to go over for a game of Tombola, or something.'

'Aye, aye, sir.'

Long before the boat had clumsily manœuvred alongside, he had seen Julia. She was standing in the wheelhouse by the skipper, wrapped in a duffle coat. As he waved to her, he felt the now familiar lurch of his inside, the overpowering sense of longing. He saw her wave back to him.

The next instant, he found his small decks crammed with visitors. Benjy Watson and Jock Murray were well to the fore, in company with two Wren officers from the Operations Section ashore. Page and his Number One, and young Crispin, Kirby's new Second Hand, whom Royce had made a special point of inviting. It was extremely rare for Kirby to allow him much free time, and by the look of extreme joy on his pale face, it looked as if he was going to make the most of it. A brightly-painted little girl, in a somewhat improbable fur jacket, and a tall, aristocratic W.A.A.F. Officer, completed the party, so far. Carver bustled around, and shepherded the uninitiated below, away from the probing fingers of the rising wind. Royce muttered welcomes in every direction, but made straight for Julia.

'Welcome back,' and he took her hands in his, 'let's get below quickly.'

Coats and caps were shed, and the ladies retired to Royce's cabin, which was to be the unofficial "powder room".

Bottles clinked, and the men lifted their glasses thankfully.

'Blimey, I need this,' gasped Benjy. 'Blessed wind took me breath away!' He drained it at a gulp, and looked round approvingly.

'Glad we decided to come here, Clive. Can't get many bodies in my little paint-pot.'

Page, who was carefully examining the Christmas cards, chuckled suddenly.

'Heard about you and old Kirby, this morning, you rascal! Fancy you managing to get him bottled. Little Mister Perfect!'

Benjy's eyes creased. 'Yep, gave him a treble gin with a drop of high-octane in it. Boy, he went off like a bomb! Still,' he sighed heavily, 'he got it on me this morning. He's made mine the Duty Boat!'

'But for Pete's sake, all your lads are as drunk as coots!' exploded Murray. 'Ye're a fine Duty Boat. Suppose the *Tirpitz* comes out to bombard the White Hart. A fine protection you are!'

Royce laughed. 'Have you seen the weather? There'll be no Jerry activity today. Old Benjy knows his onions!'

The tall Waaf entered, guiding the small girl, who smiled shyly at the wardroom in general.

Carver and Leach hurried forward.

'This is Jean Mannering, an old friend,' announced Carver, as he introduced the girl in immaculate air force blue. 'Used to be a model, didn't you, dear?'

Benjy's eyes lit up with sudden interest.

'Well, now, that's very interesting. I'm sure we shall find a lot to talk about later on!'

She smiled, and looked faintly bored.

'I can imagine. By the way, this young lady is Ann Hardwick.' She pushed the girl into the limelight, and Royce realized that this must be Leach's latest conquest.

'Pleased to meet you, I'm sure,' she cooed, and took the gin from Leach's hand with alacrity, while he studied her with dumb admiration.

God, that must be what I look like, thought Royce ruefully.

The two Wrens were on familiar ground, and quickly made themselves at home, but Julia seemed to bring all festivities to a temporary halt. When she entered, Royce knew that, like himself, the others were just standing, drinking in her beauty. She was wearing a plain, flame-coloured cocktail dress, which was devoid of jewellery, but whose simplicity accentuated the breath-taking curve of her body.

She paused, a little uncertain of her reception.

'Thank goodness, my guest has arrived!' roared Benjy suddenly, and ushered her solemnly to a chair. 'I'm afraid you aren't going to get a look in, Clive!' he laughed, with a wink.

'I was afraid of that,' groaned Royce feelingly.

Already he had the impression that events were moving too fast for him to keep control. He turned to the messman, who was carefully tasting a large bowl of punch. He jumped, as a slim, brown arm slipped through his, and turned to look into her laughing eyes.

'You see, I'm here, Clive. Don't look so gloomy,' she said softly. 'Happy Christmas to you.'

Royce was transformed. He wanted to seize her, here and now, instead he grinned sheepishly. 'Sometimes I feel just like a blessed schoolboy!'

'And so you are. And that's just how I like you!'

'Here, you two!' bellowed Benjy. 'That'll keep till later. Here come the eats!'

The ice was broken, if it had ever existed, and noisily they jammed themselves around the table, and its extension, which was constructed of disguised ammunition cases.

How they struggled through the mountains of food, Royce couldn't say, but eventually they lay back in their chairs, sighing contentedly.

"That was a real fine do,' sighed Murray, as he glassily watched the messman whisking away the table, and piling the plates through the pantry hatch.

The gramophone was lifted into place, and Carver and the messman soon had the air ringing with suitable background music.

Through the scuttles Royce saw that the sky was darkening angrily, and the bucking water was turning into an unreal purple. He turned away, feeling unnaturally snug and contented.

Carver brushed by him, and hissed in his ear. 'Don't forget the present!'

Royce nodded, and turned to Julia, who was having a deep conversation with Page.

He let his glance caress the warm, soft curve of her slender neck, the smooth cheek framed by a raven's wing of shining jet hair, and he swallowed hard.

Benjy lurched to his feet, and grabbing one of the Wrens, heaved himself over to the gramophone.

'C'mon, Dorothy, let's shake a foot!'

'I'd love to, Benjy. But my name's Alice!'

Royce leaned forward. 'Care to take a chance, Julia?'

Together they moved across the tiny cleared space, while the others called encouragement. He was not only aware of her nearness, but of her elusive lightness in his arms. A breath of perfume made his head spin, and coupled with the uneasy sway of the M.T.B.'s deck, he wanted only to hold her close.

He was aware that some of the others had started to

dance, and now, the pressure of bodies around them forced them together.

Protectively his arm encircled her waist, and through the thin material of her dress, he felt her body stiffen. Then, as he wondered whether to release her or not, she suddenly relaxed, and moved in close against him. He could sense the gentle pressure of her body willingly cradled in his arms, and the overpowering feeling of desire which engulfed him at that moment made him bury his cheek in her hair. He didn't trust himself to look into her eyes.

The music screamed to a halt, as a sudden lurch by the boat made the needle screech across the record. Benjy and his gasping partner collapsed, helpless in a chair, hooting with laughter, while the others sorted themselves out by the gramophone. Leach was trying to pacify his small friend, she was already looking a little the worse for wear. Only Royce and Julia remained, motionless, in the middle of the throng, and he knew then, that he would never let her go. He put his hands on her shoulders, to steady her against the roll of the boat, and she lifted her eyes to his. They were very large and very near to his. They seemed to be filled with violent and mixed emotions, as if she too felt as he did, yet at the same time imploring him to use his control, for both of them. He felt hot and cold in quick succession, and then, with a quick, almost apologetic smile, he dropped his arms to his sides, and motioned her to the settee berth at one side of the wardroom.

'Phew, let's take a breather,' he said unconvincingly.

She nodded, without speaking, her eyes shining.

With a squawk, the music started again, and immediately the others proceeded to sway noisily together in the semblance of a dance. They sat in silence, watching, Royce not daring to look at her. She put a cool hand on his, but when he stole a glance in her direction, she was staring ahead. Seeing nothing but her thoughts.

He listened to the faint but persistent moan of the wind against the wooden hull.

'Pity it's not summer, we could have had a walk round the upper deck.'

As he said it, he saw a distant vision of a lonely, sun-drenched beach. He was lying at her side, while she lay in a sleek bathing costume, her head pillowed on his arm, gazing up at an azure sky. It was a long time since he had dared look so far ahead. Any future had always seemed far too improbable.

Without realizing it, he said quietly: 'I've got a present for you, Julia.'

'Clive! What a terrible thing to do! I didn't bring you one. How sweet of you.'

She was smiling at him, her eyes searching his face. He stood up stiffly, the drinks and the atmosphere making his head whirl. He felt reckless.

'It's in my cabin. Will you come and see it? I can't let you open it here.' He gestured towards the others.

'All right, but I shall feel awful about not bringing you anything.'

You'll feel awful anyway when you've seen it, he thought desperately. He helped her to her feet, and as her hair brushed his cheek, the feeling of longing stabbed him, so that he wanted to cry out.

As they pushed their way to the door, Carver, who was slopping gin into the Waaf's glass, looked up sharply, but his look of encouragement was wasted. Royce didn't see him. Nor did he heed Benjy's throaty, 'Oi, oi, then?' He hurried her into the comparative quiet of the narrow passageway, feeling his way past the familiar obstructions, until he felt the door of his cabin. The light revealed the piled clothing of his guests, littering his bunk and chair, and for a moment he blinked uncertainly. It was as if his one private place had been invaded.

'I like your little hide-out, Clive. It's quite cosy.'

She stood framed against the white bulkhead, a vision of flame and cream, touching the simple fittings lightly, while he looked at her dumbly.

His eye fell on the bureau at her side, and hurriedly he jerked open a drawer, and held the parcel delicately in his hands.

'Before I give you this, there's one thing I must make you understand,' he started, watching her face. 'I wanted

228

to give you this, but . . .' he faltered. 'It's a present that you might take offence at, if you didn't know that I'm no hand at this sort of thing, and that my intentions, all my intentions where you are concerned, are completely sincere.'

That was not what he had wanted to say at all, but he stopped; his mind had dried up. He held out the parcel to her.

She put it on the bunk, and carefully untied the wrapping, a loose lock of hair falling over her smooth brow.

Royce braced himself, and watched, fascinated, as with a gentle movement she drew the nightdress from its paper. He heard her quick intake of breath, as she held it at arm's length, her face entranced. Slowly she lifted her head, and then he saw that there were tears in her eyes.

He clenched his teeth. 'You're not too angry, are you?'

She shook her head violently, and suddenly held the black wisp against her body.

'Angry?' she asked, and there was a sob in her voice. 'I think it's wonderful. And I know exactly what you were thinking when you got it. Oh, Clive. It's beautiful, and I love it.'

A surge of elation lifted him, and he took two steps across the cabin towards her. When he put his arms round her, she buried her face in his chest, crying quietly, while he stood happy but uncomprehending.

'Don't mind me, Clive, just hold me. It's just that you make it so difficult . . .'

He stroked her hair gently, and held her close, shutting his eyes with a feeling of great contentment.

There was a sudden and violent commotion outside the door, and he heard Benjy's loud voice calling him. He cursed inwardly, and giving the girl a reassuring pat on the arm, he stepped into the passage.

'Well?' he asked, trying to appear more normal than he felt. 'What's the matter now?'

'Matter? Matter?' Benjy's face was purple, and for once, worried. 'I'll tell you the matter. My dear old chap, I've just had a signal.' He brandished a soggy piece of paper. 'I've got to go to sea! Now!' He paused, gasping

229

for breath. 'As you know, I'm the duty boat,' he added, as if that explained everything.

Murray appeared behind him.

'Ah told you, Benjy boy, you shouldn't have let your boys get bottled, even for Christmas,' he said grimly.

Royce mustered his thoughts. 'But what the blazes have you to go out *for*? The weather's like hell.'

'That ruddy R.A.F. rescue launch has broken down off the Mullion Flats, an' I've got to tow her in!' he wailed. 'What the hell am I going to do?'

Royce took the signal from his limp hand and glanced at it, a wild plan forming in his brain.

'Leach, get the Quartermaster and the Coxswain,' he shouted. 'I'll go, Benjy, and as I'm on the end buoy, we can get out without disturbing anyone. Make a signal to *Royston,* Number One. Explain that Benjy's developed an engine defect, or something.'

The others were looking at him in wonderment.

'Man, ye're a marvel,' muttered Murray. 'But what about the guests?'

Royce rubbed his chin thoughtfully. 'Hmm, well, we can drop those on Page's boat by the oiling wharf as we go out. We'll only be about half an hour, all being well. Unless——' He looked at Julia, his eyes bright and slightly wild. 'Care for that trip I promised you?'

She had her hands behind her, concealing her present from the others, but her face lit up, and she nodded.

'It'd be wonderful, but wouldn't you get into trouble?'

'If he's found out, he will,' grinned Murray, 'but he has the luck of the devil. Anyway, we'll be coming too, to see that he doesn't get up to anything!'

Raikes stepped forward, his hair dishevelled.

'Do I understand we're going out, sir?' His voice was quite steady.

'Can we, Cox'n? How are the hands?'

' 'Bout fifty-fifty, sir. But enough to get to the Mullion an' back all right.'

'Right, tell Anderson to start the engines now, and take as many sober blokes as you can find on to the

230

fo'c'sle, and get ready to slip. Don't worry about those on the *Royston*, let 'em enjoy themselves.' He waved his hand towards the other officers. 'We've pressed some more help into service!'

Raikes clucked, and shook his head sadly. 'If you don't mind me sayin' so, sir, I don't think the Andrew'll ever be the same after the temporary gentlemen 'ave finished with it!' And grinning hugely, he hurried away.

Benjy wiped his face. 'Gosh, I need a drink. That was a narrow shave!'

'You always need a drink,' said Murray wryly, and led him back to the wardroom.

Royce slipped on an oilskin, and wrapped a towel round his neck.

'Here, put on a duffle, and an oilskin, and anything else you can find suitable in the cupboard, and I'll go and explain to the other girls.'

As he turned to go, his head spinning with calculations, she checked him, but as he looked questioningly at her, she stepped back, her expression one of suppressed excitement.

'No, no, you go now,' she said quickly. 'You're a captain again. I'll tell you later.'

He gave her a puzzled smile, and ran for the wardroom, colliding with Leach.

'*Royston* says "Proceed", sir,' he gasped.

'Very good. Now you tell your friend Ann to get her coat and hat. I'm dropping the guests on Page's boat until we get back. You go with them, and keep the party going until we get back.'

Leach was aghast. 'But all those women!'

'It's all right. Page's Number One'll be coming with you. If he can still walk!'

He laughed wildly as he hurried for the bridge, at the excited squeaks from the girls, at the sight of a glassy-eyed seaman standing on the rain-lashed deck in his underpants, and, above all, at himself.

The engines roared belligerently into life, and the boat trembled with anticipation.

Carver stood at his side. 'Which chart, sir?'

'Don't want one,' he shouted. 'It's only round the corner!'

He peered over the screen at the dim, shining figures on the fo'c'sle. One of them waved. 'Ready to slip, sir!' Raikes' voice carried like a foghorn.

'Here, Number One, take the wheel. Leave old Raikes to manage that lot down there.'

The night was as black as pitch, and the rain was driven like icy darts into their faces, as it lashed the exposed decks.

'Slip!' he yelled hoarsely, and as the wire rasped back through the fairleads, he felt the boat borne sideways by the wind, wallowing uncomfortably.

'Ahead together, half speed,' ordered Royce carefully, and was rewarded by the engines' change of tempo, as with a purposeful thrust they pushed the boat forward into the teeth of the weather.

Squinting into the darkness, he could just make out the dim shape of the solitary M.T.B. against the wharf, and slowly he jockeyed towards her.

He took a quick glance down to the waist, where he saw the huddled group of guests waiting to change boats. Page's Number One waved what looked like a bottle in his direction. 'Ready to go!' he called. Right, this had to be just so, and with great precision he brought the boat under the lee of the stonework, and alongside the other vessel, where the forewarned crew gathered eagerly to welcome their visitors.

'All gone, sir!' And with a throaty growl they swung round and motored for the boom-gate. A green light winked brightly ahead, and Royce grabbed the Aldis to shutter a reply. Then, gripping the rail and rocking back on his heels, he let the weather hold him in its grasp.

'Here we go, then. Full ahead both!'

Once outside the shelter of the headland, the boat shuddered to the wind's mounting punch, and solid sheets of spray swept up and over the masthead. It was like racing into a solid black void, with nothing to guide them but the swinging compass card, and a distant winking wreck-buoy.

Raikes clambered on to the bridge, breathing heavily, his oilskin streaming.

'All secure on deck, sir.'

'Very good, take over the wheel.'

Carver willingly relinquished the helm, and steadied himself against the chart table, wiping his face with a sodden handkerchief.

' 'Strewth, what a night! Still, it's better than going out for a game of "catch" with Jerry,' he called.

'Better go below, and make sure the wardroom's all right. We don't want everything smashed before we get back!'

Carver waved, and ducking his head, scrambled down along the glistening deck.

'You know the place, 'Swain?' asked Royce, peering at Raikes's bulky shape.

'Aye, sir, we'll be up to it in about ten mintes, I should think.'

'Right, we'll get the new towing hawser out on deck. And a few fenders too. Just in case!'

'Already done it, sir,' chuckled Raikes.

It was at that moment Royce became aware of the girl standing at the rear of the bridge, clutching with both hands at the signal locker for support. He reached her in a bound, and helped her to the lee side, behind the glass screen.

'Did you come up alone?' he yelled, his voice anxious.

'No, it's all right. A sweet little seaman wanted to help me, but I practically had to carry *him!*'

He shook his head almiringly. She made a heartening sight, clad in an oversize duffle coat and oilskin. Protruding from beneath these billowing garments, he saw an ungainly pair of rubber boots. She stood now, laughing at him, her hair whipped back by the wind, her face running with spray, while she struggled to keep her feet.

'Well,' he said at length, when he realized he was staring rather hard. 'What do you think of her?' And he waved his arm, embracing the darkened boat.

'Marvellous! She's all you said, and more. I never realized how fast they were, before. But you will be careful, won't you?'

He smiled. 'Don't worry, I'll not take any risks with you aboard.'

An extra-big wave slapped angrily at the boat's lifting bows, and Julia slipped sideways across the canting deck, her clumsy boots skidding helplessly. Royce roughly encircled her waist with his arm, while he grabbed the rail with his other hand, pulling her safely against his body. Then he stood behind her, gripping the rail on either side of her, and acting as a cushion for any further sudden lurches.

'Phew, thanks very much,' she laughed shakily. 'You nearly lost your passenger, just then!'

He smiled happily and pulled her close, peering over her head at the angry waters approaching them, while her damp hair rippled against his chin. Her nearness, the boat, and the wild exhilaration of the weather intoxicated him.

He gripped her tighter, and pointed suddenly, as a lazy red flare arched over the black wastes, and fell slowly, spluttering into the sea.

'There she is! Right on the button!'

She twisted in his grasp, looking back at him.

'What are you going to do now?'

'Tow him. That's about all we can do at the moment.'

Carver and Page had joined the knot of seamen behind the bridge, and Royce could vaguely hear their shouted orders, as they struggled with the heavy hawser, which, like all its breed, had a mind of its own. He turned his attention back to the Rescue Launch, for as Raikes swung the M.T.B. round in a semi-circle, with the engines' roar slowly diminishing, he could plainly see her bright yellow upperworks swaying sickeningly, as the helpless boat jerked to a canvas sea-anchor, her decks awash.

The girl felt his body tense, and when he spoke to Raikes, his voice, too, was different, hard and cool.

'Near as you can, Cox'n. Don't crowd her. I'm going to speak to the skipper.'

'Aye, aye, sir.' The hands turned the spokes, almost gently.

Royce blew into the mouthpiece of the loud-hailer, and it whistled plaintively.

'D'you hear, there? Are you still intact?'

'I think so!' The answering voice was distorted by the wind. 'Thank you for leaving your party just for little old me!'

Royce could easily read the agony of worry behind that jocular greeting. He knew too well the shortcomings of such a boat, left engineless in such a sea.

'I'm going round again, then I'm passing a line to you, for the towing warp. O.K.?'

'Aye, but watch you don't get it round your screws!'

His next remarks were drowned by the roar of the M.T.B.'s engines, as Raikes swung her neatly away, to avoid being flung against the other boat's side by a white-hooded wave which reared with sudden fury.

Unconsciously, Royce had taken out his pipe, and clenched it grimly between his teeth, while he weighed up the situation. Julia moved away, and clung quietly in the corner, watching him, heedless of the spray which stung her cheek.

'Port side to! Get ready with the lines!' bellowed Royce, hoping that Carver's head was now properly clear. He found time to smile at the thought of Benjy, who, shorn of responsibility, now lay comfortably in the ward-room with Murray, singing discordantly.

There she was again. He could see the white numbers on her flat stern, rolling through a ninety degree arc.

'Stand by!'

The boat moved in fast, like an experienced boxer, then, as they stood stem to stem, barely twenty feet apart, the engines stopped, and a burly seaman sprang to the rail, gauging the distance.

'Let her go!' roared Royce, and the seaman's arm soared, sending the line snaking into the darkness. There was a faint tinkle of glass.

'Right through her blasted wheelhouse winder!' breathed

235

Raikes admiringly. There had been a seven pound wrench on the end of the line.

'Heave away lads! Roundly!'

He was rewarded to see the airmen whipping in the slack of the line as fast as they could manage under such desperate conditions. It seemed an age before the eye of the hawser was reluctantly swinging across the gap, and all the time, Captain and Coxswain used every knack and every trick of engines and rudder, to stop the boats colliding.

'All fast, sir!' Carver waved his dripping cap wildly.

Slowly, painfully, they drew ahead, holding their breath as the hawser rose out of the sea, tightening, throwing off a shower of drips like a wet dog, and then settled down to take the strain. The Rescue Launch veered round, fell in behind them, and obediently allowed herself to be taken home.

Royce didn't take his eyes off her, however, until they crawled through the protective arms of the boom, and under the shelter of the wind-swept jetties of the base.

They eased their charge alongside, and as the lines snaked ashore, the M.T.B. slipped the tow, and made for her own moorings.

'Many thanks, Navy!' The "Fisherman" waved after them thankfully.

'It was a pleasure!'

Royce breathed out deeply, and stretched.

'Not too bad, eh, Cox'n?'

'Not bad, sir.'

Carver and Page appeared on the bridge, grinning like schoolboys.

'What an original party you give,' Page chuckled. 'Nothing like a bit of excitement. I wonder what old Kirby would have said about it?'

'Funny you should say that. I was just thinking, a few months ago we couldn't have done anything like it. Any of us. You've got to hand it to old Kirby, he's taught us a lot, and I think he's learned a bit from us.'

He watched narrowly, as the seamen picked up the buoy-ring, and hooked on.

'Stop engines.'

The tide gripped the boat, and swung her firmly into line with the other moored craft.

'You're probably right,' confessed Page, 'But I still say he's an awkward cuss.'

'Well, let's go and finish the party,' said Royce sadly, 'I think I see our other guests coming over in a motor-boat. Number One, make to *Royston*, "Mission Completed".' In his heart he knew he was only trying to spin out the time, to put off the moment of her departure.

'Come below, Julia. You must be frozen.'

She shook her head vigorously. 'Not a bit of it. I'll bet the others will be terribly jealous.'

Below, in the snug atmosphere of the wardroom, Royce suddenly wanted to be rid of his friends, of everyone else but Julia, but he grinned ruefully, and submitted to the mounting noise of enjoyment.

Julia's face was fresh and alive from her boisterous sea trip, and she hung back from the door, a finger on her lips.

'I'm not coming in like this,' she whispered, 'I'm going to put a new face on, and get rid of your sea-going robes.' She faltered, and turned back to him, her face suddenly serious, and Royce stepped into the passage, his face inquiring.

'I think you were superb,' she said, her eyes warm, 'I shall always remember you like that. It helps me to understand, to realize what you are going through, when you are out there——'

'I was just trying to make an impression on you,' he grinned awkwardly. 'After all, I did promise you a trip, when I came up to Rosyth.'

She wrinkled her nose prettily. 'Don't try to fool me. Now you go and fix me a nice drink, because I expect I shall suddenly start to feel a bit weak, in a minute.'

He stared after her. "I feel a bit weak now," he thought.

They sat for the rest of the time, side by side, hardly speaking, yet each fully conscious of the other, and only dimly aware of the din and clamour.

Murray was trying grimly to stand on his head in one

237

corner, and drink a pint of beer at the same time, until Benjy took the opportunity to empty a soda syphon down his leg, to the hilarious delight of the two Wren officers.

Leach and the small girl, now looking completely dazed, were dancing slowly and dreamily in the middle of the wardroom, although the gramophone had long since ceased to play. Of Carver and the Waaf there was no sign.

Page lurched happily over to them, and sat heavily on the table. He grinned vacantly at Julia.

'Some party, eh?' He helped himself to another drink, and nodded drowsily. Then, with a jerk he looked at her again.

'By the way, are you coming to see the boy here get his gong next week?'

'Gong?' she queried, looking strangely at Royce. 'Tell me about it.'

Heedless of Royce's frown, he chattered on. 'Well, he's going to get his medal officially from the top brass, that's what,' he confided.

She looked at Royce seriously. 'Is that true?'

'Yes, I forgot to mention it,' he mumbled uncomfortably.

She let her eyes fall to the small ribbon on his chest.

'I'd very much like to be there,' she said quietly. 'But I don't think I can manage it so soon after my leave.'

'Between you and me, it terrifies me,' he confessed. 'And I'd put it out of my mind for a bit, thanks to you.'

'Write to me about it, won't you?'

'About everything, Julia, it's been so wonderful, having you here.'

They sat looking at each other, and only came back to reality, when a red-faced Petty Officer thrust his head into the doorway.

'Anyone for the shore, please?' he boomed. 'I'm collecting all guests, and this is the last boat.'

'Give him a drink, quick!' hissed Royce, banging Page to life with his elbow.

He stood up heavily, the joy draining out of him. 'I'll help you get your things.'

He watched her putting on her borrowed duffle coat,

and tying the silk scarf over her head, heedless of the other girls, who were laughing and chattering gleefully.

Carver had appeared, a trifle sheepishly, with the tall Waaf, and he noted that his collar was smeared with lipstick.

They let the others go ahead, both dreading the moment of parting.

'What time do you leave tomorrow?' he asked, although he already knew the answer.

'Eleven o'clock. I shall get back to Rosyth in time for the forenoon watch the day after.'

The keen night air seemed hostile.

He put his hands on her waist, and pulled her to him.

'I do so wish you'd reconsider, Julia. Please believe me when I tell you that there'll never be anyone else. Ever. I know I've only known you such a short time, and I know too that you could get any man, just by raising your little finger. But I want you, so very much.'

For a moment she stood still in his arms, then, with a sudden force, she put her arms round his neck, pulling herself closer, her eyes bright.

'That was what I was saving to tell you,' she murmured, 'I know now what I want.'

He felt her body tremble, and her hands gripped his neck fiercely, 'I do love you, Clive, I love you so much.'

A starshell seemed to burst before his eyes, blinding him, and there was a great roaring in his ears, and the next instant they were clinging to each other, and she was kissing him hard. As she broke away from him, he tasted the salt from her cheek, the spray of tears, he couldn't say.

'No, don't hold me again, Clive, I must go,' she cried. 'But if you want me, I'll come to you again, somehow.'

Blindly, they ran out on to the deck. A fat harbour launch, crammed with noisy passengers, was bumping alongside, while her coxswain leaned impatiently over the rail.

She was half-laughing and half-crying, and Royce was in a dream. She stepped down on to the crowded boat, and immediately the ropes were cast off, and a widening gulf of water grew between them. He shouted wildly, following the boat the full length of the M.T.B., to the delight of the passengers.

'I'll try to get to the station tomorrow!'

But he couldn't be sure if she had heard him, although she waved until the boat was swallowed up in the blackness. He was sure of only one thing. He was the happiest, luckiest man alive.

10

WHEN a country decides to go to war, it is not just the people who, willingly or unwillingly, take on a new and uncertain guise, and as in the case of England, draw together in some sort of uniform and hopeful tolerance of enforced discipline, its very way of life alters. From Buckingham Palace to the humblest home with its black-out curtains and pathetic backyard air-raid shelter, from the schoolhouse which has become a casualty station, to the church hall which has changed overnight to a Home Guard headquarters. Or the Southend paddle steamer now sweeping mines, alongside the millionaire's yacht marshalling a convoy in Weymouth Bay. All these, and more, become part of the pattern.

What had once been the rambling clearing house for fish, brought in by the trawler and drifter fleets of the east coast, had suddenly suffered such a transformation. It was a high-roofed building, over a hundred yards in length, with a smooth concrete floor, and two of its walls open to the elements and the wharf fronts. The comfortable peacetime untidiness had been changed to one of ordered neatness, with whitewashed bricks, loading bays for lorries, carefully marked with coloured signs and helpful arrows. At the far end, where the girls of the port used to tear with gory relish at the vast piles of herrings, a mountain of ammunition boxes awaited disposal, while in a dark corner on trestles, a headless torpedo, liberally smeared in golden grease, was nearing the end of its long journey.

Normally, the "Shed" as it was known by the naval population, was a turbulent centre of activity, a constant whirlpool of men and material which swept from office to shipyard, and from ship to sea. Today was different. It was one of those special days, which every so often the Navy earmarks, and puts aside for a suitably special occasion. One moment the Navy's private world is full of bustle and noise, with sweating men in shabby clothes working desperately, always with time against them, and then, quite suddenly, all that is changed. Here, at this moment, all those same men are drawn up in neat lines, smartly dressed in their best uniforms, the blue ranks forming three sides of a square. A silvery sun is forcing its way through the unsettled banks of cloud, to settle briefly on the set faces, and to reflect but momentarily on the gold badges, and the gleaming bayonets of a Marine guard. They have come together just for this short while, knowing full well that in a few hours they will be back at their work again, cursing the Service, and the war. There are all sorts of sailors present, ranging from the base personnel, to the hardened veterans of the destroyers and minesweepers, whose shore-time can be counted in hours. The bulk of the men, however, are the crews of the Light Coastal Forces, lined up with their officers, and quietly waiting to witness the nation's appreciation of their valour. For although but a few medals are to be presented, every man here knows, be he captain or signalman, gunner or cook, stoker or lieutenant, that he can share in their winning, and feel a just pride in the deed which has gained the small piece of gleaming metal.

Royce and the others stood in a self-conscious line, abreast of the dais, he with his heart in his mouth. He tried to focus his eyes ahead, on the slender mast of a distant frigate, but each time he found himself glancing furtively at the sea of seemingly unfamiliar faces around him, or at the single squad of Wrens, as if to gain their moral support.

Vice-Admiral Sir John Marsh, as Flag Officer, was representing the King for the purposes of the presentation, and he stood small and erect on the dais, his head thrust slightly forward, the pale eyes darting piercingly and searchingly over the faces before him. He was in the process of winding up a brief but carefully worded speech.

'And so,' he barked, his voice echoing round the iron girders of the roof, 'we have come to the bitterest part of the struggle, when all, each and every one of us, has to make the all-important decision.' He paused, allowing his words to sink in. Across the harbour came the clank of a winch, and somewhere overhead an aeroplane droned lazily. 'We must decide, here and now, to work harder, longer, and if necessary, to give the last drop of blood to the common end. Many of us have fallen, and will fall on the way, but that is the way to victory.' He stopped, and cleared his throat.

Royce's eye fell on Benjy, standing at the head of his crew, a tight-lipped, grim-faced Benjy, looking old before his time.

The Admiral turned to his Staff Captain, who held a sheaf of papers in a leather folder. Royce steeled himself. This was the moment. The other two lieutenants who were with him were first, they were both Motor Gunboat captains. Royce found himself listening with awe, as the Admiral read the citations. Surely these two youthful figures could not have achieved so much. He saw the Flag Lieutenant step forward and hand the little box to the Admiral. There was a great hush, as if the world was holding its breath, and then he pinned the small silver cross on the first officer's jacket, and shook him by the hand. Royce chilled as the second man stepped up. One side of his face was like a wax mask, smooth and dead. The one remaining eye stared steadily ahead, as the cross was pinned to his chest, but as the Admiral began to speak to him in a low voice, the lieutenant lowered his head, and his body shook violently with a paroxysm of violent sobs. Royce turned his face away, as the two sick-bay attendants led the officer gently from the building. Such was the price.

'Lieutenant Clive Royce,' the sharp voice broke into his thoughts, and clenching his teeth he marched quickly to confront the Admiral. The pale eyes regarded him coldly, as the Staff Captain read loudly from his papers, but Royce was only dimly aware of the context. He was still thinking of that other lieutenant. It might have been him. 'Did, in the face of extreme danger, under the aforementioned circumstances, and without regard for his personal safety, carry out the destruction of the enemy, in a manner over and above the line of duty.' The voice had stopped, and he felt, rather than saw, the Admiral affix the decoration.

'Well, my boy, I said we should meet again, eh?' The eyes were now smiling, the lined face relaxed. 'Congratulations.'

'Thank you, sir.'

It was all a dream. He saluted and marched to the side, where, with real pleasure, he watched as Raikes received his hard-earned D.S.M.

The base padre said a few words. The Marine band struck up "Hearts of Oak", and with an almost eager haste the blue ranks wheeled round and marched out into the salt air. Back to the war.

Royce and Raikes walked slowly along the main jetty, towards the landing-stage, each immersed in his own thoughts.

'Didn't take long, did it?' said Royce at length.

Raikes thought for a bit, his eyes dreamily watching the gulls dancing over the water, swooping and screaming at the flotsam.

'I dunno, sir. I aged about ten years in there!'

Royce slapped him across the shoulder, brought back to reality by Raikes's simple forthrightness, which had done so much to draw them together.

'Bit of luck the Admiral doesn't know about our Christmas escapade,' he laughed. 'I don't suppose he'd approve of Wrens in M.T.B.s!'

Raikes whistled shrilly and waved in the direction of the idling motor dory.

'I shouldn't bank on him not knowing!' he answered wryly. 'That's 'ow you become an Admiral, knowing them things!'

* * * * *

'Starboard twenty.'

'Starboard twenty, sir. Twenty of starboard wheel on.'

'Steady.'

244

'Steady, sir, course south-thirty east.'

'Steer south-forty east.'

There is a pause, and the steering chain rasps and rattles, as the Quartermaster, his eyes straining to watch the dancing compass card, floating under its feeble lamp, eases the wheel over spoke by spoke. When he speaks, his teeth are clenched because of the cold, and because the dawn is still a whole night away.

'Course south-forty east, sir.' The whisker of the lubber's line has halted opposite the required point.

'Very good.' Carver's tone is one of strain. He levels his glasses ahead, searching the invisible horizon.

Jenkins, on the wheel, curses quietly, as a feather of white spray jumps the screen and plunges itself wetly beneath a gap in his muffler. He is thinking about his mother, and her fish shop in Brighton. They'll just be closing now, and the air will be filled with vinegar and hot fat. He smiles secretly, and licks his lips.

'Watch your helm.' Carver is worried and angry. Somewhere ahead is the Motor Gunboat flotilla they have been sent to contact. Somewhere astern, Kirby will be fuming impatiently.

Paynton hums happily amid his flags and lamps, while Leach is invisible, save for his buttocks, as he pores over the chart. Thinking of his girl, thinks Carver, allowing his mouth to soften.

The bridge is like a small stage in a vast, empty and darkened theatre, where the players are waiting for a final rehearsal. Except that here there is no time to rehearse.

Above the spiralling mast, the clouds are solid black things, slashed with silver valleys, as a baffled moon tries to show them the way. As it sheds its beams briefly, the sea too is revealed, a powerful, menacing desert of heaving jet dunes, with the occasional white crust torn free by the biting wind. This is the North Sea.

There is a sharp clink from the Bofors mounting, and a scuffle of feet. Someone laughs, and Denton's throaty voice quells them with threats.

'Bridge?' A tiny voice floats questioningly up a voice-pipe.

'Bridge,' snaps Carver, wondering what it must be like, bouncing about in the engine room, between those thundering giants.

'Permission to send Stoker Barker to the mess-deck to bandage 'is 'ead, sir? 'E's bumped it on number one pump.'

'I suppose that makes a difference from, say, number two pump?' Carver's voice is heavy with sarcasm.

'Pardon, sir?'

'Skip it. Yes, send him up.'

God, I'm tired, he thinks. That girl'll kill me. There is a soft snore from the chart table, and Carver kicks savagely at the Midshipman's curved stern.

'Wake up, Colin! You lazy bastard!'

The watch is proceeding as normal.

* * * * *

Below in his cabin, Royce lay lazily and dreamily in his bunk, his mind and body unwilling to return to the ways of duty. He squinted down his fully-clothed body to his large sea-boots, which stuck into each corner of the bunk, to stop him rolling on to the deck. From a hook on the door, his dressing-gown hung out at an angle of forty-five degrees, as if on a bracket, and then swung back eerily to another improbable position. Royce watched it idly for a while, and then returned to Julia's letter, which he rested on his chest, to catch the lgiht from his bunk lamp. He sighed contentedly, and started to read it again:

'. . . and so the transfer has been arranged. I shall be moving down to Harwich, almost at once, to attend an advanced signal course there. I don't even mind that. Any excuse to be near you again.'

He smiled, and felt the strong stirring within him. He turned over the page, drinking in her round, neat writing.

'I shall come and see you as soon as I can, to let you know the arrangements at Harwich. As I said before, we *all saw your picture in the paper the other day, getting your medal. I was very proud, and cried a little bit. Must close now, as I am certainly not going to miss getting transport to the station, to come to you again.'*

It was signed, simply, "with love, Julia". He stretched contentedly. It was still like a miracle. He wanted to have some little thing of hers to touch and hold, just to prove he was not dreaming. He glanced round the disordered cabin. She was here in this place, just a week ago, he marvelled. He could still picture her, still sense her perfume, he nearness.

'Captain, sir?'

He swallowed hard, and rolled over to the voice-pipe. 'Yes?'

'Gunboats ahead. 'Bout half a mile.'

'Very good. Get the Coxswain on the wheel. I'm coming right up.'

He swung his legs to the deck, and slipped his glasses round his neck. At the door he paused. Her vision was still there and, smiling inwardly, he climbed the ladder to the main-deck.

He nodded to the others, and followed his usual painstaking routine. Compass, chart, weather, speed. Right. He turned his attention to the dark shapes, revealed only by their creaming bow-waves, which were looming on the port bow.

'Made the challenge?'

'Yes, sir. Their Senior Officer is coming alongside to get the gen.'

Even as they waited, one of the gunboats swung out of line, and sidled alongside, her engines idling. Royce could see the white blobs on her bridge, and shining oilskins.

'Ahoy there! This is S.N.O. here. Give me the message, and we'll get cracking!'

Royce raised his megaphone. The loud-hailer would be a bit too much, in the enemy's back garden as it were.

'Lieutenant-Commander Kirby's compliments, and he says for you to go straight in now, without waiting for any further confirmation. As you know, the story is that the two enemy transports are coming up the coast fast, with one escort ship. A Hans-Lody class destroyer.' He paused; the salt was making his throat like sandpaper.

'What about the bloody E-boats?' The booming voice was testy.

'Yes, they'll be in a covering sweep, about five miles ahead of the convoy. You're to go in, as if you were making a normal sweep, and draw the E-boats off. You're to start the sweep at oh-one-oh-oh.'

There was a pause, while the water swished and slopped between the two boats.

'Okay! I hope the Intelligence reports are right for once! Good huntin'!'

The gunboats milled round their leader and then, after much gear-changing, they prowled off into the night, in a tight arrowhead formation.

To Carver's ill-concealed relief, Royce took over the con, and when they eventually picked up Kirby's cautious signal, he breathed a deep sigh of admiration.

'Jolly good, Skipper. I don't know how you manage to get the exact rendezvous like that.'

'It's dead easy, Number One. He signalled, so we know it's the S.O. If he'd fired, we'd have been at the wrong place, see?' said Royce drily.

They cruised steadily towards the hidden coastline, the engines throttled down, and grumbling throatily.

Raikes, who had been moodily studying the bobbing stern of Cameron's boat, started suddenly.

'Good 'eavens, I forgot!' he exploded.

The others peered at him uncertainly.

'A' Appy New Year, gentlemen!' he said solemnly.

Carver laughed. 'So it is. God bless us, every one!'

They reached round in the darkness and shook hands. Carver called out the news to Leach, who had gone aft to his Brownings, and there was a stifled cheer.

'The last year of war, perhaps,' said Royce thoughtfully. 'Who knows?'

On the horizon there was a sharp crackle of automatic fire, and an impressive display of tracer shells. The gunboats were putting on their show.

'We've struck oil!' jerked Carver excitedly. 'Now where is the——'

He was cut short by Kirby's action lamps flashing urgently, and the quickening roar of engines.

'Full speed ahead! Stand by torpedoes!' barked Royce. 'Okay, John, get forrard. And keep your head down!'

The convoy was completely taken by surprise, as the lean hulls tore down upon them. They had confidently watched the E-boats tear after the gun-boats, and settled down thankfully behind the powerful bulk of the destroyer.

Kirby's blackboard tactics swung smoothly into operation. The destroyer was to be first, and less than twenty seconds after the first gun had fired, two torpedoes burst in her engineroom, and another reduced her fo'c'sle to a flaming hell.

Frantically she fired her secondary armament at the M.T.B.s as they flashed into the gleam of her own funeral pyre, and the night was ripped apart by the clatter of machine-guns and cannon. Yet another steel fish struck home, and with an eye-searing flash, she rolled on her beam-ends, the fires hissing and shooting out great geysers of scalding steam.

Royce saw the tracers rippling and bouncing along her upturned and streaming bilge keel, and then, with a frightful scream of rending metal, she vanished, leaving a small, glittering pool of burning oil.

The two transports were turning for the coast, but the leading vessel was hit twice by torpedoes before her rudder could be brought round. She listed heavily, and was shrouded in escaping steam.

Royce brought the boat slewing round, and fired his own sleek charges into the blackness. As he altered course, the engines racing, the night lit up with a thousand multi-coloured hues, as the ship broke in two and exploded.

The remaining ship was firing her guns frantically, and appeared to be out of control.

One M.T.B. was also in difficulties, with flames flickering out of her bridge.

Another great roar, and the last of the transports lifted her bows, and slid to the bottom.

In a welter of plunging wakes, the M.B.T.s tacked back into line, the sea dark again, but for the blazing M.T.B., now two miles astern.

Benjy's boat went about, and his voice boomed across the water.

'Kirby's bought it! Nip back and take off the blokes, will you? But don't hang about, Clive!'

Royce waved, and watched grimly as Benjy took over command of the flotilla, and led them, roaring away, towards safety.

'Stand by on the fo'c'sle, Number One. I'm going alongside. Get ready to pull the wounded aboard. We won't have a lot of time. The fire's got a good hold!'

He swung to the aft rail. 'First-aid party, Mister Leach! Lively now!'

Raikes sucked his teeth, his eyes fixed on the blazing boat, looming closer and closer.

'Gently does it,' breathed Royce. The stench of petrol, and the warm breath of fire on his cheek, made his throat contract.

The seamen lined the rails, and he saw Carver leap on to the other boat's slanting deck as they scraped alongside.

The bridges of the two boats were side by side, and as the other one listed over, slowly and wearily, he saw the shambles clearly revealed by the growing flames.

Men were leaping wildly across the narrow gap to safety, while others were dragged ruthlessly over the rails, their injuries making them cry out pitifully.

He saw Kirby step stiffly from the wrecked bridge, his clothes in rags, his face a torn nightmare.

He seemed to see Royce looking down at him, and for a moment he stood there motionless. Then, he slowly bent forward, in a grotesque curtsy, his torn scalp gleaming dully, and pitched over the side between the two grinding hulls. Royce retched.

'All off, sir,' yelled Carver, and with a quickening tremble they moved clear and, with bows lifting, speeded after the others.

* * * * *

Commander Wright strolled along the deserted jetty, sniffing appreciatively the crisp morning air.

In the harbour, a bugle sounded sadly, and one small harbour launch scudded across the anchorage, disturbing the nodding gulls perched on the buoys. He could taste the coffee on his tongue, and he hummed absently to himself as he scanned the clear, colourless sky. It had the makings of a fine day. When he reached the steps at the foot of the Signal Tower, he stared across to the heavy bulk of the *Royston*. Her moorings were still empty. He frowned, and consulted his watch, then looked out at the glittering line of the sea, towards which a dirty trawler puffed with slow, graceless rolls. They should be back now, he thought, and strolled into the signals office. The Yeoman was sitting back in a chair, his eyes puffy from too little sleep. Wright waved to him cheerily.

'Don't get up, Yeo', I'm just going to wait in the office here for a bit. The 'T.B.s'll be back soon. Any news?'

'As you know, sir, they got their objective all right. We had a signal from the gunboats two hours ago. I expect the M.T.B.s took a bit longer to find the destroyers that were going to escort 'em back.' The man yawned.

'Hmm, quite so,' mused Wright, and walked out on to the steps again.

A naval bus drew up by the gates, with a squeal of brakes, and Wright smiled, as about twenty Wrens climbed down, and made their way to the dockside canteen.

The pensioner driver called lustily after them: 'Nah don't you be long, my cherubs. 'Alf an hour fer breakfast, an' we're off.'

He noted with surprise that one of the girls had detached herself from the group, and was walking uncertainly in his direction. As she drew close, his smile of admiration was replaced by one of recognition. She saluted, and he noted warmly how her jaunty cap had difficulty in controlling her delightful curls.

'And a very good morning to you, my dear,' he boomed jovially. 'A Happy New Year, too.'

'Good morning, sir.' Her smile transformed her face. 'I hope you don't mind, but I've got something to send over to Lieutenant Royce's boat.'

He saw she was holding a brown paper parcel.

'We're just passing through, you see,' she explained. 'Going to the new Signals School.'

Wright grinned roguishly. 'He told me you were coming down. The lucky young devil! But I'm afraid he's out on Ops at the moment. Should be back any time. Then you can give him the parcel yourself.'

Her face clouded, and her eyes glanced fearfully to the vacant buoys by the *Royston*.

'Nothing too dangerous, is it, sir?' There was an edge to her voice.

'Course not, my dear. Now you come into the S.D.O. and have a cup of tea, and I'll send someone to fetch you something to eat. Then we can wait for him together.'

She smiled gratefully, but he saw the haunted look in her eyes. As he leafed through the signals, he watched her standing by the windows, her slim body taut. He shook his head and sighed. If he had a girl like that, now—— A bell jangled harshly.

'Captain C-F on the 'phone, sir,' said a rating, his hand over the mouthpiece.

'What the devil—oh, all right.' He took the instrument and listened intently. The Captain's voice was crisp.

'Had a signal from Coastal Command, you'll be getting it about now, but I can't wait. One of the boats has bought it, so you'd better arrange for all the usual stuff.'

'Was there some trouble then, sir? I thought the operation was pretty clear cut.'

The girl turned from the window, stiffening, her face white.

'Don't know anything else yet, Commander. But inform the hospital at once to get ready.'

The line went dead, and he slowly replaced the receiver.
'Bad news, isn't it?' Her voice was hoarse.

'We don't know yet,' he said grimly. 'Come on, we'll get up to the main jetty where they come in.'

In silence they hurried along the foreshore, the plump, red-faced Commander, and the small Wren at his side, until they arrived at the old harbour entrance. There was a strong smell of seaweed and fuel oil.

Wright tensed, a string of flags rose to the yard of the boom vessel.

'Damn my eyes! They must be able to see the boats. Can you see 'em, girl?' He gripped her arm tightly.

The sea was smooth and glassy, and in the far distance she saw the fast-moving craft sweeping defiantly across the early-morning stillness, ploughing up great rollers of crested foam. The air trembled and slowly filled with the vicious snarl of the racing engines, until all other sounds were swamped, and the very wharf seemed to vibrate under their feet. Nearer and nearer they came, in a perfect formation, the ensigns flapping wildly, making a splash of colour against the sombre grey hulls.

Wright was counting, 'Five, six, seven. Just one missing.'

She clenched her hands until the nails bit into her palms. It mustn't be, it can't be, her heart cried out. Not now. Oh God, spare him. Her eyes smarted, so that she could hardly see the slim shapes as they roared round the headland and into the harbour reach. The first boat bore a line of scars along her fo'c'sle, and two still shapes lay on her stained deck, covered by their blankets.

Good old Benjy, thought Wright, he's made it again.

One by one they nosed up to the jetty, where the ambulances stood patiently.

'By God!' roared Wright deafeningly. 'There he is! There's your boy!'

M.T.B. 9779 screeched alongside the rubber fenders of the jetty, and the ropes snaked ashore to the waiting hands. The engines sighed away to stillness as the stretcher-bearers went aboard.

253

She was running now, blindly stumbling over the slimy, uneven stones, her eyes bright, and her lips parted.

Royce stepped slowly on to the jetty, his waterproof suit stained and blackened, his shoulders heavy, as he watched the wounded survivors going away.

Then, with a gasp of dazed recognition, he saw her. She didn't stop running until she fell breathless into his outstretched arms.

'Julia, what are you doing here?'

He held her tightly, shielding her from the scene behind him.

'I brought you your present, darling.' There was a sob in her voice, as she pulled the parcel from under her arm.

'You're safe, you're safe,' she murmured.

With his free hand he tore open the parcel. It was a bright yellow scarf. He laughed and wrapped it round his neck, then, gently, he lifted her chin, and studied her face seriously.

'Are you happy now, darling?'

She nodded, and together they walked up the jetty.

Behind them, the little ships lay quiet and still.

DOUGLAS REEMAN

★★★ ★★★

Alexander Kent

Read Alexander Kent's stirring historical novels of courage and daring in battles at sea featuring stalwart Captain Richard Bolitho! Author Kent brings the past to glorious life in novels you won't be able to put down! Read them all.

05498-4	COMMAND A KING'S SHIP	$2.25
05375-9	ENEMY IN SIGHT!	$1.95
05349-X	THE FLAG CAPTAIN	$1.95
05437-2	PASSAGE TO MUTINY	$1.95
05719-3	SIGNAL—CLOSE ACTION!	$2.25
05370-8	SLOOP OF WAR	$1.95
05732-0	TO GLORY WE STEER	$2.25